W9-BYF-026

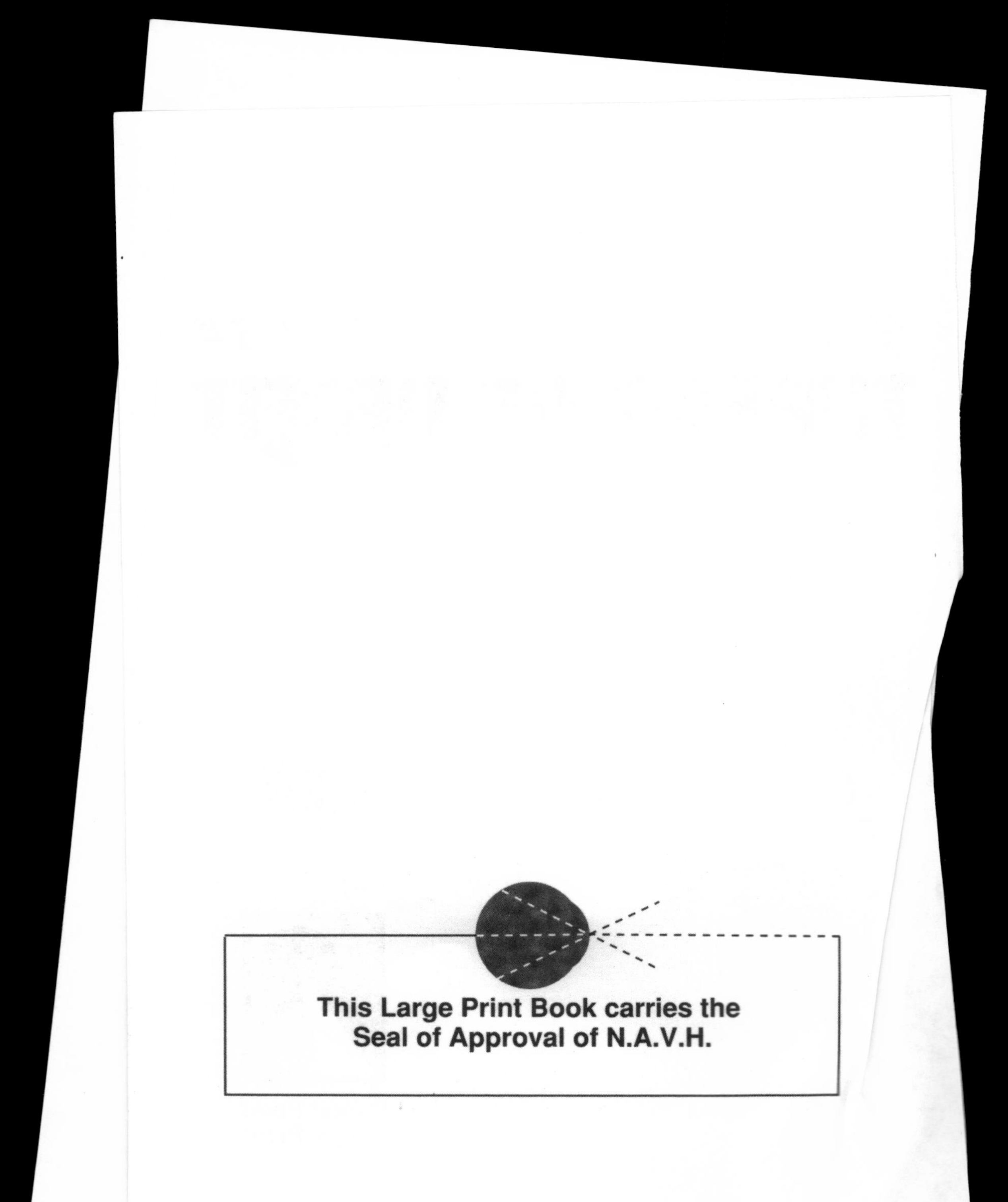
This Large Print Book carries the
Seal of Approval of N.A.V.H.

CATHERINE PALMER

CENTER POINT PUBLISHING
THORNDIKE, MAINE

This Center Point Large Print edition
is published in the year 2008 by arrangement with
Harlequin Books, S.A.

The text of this Large Print edition is unabridged. In other aspects, this book may vary from the original edition.
Printed in the United States of America.
Set in 16-point Times New Roman type.

ISBN: 978-1-60285-230-3

Library of Congress Cataloging-in-Publication Data

Palmer, Catherine, 1956-
Thread of deceit / Catherine Palmer.--Center Point large print ed.
p. cm.
ISBN: 978-1-60285-230-3 (lib. bdg. : alk. paper)
1. Large type books. I. Title.

PS3566.A495T49 2008
813'.54--dc22

208008978

For the least of these

Chapter One

" 'Come, you who are blessed by the Father,
inherit the Kingdom prepared for you
from the foundation of the world.'
For . . . I was naked, and you gave me clothing."
—Jesus Christ, Matt. 25:34,36

"*Paint?* You're kidding, right?" Anamaria Burns set one hand on her hip and the other on her editor's desk. "Carl, you hired me because my investigative reporting took a first-place award from the Texas Press Association. I moved from Brownsville to St. Louis to cover hard news for the *Post-Dispatch.* So far, you've asked me to write about a neighborhood beautification project, an ice cream stand, a sports arena and a parade. Oh yeah, and sewage. Now you want me to do a story on paint?"

City editor Carl Webster leaned back in his chair, took off his glasses and rubbed his temples. With budget cuts, a glaring error on the Sunday edition's front page and three new interns to break in, his Monday-morning staff meeting hadn't gone well. A heavy smoker, who existed on a diet of black coffee and doughnuts, he looked tired.

"Not every article can be a prizewinner, Ana," he said. "You know that."

"But *paint*?"

"Lead paint. It's a problem here." He took a moment

to huff a breath onto each lens and rub with a white tissue. “St. Louis County just got a two-million-dollar grant—”

“You shouldn’t do that, you know,” she inserted. “Clean your glasses with a tissue. The paper fibers scratch the lenses. You should use a soft cotton cloth.”

Carl set the glasses back on his nose and scowled through them at his latest hire. “As I was saying, the Department of Housing and Urban Development awarded St. Louis County a two-million-dollar grant to seal or remove old lead-based paint. The county will add a half-million bucks. This is their third HUD grant, and the money always goes to owner-occupied single-family houses or to apartment buildings. So there’s your story.”

“I don’t see it. Maybe a couple of inches in the Metro section—HUD gave the grant, and now the county is going to paint houses.” She scooped up a scattered pile of press releases, tamped them on Carl’s desk and set them down again. “How is that news?”

“What draws readers to a story, Ana? Money, sex, power. And kids.” He lifted a corner of the paper stack with his thumb and riffled it like a deck of cards. “See, children are eating the paint chips that fall off the walls in these old buildings downtown. They’re breathing in dust from crumbling paint. And lead-based paint—which was used in every building constructed before 1978—can cause brain damage in children under six years of age.”

"Okay, that's bad."

"That's not all." He pushed around the papers she had just straightened until he found the one he was looking for. " 'Breathing lead dust and consuming lead paint chips,' " he read, " 'can cause nervous system and kidney damage. The affected child can exhibit learning disabilities, attention deficit disorder and decreased intelligence. There may be speech, language and behavior problems, poor muscle coordination, decreased bone growth, hearing damage, headaches, weight loss—' "

"I get it, Carl. I do." She paused a moment, chewing on the nail of her index finger. Nail-biting was her worst habit, Ana admitted, evidence of the stress in her life. In a constant quest for perfection, order and control, she had nibbled her nails down to nubs. Not even pepper-laced polish had helped.

"But the county has the money now," she said. "They'll fix the problem."

"In houses and apartments."

"I'm sure they've already taken care of school buildings."

"Is that the only place kids spend time?"

She lifted her head, feeling her news antennae start to tingle. "How about day cares?"

"Small, non-home-based day cares are slipping through the cracks."

"Churches?"

"Basement Sunday school rooms. Vacation Bible School areas."

She thought for a moment, tapping her lower lip. "Restaurants?"

"Mostly taken care of."

"What about after-school clubs? We had several in Brownsville. Kids of all ages showed up. If their parents couldn't afford day care, some little ones spent the whole day there. They had basketball courts and crafts programs, that kind of thing."

"Now you're with me." Carl nodded. "I'd like three or four articles, maybe a sidebar or two. And put some heart into it, Ana."

Wrong body part, Ana thought. She had made a name for herself with her nose.

Ana Burns could sniff news a mile away. Since coming to St. Louis five months before, she had left several strong story ideas on Carl's desk. No doubt they were still there—lost in the clutter. Instead of letting Ana follow her nose, the editor had assigned a bunch of boring, fluff pieces and then buried them in the Metro section.

She didn't want her work to show up in Section B. She was a page-one woman. P-I, that's where her byline belonged. The other reporters kidded her about this quest for perfection—as had her colleagues at the *Brownsville Herald.* She was used to scoffers, and she paid no attention to them.

Carl leaned across stacks of files and unopened mail to hand her a sheet of paper. "Here are the names of some places to get you going. Start with Haven—it's a recreation center not far from here. Our publisher's on the board of directors, so they'll cooperate."

"Why wouldn't they?"

"Unflattering publicity. The Health Department is on their backs. Family Services, too, I imagine. Most of these small operations survive on a shoestring budget and can't afford to fix the paint problem."

Anticipating endless treks from one tedious interview to another, Ana shook her head. This was so far from her vision of big-city journalism she could scream. Instead of reporting breaking news, investigating political shenanigans and digging into the affairs of the city's high and mighty, she had been reduced to covering issues a new journalist would cut her teeth on.

"Carl, can't you give this story to one of the interns?" she asked. "Let me write something with meat on it. I heard the mayor is—"

"I'm giving the project to you, Ana. You've got two weeks."

"An entire series in two weeks? But I've got assignments on my desk already."

"This is life in the fast lane, Ana. You're not in your sleepy little Texas border town anymore. Everyone on the city staff has to pull their own weight."

"I want the fast lane," she said hotly. "That's why I left Brownsville. I crave excitement and challenge. But a story on lead paint doesn't cut it."

"Ana, if you're unwilling to complete your assignment, I've got ten reporters lined up waiting to take your job."

Carl turned away and began punching numbers into his phone. Shutting the door of his office, Ana gripped the list in her hand and tried to make herself breathe. Her sandals felt as if they'd been lined with lead as she made her way back to her desk.

Lose her job? Impossible. She would have no choice but to go home. Back to Brownsville and the house where she'd grown up. Back to her parents, whose phone calls and e-mails still were filled with grief. Their pain became her guilt, and it lay squarely on her own shoulders.

Sinking into her chair, she slid open her desk drawer and lifted out a small, porcelain-framed photograph of two little girls smiling from between their striking mother and their tall, strong father. That day at the beach had seemed so perfect. Ana and her younger sister had played in the sand, digging moats and building castles while their parents lounged beside them on red-and-yellow-striped towels.

Bending closer, she gazed into the face of the child she had been. How old? Maybe ten. An expression of calm, of outward confidence, of self-assurance on the girl's face in the photo belied the haunted terror mirrored in the brown pools of her eyes. Ana's sister was smiling for the camera, but she, too, had been filled with anxiety at that very moment. How frightened the two little girls had been during that year and the years that followed, how filled with confusion and despair. Helplessness filled both children even as loving arms surrounded them.

Her heart clenching, Ana slid the frame back into the drawer and set a file folder on top of it. She could not go home. Ever. Brownsville and all that had happened there was in the past. And she would do everything in her power to keep it there.

Two weeks—that was all the time she had. Two weeks to write the lead paint series, while keeping pace with the regular flow of daily assignments that landed on her desk.

Fortunately, the short pieces could be handled on the phone. Determined to start on the new project without delay, she opened her purse and checked her supplies. Two notebooks, five pens, a small tape recorder, cassette tape. Cinnamon breath mints. Lipstick exactly three shades darker than her lips. Spare contact lenses and wetting solution. Cell phone. A can of pepper spray.

Feeling better, she snapped the bag shut and surveyed her desk. The assignments file lay in her top drawer. Her in-box held three letters, which she opened, skimmed and tossed into the wastebasket. Her out-box was empty, of course.

Ana always had liked order, structure, neat borders. At the University of Texas at Brownsville, she had turned in term papers early. She tried to do the same with her articles. In grade school, she kept a container of antibacterial wipes in her backpack so she could clean the top of her small desk. That habit had traveled all the way to St. Louis with her, and she never set foot out of the *Post-Dispatch* building at the end of each day without first giving her desk a good scrubbing. Clean, neat, orderly. As perfect as she could make it. Yes, that was her life.

Ana knew her first stop should be "the morgue"—the newspaper's archives—which no doubt had a thick file on lead-based paint. But she wanted to get started with her interviews. She settled for e-mailing the newspaper's librarian to request copies of pertinent articles.

Standing, she shouldered her purse and pushed her chair under the desk. Two sites on Carl's contact list had addresses in the inner city. Following her editor's suggestion, she would start at the recreation center and move on to the day care.

Avoiding the elevator, Ana headed down the windowless stairwell, her thoughts on how she could dig up enough information to fill out a series. She increased her speed, now racing down the steps, feeling the burn in her thighs, expanding her lungs to take in air. Earlier that morning she had run five miles from her apartment to the Gateway Arch and back. This was barely a skip, but the exercise filled her with confidence as she burst out into the parking garage and jogged toward her car.

By the end of this year, she planned to run her first marathon. Within five years, she had to claim a Pulitzer. But first she needed to pull three great stories off a wall of crumbling lead paint. She had two weeks. No problem.

"Please sign your name on this list, ma'am." The teenage boy standing under a tattered green canvas awning held out a clipboard. “And write down your reason for visiting Haven.”

Despite her best intentions, Ana felt a jolt of trepidation as he took a step toward her. Tall and brawny, with deep chocolate skin and shoulder-length dreadlocks, he wore a plain white T-shirt, baggy denim shorts and new Nike high-tops with the laces hanging loose. She often saw such apparel on young men loitering near the *Post-Dispatch* building or playing basketball in the parks. Tattoos, graffiti, even the color of a baseball cap could be signs of gang affiliation. Though she had taught herself to walk the streets of downtown St. Louis without constantly looking over her shoulder, Ana knew enough to be careful.

As she handed back the clipboard, the youth smiled broadly. Amid a row of straight white teeth, a single gold one glinted in the July sun.

“Thank you, Miss Burns. My name is Raydell Watson. Welcome to Haven. You can walk through now. If you got anything metal in your bag, hand it to me.”

Masking her surprise, Ana glanced at the club’s door. A metal detector blocked the entrance. “Tape recorder?”

He nodded, and she handed him the device, stepped through into the cool building and blinked in the dim light. Laughter, balls bouncing, a referee’s shrill whistle, the smells of perspiration and popcorn assailed her.

“Good afternoon, ma’am.” A girl’s voice drifted up

from the gloom. She handed Ana the tape recorder. Petite, with elaborate braids swirling around her scalp, the teen flashed a bright smile. "This is Duke. He won't bite."

A German shepherd padded forward from the darkness. Ana gave an involuntary gasp as the animal circled her. She went rigid, elbows high, shoulders scrunched, clutching her bag to her chest.

The girl giggled. "He sniffs for drugs, but you clean. C'mon, Duke. Heel, boy!" The dog trotted to her side and sat down, tail swishing the floor. "You gotta put on this T-shirt, Miss . . . um . . ." She glanced at the clipboard, which had somehow materialized in her hands. "Miss Burns. You got on a red blouse, and we don't allow no gang colors at Haven. Here you go. And don't roll up the sleeves. That's a gang sign, too."

Unaccustomed to taking orders from teenagers, Ana couldn't summon the will to protest. She set down her bag, glad her khaki skirt had passed muster, and tugged the T-shirt over her blouse.

A drug-sniffing dog. A metal detector. What was going on here?

"I've come to see—"

"You gotta talk to Mr. Hawke or Mr. Roberts," the girl cut in. "That's the rule." She spotted another teen dribbling a ball in their direction. "Hey, Antwone, go get Uncle Sam or T-Rex!"

The boy swung around and headed off toward a group of youngsters shooting basketballs at a backboard that hung from the ceiling of the large room.

Ana eyed the dog and let out a breath. "This is quite a place. Haven. Wow."

"Yes, ma'am. I'm on Duke today." The girl's chin rose with pride. "You only get to be on Duke after you earn fifty points. And you get trained at the police station."

"So Duke is the . . . uh . . . dog. Well, I'm sure that's quite a responsibility. How did you earn fifty points?"

"Volunteered for stuff like latrine or KP or laundry. And good behavior. You gotta have that or you get your name put on the list, and then you can't come back." She straightened as someone signaled to her from a distance. "Okay, you can go over to the offices, Miss Burns. See that door right there with the glass window?"

"With the duct tape?"

"Yes, ma'am. Go on inside and sit down. Somebody be there in a little bit."

"Thanks." Ana took her time crossing the room. The building must have been a warehouse at one time. Or maybe a department store. The ceiling wasn't high enough for regulation basketball, but the kids seemed to have devised a new set of rules to deal with that. They played hard, shouting, scuffling, pressing, forming and reforming as the ball slammed against the concrete floor. Athletic shoes squealed. A whistle pierced the air. The smell of sweat hung like a heavy cloud over the players.

Ana reached the office and noted the silver tape holding the glass together in a broken windowpane.

Poor lighting, bare floors and walls, inadequate ventilation. How had this place met municipal codes and been permitted to open in the first place? She could hardly blame the health department for seeking a reason to shut it down.

Stepping into the office, she noticed a boy with brown curly hair and the requisite white T-shirt. He sat hunched over a computer.

"Excuse me?"

He didn't look up.

"I'm from the *Post-Dispatch.* I'd like to speak to the director of Haven."

"Sec," the youth muttered, peering into the screen as if he could see through it to the inner workings. Ana gingerly took a place on an old red vinyl restaurant booth that served as seating.

The office was a wreck—motivational posters peeling off the walls like dried onion skins, balls of every type scattered on the floor, damp white towels piled high in a corner, a desk covered with broken trophies. Bowling? Archery? The old statuettes had names and dates engraved on the front, and several bore the ignominy of missing arms or broken tennis racquets. What good was a beat-up tennis trophy in a place like this?

"Rats!" the boy said suddenly, slamming his palms down on the card table and pushing away his chair. He rolled backward five feet, his fingers knotted in his curls. "Rats and double rats! This computer is a piece of junk!"

"What kind is it?" Ana asked. She had taken out her reporter's notebook and was testing her pen.

"An old geezer. Take a look at the size of that screen. Have you ever seen one so small?"

Ana stood and leaned toward the grimy tan computer. "Were you even born when this thing came out?"

"No way. But I can fix it. It's just going to take some time."

"You have a lot of confidence. I guess that's par around here."

He looked at her for the first time. "Oh, I'm not from here. I'm a summer volunteer. My church sent seven of us from our youth group to work in the inner city for two months. I'm setting up Haven's computer system."

"With that old thing?"

He shrugged. "You use what gets donated. My name is Caleb."

She shook his hand. "Ana Burns. Nice to meet you, Caleb. Any idea where I can find the club's director?"

"They're both out with the kids. Uncle Sam and T-Rex—that's who you need." He glanced up at a clock with a cracked face cover. "It's almost time for activity change. One or the other should be in soon."

"Activity change?"

"Yeah, the place runs like a military camp. Organization, discipline, respect, all that. Everything on the minute. Spit and polish. It's awesome."

Ana nodded, unconvinced. "So, are there a lot of volunteers?"

"Not enough locals. Our group came all the way from New Mexico. My friend Billy is working construction upstairs with another guy who knows wiring. They run groups of kids through the rooms they're rehabbing and teach them about electricity, plumbing, patching cracks and stuff like that. You couldn't spend more than a couple weeks at Haven without learning something new. Sam's goal is to give everybody a job skill by the time they're an adult."

"Uncle Sam?"

"Better not use that name in vain."

The voice behind her drew Ana's attention. She turned to find a broad-shouldered man silhouetted in the doorway. Well over six feet tall, he wore the usual white T-shirt—this one transparent with sweat. As he stepped under the fluorescent light, she noted that he had short brown hair, deep-set blue eyes and a grin that carved a pair of parentheses into the corners of his mouth.

"Sam Hawke." He stuck out his hand. "What can I do for you, ma'am?"

Ana stepped forward and met his hard grip with one of her own. "Ana Burns with the *Post-Dispatch.* I understand the health department has contacted you about a problem with lead paint."

The grin vanished. "We're working on it."

"Would you mind if I asked you a few questions, Mr. Hawke?"

"I just told you everything you need to know." He stepped around her, his damp shoulder brushing against hers. "How's the computer, Caleb?"

"The motherboard may be fried."

"You'll fix it." He opened a narrow door Ana hadn't noticed, stepped through it and shut it firmly behind him.

Caleb's dark brows lifted. "I guess that's all he has to say about lead paint."

"I don't think so." She tried the door handle and found it locked. This was getting a little more interesting. Was the guy hiding something? She knocked.

"That's . . . uh . . . the bathroom," Caleb told her.

Blushing, Ana stepped back. "It ought to have a sign."

"Well, it's private, you know. For staff and volunteers. Sam's office is down that short hall, if you want to wait for him there. He usually stops in and checks the schedule during activity changes."

Ana folded her arms. "I'll wait right here."

Caleb shrugged. "You might not want to mess with Sam.

Maybe you could get something out of Terell."

"I'll mess with Sam first."

He gave a low whistle and rolled back to his computer. The bathroom door opened and Sam emerged, ducking his head to avoid the top of the frame.

"Still here?" he mumbled, shouldering past her again. He walked to a row of gray lockers that must have come from an old high school gym, jerked one open, stripped off his T-shirt and grabbed a towel. After blotting his face and chest and applying stick deodorant, he tugged a dry T-shirt over his head. Finally, he tossed his dirty laundry onto the massive pile in the corner and turned those blue eyes on Ana.

"Ma'am, Haven is all about respect, and I'd be glad to talk to you if I had anything to say." He glanced at his watch, then looked around her to check the clock in the gym. "I told you all there is. We're working on the paint."

"Mr. Hawke, I have only two weeks to complete this story, and my editor assured me you'd cooperate. In fact, Haven is at the top of my list of sources. I believe our publisher serves on your board of directors."

He paused a moment. "Davidson's a good man. We appreciate his dedication."

"So, are you planning to remove the lead paint or seal it?" she asked.

"Whatever it takes."

"Exactly where is the paint?"

"It's around."

She flipped open her notebook. "How many rooms at Haven have lead paint?"

"A few." He reached out and pinched the notebook between his thumb and forefinger, slid it from her hand and folded it shut. "We're dealing with it. That's all. No story."

Returning the notebook to her, he smiled. The parentheses were absent. "Thanks for dropping by Haven, ma'am.

Now if you'll excuse me, we're in the middle of activity change, and I need to check on my crocheters."

"Did you say crochet?"

She followed him out of the office, scrambling to reopen her notebook and get the cap off her blue ink pen. He lifted a hand as a new group of youngsters took to the makeshift basketball court. Several waved back, some shouting, "Hey, Uncle Sam!" He strode toward a row of doors that Ana suspected had once led to offices. Stopping at the first in line, he peered inside the small room. "Hey, Terell, how's finger painting?"

"Good. We got six today." A large man looked up from a table spread with newspapers. Like Sam, he had a military haircut and arms sculpted with muscle. His long legs, bare and ebony hued, ended in white socks and a pair of the largest sneakers Ana had ever seen. A half-dozen children clustered around him, their fingers and faces smeared with blue, red and yellow tempera paint.

"You showing around a new volunteer?" Terell asked.

Sam glanced over his shoulder at Ana. "Didn't know you were still here."

"I'm taking the tour."

He turned away, the big shoulder in her face, and addressed the children. "She's a newspaper reporter. Her name is Miss Burg."

"Burns."

"Terell Roberts is my partner," Sam told her. "T-Rex, who've you got there?"

Ana shifted her focus to the little girl on Terell's lap. Fairytale princess golden curls crowned her head, but there the image ended. Thin and dirty, the child wore a small white T-shirt and a pair of badly stained purple shorts. Her feet were jammed into sandals at least two sizes too small, crowding her tiny pink toes. Nestled close to Terell, she leaned her head against his broad chest. His arm circled her as she turned sad blue eyes on Ana. Noting that one cheek appeared swollen and tinged with hot pink, Ana's instinctive alarm system went off. Someone had slapped the child—and not long ago.

"This is Brandy," Terell said. He bounced her on his knee. "She's not feeling too happy today. But we're gonna fix that, huh, sugar-pie? Do some painting, maybe eat a bowl of popcorn."

The child stretched up and planted a kiss on the man's cheek. Ana felt queasy.

"Who hit her?" she demanded.

Terell's head shot up, his eyes suddenly hooded. "Ma'am, I'm taking care of that," he said in a low voice. "You all get on with your tour now."

"See you at the next activity change," Sam told his partner as he shut the door. Before Ana could speak again, he marched on to another room.

"Hey, Lulu," he said, leaning through the open door. "What are we up to this afternoon?"

Ana peered around his shoulder. A woman with light brown skin perched on a green plastic chair that sagged precariously under her weight. Eight children sat cross-legged at her feet on the concrete floor. "We're reading *Peter and the Wolf*," she announced, holding up a large book. "Then we'll listen to the music."

"You kids be good for Lulu," Sam said, stepping away from the room.

"Hey, did you see that child's face—back in the other room?" Ana demanded, hurrying to keep pace with him. "The little girl named Brandy? Someone had slapped her."

"Listen, Miss Burns." He swung on her. "I appreciate your interest in Haven and our children. If you want to write an article about lead paint, I can't stop you. But I have nothing more to say."

Ana pursed her lips as she followed him to another room. She knew she had not imagined that bruise on Brandy's face. And the way Terell Roberts had been holding the child unsettled her. Vulnerable children hidden away with grown men inside small rooms did not paint a pretty picture in her mind.

Her heart hammering, Ana paused at the third in the line of classrooms. A young man sat with a group of older children at a round table littered with hammers, nails, blocks of wood screwdrivers and various lengths of wire. Spotting Sam, he shrugged and threw up his hands.

"Same bunch," he said. "Granny didn't send hers over at activity change, so I kept these I already had. It's no big deal, sir."

"That's a great attitude, Abdul, but everybody gets a turn at crocheting, just like everybody gets a turn at tools." Sam gave a thumbs-up. "Let me check on Granny for you."

"Thanks, sir."

Sam walked to the last room and poked his head through the open doorway. "Well, hello there, Granny. Looks like your crew is busy."

An elderly woman with snowy curls and a black velvet pillbox hat peered at him through oversize glasses. "What's that you say, Mr. Hawke?" she asked loudly.

"I said you look busy here." He raised his voice. "Nice work!"

Ana studied the center's director as he stepped into the room and crouched down with the children. On first analysis, Sam Hawke seemed like a decent enough man. She appreciated the stringent rules and the emphasis on respect at the center. The volunteers clearly enjoyed their work, and most of the kids who dropped in appeared happy.

But her introduction to Terell Roberts still bothered her. What had been going on in that small room? Sam Hawke's presence in such a place also raised questions. What had motivated an educated male in the prime of his life to take on the job of managing a run-down inner-city operation constantly threatened with closing? If the man enjoyed sports, he ought to be coaching a team, or working at a country club somewhere. It didn't make sense.

What kind of future could Sam Hawke or Terell Roberts have here at Haven? If the recreation center had a large budget and generous donors, the lead paint might not be a problem. But Carl had called

Haven a shoestring operation, and the place obviously didn't generate enough financial support to pay two adults a decent salary. Sam and Terell would be living hand to mouth . . . unless they were using the building as a front to make money another way.

Ana's blood raced at the possibility that she might uncover a real story at Haven. Oblivious to her thoughts, Sam hunkered down on the floor and picked up a length of pale blue yarn and a crochet hook. A girl—about ten, Ana guessed—leaned against his shoulder as she tried to show him how to loop the yarn onto the hook. He gritted his teeth, the muscles in his jaw rippling as he thumbed the delicate yarn.

Why this fascination with children? Prickles of alarm shot through Ana like thin, sharp needles at the memory of the way Terell's hand had rested on little Brandy's leg. The unhappiness in the girl's blue eyes was palpable. She had kissed him, but had he slapped her only moments before?

"Tenisha, you've got me beat on this one," Sam said, handing her the crochet hook and a tangle of yarn.

"Aw, you can do it, Uncle Sam." She looked up at him. "You just have to try."

"Tell you what, young lady. You play some basketball with me this afternoon—"

"No, I—"

"Now, don't interrupt, Tenisha." He held up a big index finger. "Remember the rules? Here's a proposal for you. Try basketball this afternoon, and tomorrow I'll come back and let you and Granny help me get started on crochet."

"But I can't play basketball, Uncle Sam. I can't run hardly at all, y'know."

"Well, how would I know that? I haven't seen you ever try."

She gazed down in her lap for a moment, her face glum.

"Do we have a deal?" he asked.

"Okay," she said in a tiny voice.

"Great." He gave her a solid pat on the back, and she brightened. Then he raised his voice to the other adult in the room. "Now, Granny, it's time for activity change. These kids need to go try the tools."

"What you talkin' 'bout, boy?" The elderly woman squinted at him over the top of her glasses. "Fry the rules?"

"Tools!" he shouted, then muttered, "We've got to get you a hearing aid, Granny."

As the youngsters scampered to their feet, Ana watched Tenisha lose her balance and stumble into a boy's path. He barked in anger and gave her a shove. At that, Sam reached down and lifted the boy off his feet.

"Ladies first, Gerald," he said as he held the youth high, giving Tenisha time to pick her way toward the door. Her unsteady gait revealed cerebral palsy, Ana surmised. So why had Sam Hawke urged the girl to attempt a sport that would only cause further embarrassment? Again, she felt the twinge of alarm and distrust.

Waiting for the group to file toward the toolroom, Ana noticed a figure seated in a shadowy corner at the end of the row of doors. She took a couple of steps closer and discerned a pair of skinny legs emerging from a green skirt. The girl wore the requisite white T-shirt and a pair of pink plastic sandals. Her hair, pulled back into a long braid, gleamed like black silk. She blinked at Ana, her large brown eyes wide.

"Hi." Ana tried giving a little wave. She'd never been much good with children.

The girl looked away.

Well, that's that.

Turning back, Ana nibbled a fingernail as she waited for Sam to complete the activity change. If Haven was as positive a place as it proclaimed, an article on the center's activities might make a good feature for the Everyday section. She would suggest it to the editor.

Her own focus had to be the lead paint problem. Carl had wanted her to use Haven in the story, and she couldn't very well turn it in without a single decent quote or even a pertinent fact or two about the place. She had to find out which parts of the building still contained the old paint, whether these children were at risk, how Sam intended to fix the problem, and where he would get the money to pay for it.

If the other sources on her list proved as uncooperative as this one, she would be hard-pressed to finish the series in two weeks. The memory of her editor's promised reaction to such a failure chilled her. She tried to put it out of her mind. Why think the unthinkable?

As Sam stood at the door watching the new bunch of children settle in with Granny and her crocheting, Ana ventured another glance at the girl in the corner. Gazing back at the tall visitor, the child wore an expression of such emptiness, such sad hollowness, that Ana caught her breath. At the look on the girl's face, a painful ache stirred to life inside Ana, and despite her best effort, she couldn't immediately suppress it.

"Don't you want to crochet?" Ana blurted out. She pointed to Granny's room. "They've started a new group."

The girl turned away in silence, her profile lovely and delicately haunting. Ana swallowed, wanting to go to the girl, to touch her somehow.

"Got the room switch taken care of." Sam Hawke's voice at her ear startled Ana. "Miss Burns, I need to ask you to leave now. We don't allow anyone but volunteers and kids in the building unless they have a good reason."

"I have a great reason," she replied. "I want to interview you about your lead paint problem."

His blue eyes fastened on her, and she knew exactly how an ant must feel as someone's heel bore down on it.

"I'm not giving you an interview on Haven's lead paint problem." He enunciated each word as though she had as great a hearing loss as Granny. "Not today, not tomorrow, not ever."

"I've been assigned this story," she said as he turned his back on her and started toward the offices. She strode after him. "Haven will benefit from it. It's obvious you serve needy kids here. Like that girl in the corner—"

"What girl?" He swung around.

"Tut-tut. No interrupting, sir." She gave him a mock salute, then gestured behind her. "Back there. In the shadows. Who is she?"

He peered over Ana's shoulder. "I haven't been able to get her name. She showed up here a couple of weeks ago, but we can't coax her out of the corner. She doesn't speak English."

"Now see? If Haven had to shut down because of the lead paint, that child might not have a place to go."

"Haven is not going to shut down."

"How are you planning to fix the problem?"

His face darkened. As a boy ran past with a basketball, Hawke snagged him. "Hey, Ramone, see Miss Burns to the door, would you?"

"Yes, sir." The young man smiled. "C'mon with me, ma'am. You got to check out before you can go. And we need your T-shirt, too."

Ana glared at Hawke's broad-shouldered back as he headed toward his office. He thought he'd gotten rid of her. But he didn't know Anamaria Burns.

No, sir.

He was staring through the window, thinking about

what had happened in Springfield. Since the phone call from his associate three nights before, an acute pain had settled behind his eyes, and he had not slept well. Nothing could be resolved, of course, until he had more information.

What exactly had occurred that night? Who had done it? How much was known?

Despite the lack of details, he had begun working out his own answers to questions that might arise. He shouldn't give the issue much weight, he reminded himself, because he really hadn't been involved. The incident had occurred in another state, and he wasn't responsible for it. If people didn't take proper precautions, trouble usually found them, and they had no one but themselves to blame. Long ago, he had learned that he could not depend on anyone but himself to take care of things. No one had ever looked out for him, yet see how far he had come.

People counted on him now, and this gave him tremendous power. People feared him. They needed him. And he could demand their silence. Even if this particular situation blew up, he knew his colleagues would remain loyal. They would have no other choice.

As for himself, he would do just as he always had. Things would turn out well. He had organized everything so carefully, putting the building blocks in perfect order, setting each of the safeguards in place. He was cautious at all times, so that nothing could catch him by surprise.

Still, he jumped when his cell phone rang. Turning

from the window, he put the phone to his ear as he dropped to the edge of a chair. "Yes?" Keeping his voice low, he spoke into the receiver.

"Hey, this is Sam Hawke over at Haven. How are you today, sir?"

The light tone jangled his nerves. He frowned. Not the call he'd been hoping for.

"Fine, and you?" he responded, forcing civility.

"Good." There was a brief pause. "Listen, I thought I'd better let you know that someone from the Post-Dispatch *dropped by today."*

"A reporter?" His nostrils flared as he took in air. "Why? What did he want?"

"It was a woman. She's doing an article on our lead paint problem. I think Davidson may have put her up to it."

"Davidson? Why would he do that?"

"I don't know, sir. I can't see how that kind of publicity can be good for us."

"Absolutely not."

"Maybe Davidson doesn't see this situation the way I do, but I chose not to cooperate with the lady. We're having enough trouble raising money without the newspaper dragging our name through the mud."

"What did you tell this reporter?"

"That we're aware of the problem and plan to fix it."

"Good." He dug a handkerchief from his pocket and blotted his forehead. The pain behind his eyes was intense. "I affirm your decision completely, Sam. You

don't need reporters nosing around there, that's for sure."

"I agree. I thought I'd better let you know in case Davidson mentions it."

"Certainly. I'll make sure he understands our point of view. I may give him a call right now, in fact. We need to be on the same page."

"Great. Thanks, sir."

"Listen, Sam . . . if she comes around again, let me know."

"I doubt she'll be back. I made my position clear."

"Excellent. And again, thank you for the call. You were right to bring me up to speed. Anything like this . . . don't hesitate to phone."

"Will do. Better run."

As the phone went dead, he let out a hot breath. Lovely. A reporter. He should have gotten a name. Clenching his fist around the phone, he turned back to the window.

He stood, stretched his stiff muscles and crossed toward the door. He needed to make some phone calls, but they could wait. Right now, he was going to have to do something about this headache. He hadn't visited his special closet in many months, and he preferred to keep it that way. But commonplace antidotes didn't work for him as they did for others. He was unique in so many ways. As usual, he would have to take care of himself. He always had.

Again I see the lightbulb, and I am glad. I close my eyes.

Maybe if I close them, I can hide. I want to hide, because I am afraid. Afraid of the room. The terrible room. And the man. The good mean kind cruel love-me hurt-me man.

I say a prayer now. Thank you, God, for the lightbulb. This is not a prayer I learned in church. My mother used to take me to church, but now we do not go. I have forgotten all those prayers.

I have not forgotten God. Has He forgotten me? No. I know He is with me, because He gave me the lightbulb. When the pain begins, I open my eyes and look up at the ceiling. The white ceiling. Swirls and patterns, like a white river. Like snow on a river.

I see that lightbulb, and I am not afraid. It glows, shining into my eyes, and I stare at it. I stare and stare until my head hurts. I stare until the blackness comes. I command my eyes to travel into the light, into the whiteness of the bulb, the roundness, the glass, the ceiling, the swirls . . .

. . . and it is the sun, the bright sun, and I am running up the hill with my little sister. Come, Aurelia! Hurry up! Mama is calling. Can't you hear her? We will be late for supper! We will miss our beans and tamales.

Green grass cools our bare feet as we run. Our wet skirts slap against our thighs. We played in the stream near our house today, looking for treasures. We found a tire and a shoe. We found a plastic bottle. We found a battery. Oh, such treasures!

Hurry, Aurelia! I hear her laughing behind me, and I tug on her small hand.

We reach the lane, warm brown stones under our feet.

Hot dust swirling around our ankles. Broken glass—be careful, Aurelia! Watch where you are stepping! Don't hurt yourself!

I take care of Aurelia, and she is safe with me. She laughs and laughs, as though missing our supper is part of the great adventure of this wonderful day. She knows I will get food for her, even if we miss the supper. Even if Mama puts everything away, I will find something for us to eat. My feet bounce and skip and sing up the path, past the houses, past the wide porches and the children and the mamas and papas and the grandmas. I feel the sun shining on my face, warming my cheeks, kissing me with love. Oh, God, thank you for the sun! For the bright light. For Aurelia and the dusty path and the tamales waiting for us in our home.

Do I hear my mother's voice? She calls! The smell of roses curls around me, and I am nearly home. Nearly there. I am coming, Mama! I am bringing Aurelia! She's safe with me.

We run through the light, the heat, the brightness. We run up to our front door, out of breath, laughing, too silly to worry about tamales. I throw my head back, and my hair tumbles down behind me in a waterfall. The sun dances across my cheeks. I open my eyes and look into the sun, the bright white shining sun, the glowing glaring gleaming sun . . .

. . . and now I see that the sun is a round, white glass. It is small, and it hangs from the sky by a single black cord. It is the lightbulb. It has saved me again.

Thank you, God.

Chapter Two

Sam spotted her the moment she stepped through the metal detector at the front door of Haven.

"Great," he muttered.

Raydell Watson scowled as he followed the direction of Sam's gaze. The brawny eighteen-year-old usually asked to work guard duty at Haven's front door, and Sam had come to rely on him to keep troublemakers out of the recreation center. Despite Raydell's youth, his dreadlocks, gold tooth and massive tattooed biceps made him an imposing barrier. He loved rap music, and his foul mouth had gotten him into trouble at the center more than once. A life spent mostly on the inner-city streets had hardened the boy at an early age. But to the best of Sam's knowledge, Raydell had no gang or drug ties, and his loyalty to Haven was unquestionable.

A few minutes before, Raydell had relinquished his responsibilities to a younger boy and had come inside to cool off. Standing beside Sam, he watched the basketball game.

"It's that newspaper reporter," Sam said. "I'm supervising practice, and I don't have time to talk to her this afternoon."

Hadn't he made it clear there would be no interview? Of course he had. But here it was just two days later, and she was back, sniffing around like a hound dog on a hot trail.

"Lucius, pick up your feet!" Sam barked as a boy barreled past, nearly tripping on his own sneakers.

"What's a reporter want with you, man?" Raydell asked.

"The lead paint problem." Sam had told the youth about the situation earlier. "She's onto it. Keeps asking me questions that I don't want to answer."

"She don't even see you standing over here," Raydell observed. "Some reporter, huh."

"I hope she doesn't spot me, because I don't intend to talk to her. I've only got two weeks left to come up with the money to fix the paint, and she could write things that would scare off donors. She could shut us down."

"No way, man."

"It's possible. They say the pen is mightier than the sword."

"Yeah, that's why we carry guns in the hood."

Sam cast the youth a skeptical eye. "And look what good it's done you. No guns, my friend. And no reporters. I practically had to run her out of the building the other day. She's trouble."

"You already got enough of that."

"No kidding."

The woman headed straight for the office, head held high, dark brown hair swept up on top of her head like royalty. A queen expecting to command everyone in sight. What was her name? Burns or something, Sam recalled. She figured she was going to burn him. Splatter his sorry hide all over her newspaper. Slam the doors and lock them tight.

Not a chance. He had given his life to this place, and he believed without any doubt that God had commissioned him to the work he was doing with these children. Anything that rose against him became a part of the spiritual war he was fighting. And he certainly wouldn't allow a prying reporter to sabotage his efforts.

At least she'd remembered the center's rules and was wearing a plain white blouse. Tall and lean, she had the stride of a runway model as she crossed the floor in her belted slim gray slacks and high heels.

"Acts like she owns the place," Raydell remarked.

Sam chuckled mirthlessly. "Yeah, comes gliding in here like a Stealth bomber out to do her damage."

"Just let her try."

"Calm down, Raydell. This is God's battle."

"She better not try nothing. Ain't nobody messin' with my people."

Pumped up now, the young man was flexing his muscles and clenching his fists as if ready to knock the reporter out with a single punch. Sam shook his head and focused on the game again.

"Shoot, Abdul!" he shouted. "You're in perfect position. Go for it!"

Raydell elbowed Sam and pointed to a heavyset teenager standing flat-footed beneath the basket. "Hey, look at Natasha. She got concrete shoes, or what?"

"Jump, Natasha!" Sam called out. "Get those feet off the floor, girl!"

Raydell threw back his head and laughed. "Aw, man, that's pitiful! I'm going back outside where at least I got something interesting to watch."

"Later, Raydell," Sam said as the teen sauntered away. He glanced at his watch. Almost time for activity change. He would send Miss Burns packing as soon as he could hand over these kids to someone else. She had stepped into the office, and he could see her talking to Caleb. One hand on her hip, she leaned over and said something to the boy.

That's right, Cleopatra. Try to work your wiles on a seventeen-year-old boy. It won't get you what you want.

A moment later the office door opened and Caleb walked out. But instead of coming for Sam, he headed toward the row of small rooms where the younger children were doing crafts projects and listening to stories. The young man poked his head into one room after another. Finally, he headed up the stairs.

So that was her scheme. She knew she couldn't get anything out of Sam, so she had set her sights on his Haven partner. Young Caleb had been sent off to fetch Terell Roberts while she sharpened her claws. Smooth move, Cleopatra, but—

"Uncle Sam, I think the basketball is flat, sir." Tenisha tugged on the hem of his T-shirt. "It don't bounce good, and Gerald keeps on stealin' it away from me."

He studied the orange basketball as players maneuvered it around on the makeshift court. "It's still got air, Tenisha."

"I can't do it, Uncle Sam." Her face crumpled as she clenched her fists. "I told you! I can't play basketball. I can't run."

"Hey, now—what's this *I can't* nonsense? Is that how we talk at Haven?"

"No, sir, but I really can't. My legs don't work good 'cause of the palsy, and every time somebody throws me the ball, Gerald pushes me out of the way and takes it."

Sam focused on the skinny boy with buckteeth that stuck out so far he had a permanent groove on his bottom lip. Gerald carried a massive chip on his shoulder because he'd been bullied for years about his appearance. The kid had learned that Tenisha made a handy target when he felt the urge to take his frustrations out on someone.

"Stealing the ball is part of the game, Tenisha," Sam told her gently. "But pushing is illegal. Tell you what, next time Gerald pushes you, fall down flat and start wailing."

"You mean crying?"

"Just let out a squawk loud enough to get the referee's attention. Who's ref today?" He glanced at the court. "Okay, see Patrick over there with the whistle? If you fall down and squawk, he'll notice what's going on and call it. Before too long, Gerald will foul out of the game."

"Ain't that cheatin'?"

"Not if he really pushes you. The pros do it all the time." He paused as his line of vision centered on

Miss Cleopatra Burns, notebook out and pen in hyper-drive, having a big confab with Terell.

"Hey, T-Rex!" he hollered. Then he patted the girl on the back. "Go on out there, Tenisha. Don't let Gerald mess with you."

Before the codirector of Haven could spill the beans about their problems with the health department, Sam hoofed it over to him. "Terell, this is the reporter I told you about, and we don't—"

"Anamaria Burns," she cut in, turning to him and sticking out her hand. "How are you this afternoon, Mr. Hawke?"

"Not happy to find you back here." He took her thin, strong hand and gave it a hard squeeze. "I told you we don't have anything to say about paint."

"That's what I've been trying to tell her," Terell spoke up. "This lady doesn't listen, man."

Sam regarded his best friend. Terell was the color of rich, dark coffee, but otherwise he looked like Sam's twin. However, while Sam was the keeper of rules and the master of the clock, Terell functioned as Haven's mascot. A teddy bear.

Today, as usual, a child hugged him, small arms wrapped around the man's large leg as if clinging to a tree trunk. He held a little girl with blond hair on his back, her cheek resting on his head and her arms around his thick neck. She was asleep.

"Terell and I discussed this the other day," Sam told the reporter. "We don't think it's a good idea to talk to you."

"She won't take no for an answer," Terell said. "She keeps on saying she'll write about the good we're doing here."

"She's going to make a big deal about the paint."

"I can write the article any way I want," the reporter interjected.

"I've been burned by the press before," Terell added. "But I don't know, Sam. Maybe she could help us."

"Does my opinion carry any weight around here?" Sam shot back.

"Not as much as you like to think, dog," Terell replied. As he spoke, his face split into a grin, and his distinctive deep laugh rolled up out of his chest. He guffawed for a moment, the little boy who clung to his leg joining in with a giggle.

Sam turned on Cleopatra. "Is that the focus of your story, Miss Burns? The good things we do at Haven?"

"Well, no, but—"

"That's what I thought. You're going to write about our building, and how we don't meet city code and the health department is breathing down our necks."

"How long do you have to fix the paint problem?" she asked.

"Two weeks," Terell said.

Sam rolled his eyes. "Way to spill the beans, T-Rex."

"Two weeks is not long." She scribbled on her notepad. "Are you planning to raise funds, or do you have an account set up for emergencies?"

"An account!" Terell started laughing again. "Did you see any of these kids pay to get in here? None of our donors are handing over enough money to set aside extra, ma'am. We pulled together the start-up money from what was left after my NBA days with the Magic, and now we're basically what you'd call a charity case."

"You played professional basketball, Mr. Roberts?" she asked, writing fast.

Sam eyed his friend in dismay. "You're going to give her enough for a book, aren't you, Terell? Sure, tell her everything."

"No way, man. Not about DFS and all that."

"Division of Family Services?" Ana spoke up. "They have a problem with Haven, too?"

"I can hardly wait to read the article," Sam growled.

"Well, why don't you handle it then?" Terell glanced at his gold Rolex watch, one of the few remaining luxuries from his once-lucrative career. "It's time for activity change, anyhow. I'll take care of it, and you talk to Miss Burns."

"I don't want to talk to her. I want her to leave."

"Listen, Mr. Hawke," she said. "I already have enough information here to include Haven in my article, so you might as well fill in a few holes. I can always talk to DFS myself."

Sam stared at Terell. Terell stared back. Ever since their basketball days at Louisiana State University, the two had butted heads. Sam was intense, driven, edgy. Terell loved everyone, saw the silver lining in each situation and would give away his last dime. Sam had practiced on the basketball court for hours, honing his skills, pushing himself to his limits. Terell arrived late to practice, barely passed his college classes and led the team to one victory after another on raw talent. Sam trusted no one. Terell believed the best about everyone he met. So-called friends had conned, manipulated and cheated him out of most of his money, yet he never held a grudge. The two men loved each other like brothers.

"I'll talk to her," Sam said finally. "You've got five minutes, Miss Burns."

"Ana." She smiled, radiant and suddenly prettier than he'd realized.

"Shall we go to my office?" he asked. "It's quieter."

"Your office?" The smile vanished. "We can talk here. I don't have a problem with noise."

He studied her for a moment, observing the brown eyes and reading in them something he hadn't expected. Fear. So, Miss Ana Burns had a chink in her armor. She didn't want to go into his office. His turf. Seeing an advantage, he seized it.

"I'd like to sit down," Sam told her. "Been on my feet all day, you know. Follow me."

"But . . ." she tried. "But I . . ."

Ana matched his stride as Sam headed across the room. Unusually long legs, he noted. Most women barely reached his shoulder, but a tilt of this one's head would put her face disconcertingly close to his.

Military training had taught Sam the art of inspection, and instinct took over despite his determination to ignore the pesky reporter. Her firm chin and aquiline nose created a sharp profile, he noted, which was softened by large brown eyes and full lips. Squared shoulders eased into gentle curves. Her topknot had clearly started the morning tightly coiled. But the day had loosened it, and now wisps of dark hair trailed around her ears and down the back of her long neck. The combination of prickly and soft intrigued Sam—which in turn, irritated him no end.

A short distance away, Terell blew the whistle for activity change. Like jelly beans, kids poured out of the little classrooms, down the stairs and across the basketball court. Despite his annoyance at her intrusion, Sam felt glad that the reporter was seeing the large numbers of children and teenagers who had found a secure place to spend their summer days.

Without Haven, most would be loitering on the streets, vulnerable to the drug dealers, drive-by shootings, prostitution and gang activity that proliferated in these neighborhoods. Here, they stood a much greater chance of not becoming a statistic—one of the hundreds of young men who ended up in hospital emergency rooms with knife or bullet wounds, or one of the countless unmarried teenage girls who became pregnant each year.

Giving them hope was Sam's passion. His mission. He had blown assignments in the past. Made mistakes. Fatal flaws. This time he would not fail.

He stepped into the front office and clapped a hand

on Caleb's back. "How's the computer, buddy?"

"A pile of junk." Caleb squinted into the screen as he spoke his familiar refrain.

"Hey, get on the Internet and see if you can dig up a little dirt on somebody for me—her name's Ana Burns."

"There's no modem on this old thing, sir, and I—" Caleb glanced up, saw the woman, and then laughed in embarrassment. "Oh, hey there, Miss Burns."

"Hello, Caleb."

"I thought you wanted to talk to Terell."

"I intended to, but it looks like I'm stuck with Uncle Sam."

The teen grinned. "Lucky you."

"By the way," she addressed Sam as they walked down a short hallway to his personal office. "My name is Anamaria Cecilia Guadalupe Burns, and you won't dig up any dirt on me. I'm clean. Your dog can vouch for that."

"Your name . . . you're Hispanic?" he asked, pulling the door shut behind him and pointing her to a chair.

She stood statue-like, eyeing the room, her knuckles white on the handle of her purse. Then, moving suddenly, she turned and jerked open the door. With two quick paces, she stepped to the chair and sat, her hips on its edge as though she intended to leap up at any moment.

"I prefer the term *Latina,*" she said, flipping open her reporter's notebook. "My mother was born and raised in Mexico. My father's ancestors came from

Scotland. I grew up in Brownsville, Texas, graduated from UTB with a degree in English and worked at the *Brownsville Herald* before moving here five months ago."

"Ah," he said, taking a seat behind his desk.

"And you?"

"Wyoming."

"What brought you to St. Louis?"

"Haven." He straightened a stack of papers, tamping the edges before setting them back on his desk. "I thought this interview was about lead paint."

"And I thought you wanted a broader story."

"You don't need my background for that. Write about the kids. Most live in government-subsidized housing projects. Few have a father in the home. We have a mix of African-American and Caucasian, but we—"

"So I've observed." Her eyebrows lifted like a pair of raven's wings. "Sorry to interrupt, but would you mind if I asked the questions?"

Sam leaned back in his chair and laced his fingers across his stomach. The lady was a major pain.

"I like your office, by the way," she said, brown eyes flashing from one side of the small room to the other. Long dark lashes curled up almost to her eyebrows. "Orderly. Neat. But you ought to clean the front area. That pile of wet towels is sprouting mold."

"Would you like to take over management of our laundry room, Miss Burns?"

"It's Ana, and the posters are peeling off the walls out there, too. That office is a wreck."

"We have lead paint in our laundry room," he informed her. "I can't let the kids work there anymore, because the paint is peeling even worse than those posters out front. So our towel mass is becoming critical, and we could use an adult to help out."

"I'm not that into laundry," she said. "I send most of my clothing to a dry cleaner."

He sat back and studied her. "Ah. A dry cleaner type."

"Do you have a problem with dry cleaners?"

"I have a problem with people taking up my valuable time discussing wet towels."

She picked up her notebook. "When did you meet Terell Roberts?"

"At LSU. We both played basketball there."

"And then you turned pro?"

"He did. Played for the Magic and the Clippers. I went into the military. Marines."

"Ah," she said. "A Marine type."

He couldn't hold back a grin. "Not a Marine *type.* A Marine. I brought that training to Haven, because I believed if I could teach discipline and respect, the kids would benefit."

"So you contributed the military atmosphere, while Terell came up with the seed money to start the operation."

"Haven is a team effort. We rely on our patrons for funding. Our volunteers add their ideas to make this a better place. Nobody has all the answers to help these kids."

"So what's your motivation?"

"Like I said. Helping kids."

"Really?" She sounded skeptical. "Terell wants to help children, too, I suppose."

"Yes, he does."

"Why these kids? And why you?"

He put his head on the padded chair back and closed his eyes. How could he explain the complex and painful reasons why he had sought out Terell Roberts after so many years? How could anyone even begin to understand what had compelled him to spend every last cent he had saved, to work countless hours tearing out old plaster and making the place habitable, to come each morning knowing it might be the last day Haven's doors would open?

Lifting his head, he gazed at Ana Burns. She sat across from him, her notebook propped up and her pen poised. Her straight shoulders and long neck were held in that regal pose now so familiar to him. But for the first time, he noted a small pendant at her throat. A gold cross set with garnets.

"Your necklace," he said.

Her hand moved up to touch the cross. "My mother gave it to me on my fifteenth birthday—the *Quinceañero.* It's a special occasion."

"It's a reminder of your family . . . and your faith?"

"God is important to me." Her dark eyes pinned him. "Without Him, I wouldn't exist."

Stunned at her bluntness, Sam couldn't respond for a moment. She dropped her focus to her notebook, as if reading over what she had written, but he could see that her eyes weren't moving.

He let out a breath. "Then maybe you'll understand this. I started Haven because I believed it was what God wanted me to do."

She had stopped taking notes and was moving her pen tip around on the paper in a tiny blue circle. "You believe God talked to you?"

"In a way."

"Is it the same with Terell?"

"Terell is a strong Christian. When we were in college together, he led me to Christ."

She looked up. "Led you to Christ?"

"To salvation. I'd been raised in a Christian home and had believed in Jesus from early childhood. Terell helped me see that it's not enough to believe. A person has to commit his life to Christ."

She wrote something in her notebook. "So, your patrons . . . you run Haven as a religious organization?"

"We get some financial support from churches, and we maintain Christian principles. But Haven is non-denominational. We're not-for-profit, and we operate under those governmental regulations. We don't qualify for any exemptions as a religious group."

"You've met state guidelines in every area except this lead paint situation?"

"As far as I know. They allowed us to go ahead and open, but different agencies keep coming around to inspect. We're doing our best."

He stood, the subject touching a sore place in his gut. "The codes, the regulations . . . the whole thing is difficult. When Terell and I found this building and bought it, we thought we'd just need to clean it and then get the center going. We had big plans for the outside—turning the parking lot into a top-notch basketball court with bleachers and a snack bar, setting up a tennis court, even putting sod down for a park area with picnic tables. But we haven't had time to start on any of that because of all the work we've had to do inside—wiring, plumbing, rehabbing the whole basic structure. We had to widen doorways and enlarge the bathrooms. Had to buy special toilets. Had to put in ramps. Lights. Exit signs. Washer and dryer."

He moved across the room and began restacking the books on his small shelf. "Don't get me started on the kitchen," he continued. "We're not even close to code there. We're not certified, so we can't provide hot meals or homemade refreshments—which was one way we hoped to make a little money. At this point, all we can sell is packaged snacks, popcorn and sodas, and we do that at cost."

"I had no idea it was so complicated," she murmured, taking notes. "It sounds like an uphill battle."

"Battle is the right word for it. Right after we purchased the building, vandals broke into the main level. It was still empty, so they couldn't find anything to steal. But they smashed out windows, spray-painted walls, demolished toilets. We've had to use the bathrooms downstairs, which is a problem for our kids with special needs. Some of our volunteers have offered to build ramps, and those have to meet code. We've been working like crazy to fix the restrooms on this level, and we're nearly there. The punks destroyed nearly all our light fixtures, too, so now we're working to buy and install new ones."

"Your military background must be a help. If you see this as a battle, I'm sure you're determined to win."

"We'll win. But there are times I'd almost rather be stranded in an Iraqi sandstorm." He rubbed the back of his neck, remembering. "Terell and I can handle the kids, and our volunteers will get the building into shape. But we need more of two things we lack. Time and money."

"If Terell played professional basketball, he must have earned a huge salary." She frowned, the raven wings drawing closer. "Maybe you could convince the city to give you more time."

"Terell can tell you about his pro career, if he chooses, but he gave Haven all he had left. He's a good man. We're both willing to sacrifice everything for this place, but we can't live forever without bringing in some income. And we can't keep the doors open unless we have a solid financial operating base. The trouble is that our donors are reluctant to fork over more money until they're sure we're on solid footing with the city, the county, the state and probably the Feds."

“Makes perfect sense.” She leaned back, relaxing in her chair for the first time since she’d entered his office. “And it explains your reluctance to let me publicize your problems.”

As the light of understanding shone in her eyes for the first time, the knots in Sam’s shoulders loosened a little. He picked up a file from his desk.

“Our donors are mostly individuals or small-business owners,” he explained. “Churches have given us some money, but we don’t have any corporate sponsors. We can’t afford to pay salaries for a fund-raiser and a public relations expert. Basically, it’s up to Terell and me to carve out the time for those things.”

“Doesn’t sound like it’s your cup of tea.”

“We’re both athletes. I’m a soldier.” He dropped the file on his desk. “Nah, it’s not our thing.”

“Mind if I take a look at your donor list?”

“Why?”

“I’d like to take down the names and give some of them a call. If I can get a few good quotes about the vision these people have for Haven, my article might help you drum up additional support.”

He considered her request. “If our donors agree to be interviewed, it’s fine with me. But I don’t want you to publish names without their permission.”

“No problem.” She took the file he handed to her and scanned the list. “This is good. I know some of these people. Isn’t Richard Hayes the CEO of a moving van company?”

"He's been great. But so far, it's all been personal donations. He hasn't involved his business yet, and that's where the big money is."

"These are fairly large churches, aren't they?" she asked, jotting information as she went down the list.

"Sure, but they're in low-income areas. They send us a lot of volunteer help, but they don't have much money to give."

Her finger stopped at a name. "I know this man—Jim Slater. He goes to my church." She looked up, her face transformed by that radiant smile. "He runs an adoption agency, doesn't he?"

"It's called Young Blessings Adoption Services," he told her. "Jim's on our board of directors, and he drops by fairly often to help out with the kids. I'm assuming he must be well-off, because he's done a lot for Haven. He paid for new tile in the bathroom. In fact, I have an appointment with him later this afternoon. To talk about the lead paint problem."

"I bet he'll help. I've worked with Jim in the church nursery a couple of times. He's a gentle man, and so good with children. He lost his wife to cancer, you know."

"I didn't realize that."

"Well, this is great." She looked up from her notebook. "One more thing, Sam. Terell mentioned a problem with DFS."

Sam shook his head. "Your story's on lead paint, Miss Burns. That's all I'm willing to discuss."

"But why would Family Services be after you?"

"They're not 'after' us. You make it sound like we're criminals."

"Are you?"

He scowled. "Of course not. If you work with children and don't meet your health codes, then DFS starts sniffing. Look, I've given you all the time I can, Miss Burns."

"Ana." She stood. "So, how's the little girl in the corner?"

He thought for a moment, picturing the forlorn child who never spoke. "We've tried, but we can't get her involved in our activities. Still, she seems to feel safe with us. She comes every day."

"She's kind of a lost child, isn't she?"

"Invisible. That's the word I use. She's not the only one. We have several kids who drift at the fringes, looking on, and trying not to be noticed. They're like ghosts. Haunting. We do our best to involve them, but we don't insist that they join the activities."

He started for the door. "Why don't you talk to the girl? And put in a load of laundry while you're at it."

He was halfway down the hall before he realized he'd left her alone in his office. An unsupervised guest. A snoopy reporter. He swung around, strode back into the room and took her arm.

"This way out, Miss Burns."

"Ana."

"Cleopatra," he muttered, leading her through the front office. He gave her a nudge out into the main area, where the youngsters were playing basketball.

"There she is—in her corner. See if you can get through to her. Even a name would be helpful."

"I don't have time."

"Sure you do." He studied Ana, surprised at the pale wariness that filtered across her face. "We're not helping her. Maybe you can."

"I can't, sorry. I have to make these phone calls."

"Scared?" he asked, taking a step closer, meeting her almost face-to-face. "You're happy to announce Haven's problems in your article, but when it comes to understanding what we really do, what our mission means—"

"I'm not scared," she snapped back. "I'm just not comfortable with children."

"You work in your church nursery."

"One-on-one, I mean." Her eyes narrowed and her soft lips pursed. "Okay, Uncle Sam. I'll go talk to her. I'll talk to the other kids, too. Maybe I'll find out a few of your secrets."

"I don't have secrets," he called after her as she started to walk away.

"Yes, you do. Wyoming. You and Terell. The Marines." She shrugged. "And my name is not Cleopatra."

He watched as she headed across the room toward the shadowy corner. The little girl spotted her and quickly turned away.

The lightbulb pulls on my eyeballs as though they are attached by strings. I fear they will come right out of my head and leave me blind. Seeing nothing but the darkness. Then I will be even more afraid than I am now. Quickly, I close my eyes, hiding them safely behind the skin of my eyelids. It's black in this place, and I can feel the pain. Fear tastes like blood on my tongue. It smells like sweat. Not the good sweat of my father when he comes home from work. This is the bad sweat of thieves and murderers and my father when he has drunk too much beer. Darkness curls around me like monster shadows and demon smoke, choking me and flooding my nostrils with the evil smell.

Afraid, afraid, afraid of this pain and sweat more than of blindness, I open my eyes and stare at the lightbulb. My eyes float upward into the light, the shining and shimmering light. It is so bright that my eyeballs must surely burst open . . .

. . . and it is the sun, gleaming on my sister's white teeth as she laughs. She pulls on my hand, urging me into the light, and I run with her. We race down the beach, our feet flying across the loose sand, our toes digging into the soggy, slushy sand, and now we skip out into the water.

I call to her. Hold my hand, Aurelia! Stay beside me! A wave rolls in and slaps our legs, and we gasp and cry out in shock and delight. So cold! So wet! Oh, we love this water, and the way it beckons us deeper and deeper.

Come! Come on, my sister calls me.

No, Aurelia, I tell her. I squeeze her fingers tightly with my own. Stay close to me. Stay near the shore where it is safe! In the ocean live big fish with sharp teeth to bite us. In the ocean, coral can cut open our toes and make us sick. Sea urchins can stick their spiny needles into our feet, and jellyfish can wrap their poison threads around our legs. Seaweed can pull us under so that we would drown.

Stay with me, Aurelia. Stay near, and I will keep you safe.

We dance in the waves, my sister and me. We march up and down like soldiers. We play trumpets and guitars in our mariachi band. We chase our children, those naughty waves, as they run away from us and then back into our arms again.

Oh, we are wet, and Mama will be angry! But the sun is hot, and our skirts will be dry by the time we walk all the way home. The sun beats down on us like the drummer in our band, and we sing to it. We fling water upward into the sky like a baptism. And the droplets shower down on us, shiny crystals, God's diamonds. His blessings fall on Aurelia and me as we play in the sunshine. As we lift our faces to the sun and laugh at the light sifting through our black lashes. Oh, the sun . . .

. . . the round, glowing bulb of light. Now the pain is gone, and the fear creeps away, back into the darkness, and I thank God who brought me the lightbulb.

Chapter Three

"Hi, there." Ana approached the girl.

Brown eyes focused on the basketball game, the child sat on the concrete floor. With her legs tucked to one side, she gripped the hem of her skirt with both hands, as if she could somehow tug it over her knees. She wore the usual white T-shirt, her arms like thin straws hanging from the cupped sleeves.

"Can you please tell me where the bathrooms are?" Ana asked.

The girl said nothing. Her tongue darted out to moisten her lower lip, but her eyes remained glued to the game. Ana considered walking away. Obviously this child wanted nothing to do with her. She had chosen her dark corner, and she intended to stay in it.

Ana's palms dampened, and she smoothed down her slacks. She, too, had known the need to hide.

"Los baños, por favor?" she asked in her mother's native Spanish.

The girl's brown eyes darted to her. She had understood.

"Sabe donde quedan los baños?" she tried again, keeping her voice casual.

The child looked away. *"No se,"* she whispered.

Ana smiled. *"Esta bien."*

Taking a step closer, Ana eased down onto the floor nearby. She leaned against the cool wall and took off her shoes. "Oh, my feet," she said in Spanish. "These things are killing me! Take a look how high the heels are."

She held out a shoe. The girl shook her head, her attention back on the basketball players.

"You're smart to wear sandals," Ana continued. "I've been up and down the sidewalks today. I bet I have blisters."

She levered one leg over the other and examined the bottom of her foot. The child's dark eyes slid across, studying the woman's toes as Ana checked them.

"There's a blister. See?" She angled her foot in that direction. "That really hurts. I need to soak it in some warm water. Do you know where I could do that?"

"Down the hall," the girl whispered in Spanish. "You have to take the steps to the basement."

"I wonder if it would be okay for me to go barefoot. There are so many rules here."

"It's all right. They won't notice you."

Ana sat for a moment, absorbing the dark corner where this little one had found her private haven. Where had she come from? Why had she chosen the shadows? And what made Ana's heart beat so heavily each time those brown eyes focused on her face?

Was it possible this skinny child had a story Ana needed to tell? Carl Webster, her editor, had asked for several articles on the lead paint as well as accompanying sidebars.

The deadline was a week and a half away, and Ana had no time to detour into any other subject. In addition to the series, she had to keep up with the small assignments that landed on her desk each day. If she couldn't produce quality reporting, Carl would replace her. He had made that clear. There was no way Ana could allow that to happen.

Haunted, Sam Hawke had described the invisible children. A small girl with haunted eyes was not worth Ana's time, was she? Neither was Terell Roberts, who even now—across the basketball court—sat with one child draped over his back, a second in his lap and a third at his feet. He was rubbing the back of the little boy at his feet, and he and the girl on his knee kept tickling each other. Again she felt a vague unease, and she had to look away. Maybe it was innocent. Maybe this little girl in the shadows had nothing to tell.

Ana lifted her hand and touched the cross at her throat. As a child, she had gone to church with her parents and learned about God. But not until later, after her sister's death, had she given herself to Him wholly, completely, falling into His arms like a drowning woman pulled from the sea at the last moment. The last gasp. The final breath. In that instant, she would have died and been glad. Welcomed the end.

But God had saved her. Truth had dragged her up from the sandy bottom, the clutching seaweed, the deadly undertow. She had seen His hand reaching out to her, and she had taken it. Even now, years later, she recalled that moment when she had chosen to live. And all the way out of the depths, onto the shore and along the pathways of her life, He had stayed at her side.

Now, each morning when she opened her eyes, she searched for God, prayed to Him, and gave herself to Him again. It was the only way she could survive. Her morning run to the river, the articles she wrote, the people she encountered, each activity throughout the day until she dropped into bed at night belonged to Him.

Her faith didn't sound exactly like Sam Hawke's. He had spoken of committing his life to Christ—almost as though Jesus were a military commander who required absolute obedience. Ana saw God as the Father. She had met Him one desperate day, and to Him she belonged with her whole heart. As she studied the skinny girl in her faded green skirt, Ana prayed. Why this child, Father? Why did You draw my eyes to this little one in the corner? Has that huge man across the room harmed her in any way? Can I do anything about it? What do You want of me?

"Could you lead me to the ladies' room?" Ana whispered the Spanish words. "This is only my second time to visit Haven, and I'm afraid I might get lost."

"I can't take you." The girl hung her head. "Ask someone else."

Ana relaxed against the wall and lifted her eyes to the water-stained white ceiling. She ought to leave the child alone. Talk to some of the others in the building, concentrate on her lead paint story. Upstairs, she could interview the construction crew. They would know how many rooms had been contaminated with the deadly old paint.

She might even approach Terell again—ostensibly

to discuss his background in professional basketball. That ought to produce some interesting quotes. She slipped her shoes back on her feet and started to rise.

"Do you know La Ceiba?"

The birdlike voice stopped her.

"La Ceiba?" Ana frowned, trying to think where she might have heard the name. Wasn't that some kind of tree? She recalled her mother pointing it out in Brownsville—a tree with palm-like leaves and large fruits. Several Ceiba trees grew in their neighborhood, and when the fruit burst open, the silky fiber pulled away from the seed and drifted on the breeze like clouds you could actually touch. Ana had stuffed the fiber into pillows for her dolls' beds.

"La Ceiba is a tree," she said.

The girl looked down, her face sad. "Yes, it's a tree."

"Why do you ask me this?"

"Because . . . because I understand your words when you talk to me."

Ana wondered what her knowledge of Spanish had to do with the silk-cotton tree. "My mother is Mexican," she explained. "But I grew up in Texas. It's a long way from here."

The girl nodded, twisting her fingers together. "Yes, a long way."

"Where did you come from?"

The girl shook her head and wedged her shoulders into the corner, retreating into the darkness again. Ana ached to ask more questions. Her reporter's instinct told her to keep pressing, cajole the information out of the girl, make her give up the story. But she sensed it would do no good now. The door had closed.

"I guess I'll try to find the bathrooms," she said, getting to her feet. On an impulse, she put out her hand. "My name is Ana."

The child lifted her left hand and set it softly in Ana's right palm, as though she might suddenly decide to climb up out of the shadows and come away with this kind stranger. But at the touch of human flesh, the child snatched her hand away and tucked it behind her.

"Me llama Flora," she said softly. I am called Flora.

A surge of victory welled up inside Ana. "Goodbye, Flora. *Hasta mañana.*"

But the girl's eyes were focused on the game again. Ana stood and walked down the row of classrooms. She found the stairs, the ramp for the special needs children and eventually the bathrooms. In sad shape, they spoke of hard times in the city. Cracked white wall tiles, missing mirrors, vulgar graffiti scrawled across toilet stalls. Ana gazed at the dank room, thinking of those who had passed through before her, doing their damage, uncaring that others would follow.

How could Sam Hawke and Terell Roberts possibly pull together enough money to redeem this place? It would take gallons of paint to cover the crude messages. Repairing the floors would cost a fortune. Did the plumbing even work? She hoped so.

She turned a faucet and let the cool water trickle

over her hands. Hope. This was all any of them had. A thin stream of water. A dusty glint of sunlight. A stranger's hand in the darkness.

Ana dried her fingers on a tissue from her purse and shouldered her bag. If she hurried, she could get back to the newspaper building before Carl left. She would tell the editor about her interviews and fill him in on her plans for each of the articles. And she would mention the child—the many lost children—who straggled into Haven, put on their white T-shirts and found a place to play or rest for a few hours each day.

Pausing, she studied herself in the cracked mirror over the sink. Her heart told her to follow these children and learn their stories. Her gut told her to investigate Terell Roberts and find out what was going on behind closed doors at Haven. She could ask Carl for more time, but would he give it?

She thought of her editor, dipping a doughnut into his coffee and then chewing as his stubby index fingers punched out a memo on his computer keyboard. Carl was an old-school journalist who focused primarily on putting out the paper each day. He hadn't responded to any of the story ideas she'd left on his desk, so why would he give her time to follow a hunch now?

But how could she let it go—the invisible child and the too-friendly man and the certainty that not all at Haven was as it seemed? Ana fretted as she climbed the stairs back to the main floor. She couldn't let it go. She wouldn't.

As she passed the office, she spotted Sam Hawke, once again stripping off a sweat-soaked shirt. Unconscious as a lion in the bush, he stretched his long arms. Muscles flexed and rippled. He scratched his chest and gave a careless yawn. Then he reached into his locker for a dry T-shirt and tugged it over his head.

Ana poked her head through the door. "Hey, Sam."

He swung around, recognized her, flashed a look of surprise followed quickly by annoyance. "Are you still here?"

"It's Flora."

"Huh?"

"The little girl in the corner. Flora." Giving him a wave of fingernails, she turned away.

He pressed the phone to his ear and tried to keep his voice light. "So, Stu, what's going on up there? Any more news on our friend?"

"It's what we thought. Busted. They caught him. All the papers have the story. TV, too. It's everywhere."

Swirling his martini, he watched the olive rotate at the bottom of his glass. "Do they have any idea if anyone else is involved?"

"No leads. At least that's what they're saying." The silence on the other end broke as Stu cleared his throat. "Uh, the Feds . . . they've taken his computer. And his file cabinets."

"But there won't be any trouble with that. You set things up the way I told you, right?"

"I did what you said." Heavy breathing. "Look, I'm

getting nervous. I can't have anyone poking around here. My wife . . . she wouldn't understand at all. She'd leave me, and I couldn't handle that. She'd take the house and the car. I'd have nothing left. I mean . . . I just wouldn't want to go on, you know?"

"You want me to have a pity party for you, Stu? If you did what I told you to do, you don't have to worry. Everything will be fine. You're not lying to me, are you?"

"No, no."

He took a sip of his drink, savoring the burn as it traveled down his throat. Of course he shouldn't have relied on Stu to do things right. He ought to have set up the whole thing himself instead of trusting someone else to help out. This was exactly what happened every time he counted on people to keep their end of a bargain. They let him down. They lied to him.

"Look, Stu, I've been thinking about moving the operation," he said. "I might even retire. I could use a break."

"Retire?"

"This whole thing is beginning to bore me. Besides, I don't need the stress." He took another swallow of the martini and wondered when the alcohol would kick in. His head was killing him, and he'd had stomach problems the past couple of days. Of course, he'd hardly been able to eat, so it wasn't surprising.

"What about the clients?" Stu asked. "We've got six on the waiting list."

"I don't care about the clients," he snapped. "I care

about clearing out my house, because I don't believe a word you said about setting up the safeguards in Springfield."

"I did! I swear it."

"Good. Then you won't have any problem taking the product that's in storage here. Drive down tonight, and I'll meet you at—"

"I can't do that! What if someone's tailing me? What if they're watching my house? They could follow me."

"You idiot. You didn't set it up, did you?"

"I tried, but—"

"You'd better be here tonight to take these things off my hands, Stu."

"Don't talk to me that way. Please. I can't handle your threats. Ever since this started, I've been really down, okay? I mean today . . . this afternoon . . . I got out my gun. If things get too hot, I don't think I can take it."

"Look, Stu, can you get here tonight or not?"

He heard a sniffle on the other end. "I'll check with the client.

I have to make sure I can work the transfer. I'll do my best."

"You owe me, Stu. You owe me everything."

"Okay, okay. I'll call you later."

Fool! He dropped the phone into his pocket and slammed his fists on the arms of the chair. This was so typical. Stu was just like all the others—clients and colleagues—thinking only of themselves and what they could get out of him. If trouble erupted, it would be Stu's fault, that pathetic liar.

No one understood how hard it had been to set everything up. The whole process functioned like clockwork, and all because of his careful planning. He had figured it out, he had put it in place and he ought to reap the benefits.

Instead, he was spending every waking moment watching his back. If the Feds tracked him down, it would all be over. They would make an example out of him, as they had before. Holding him up like some kind of monkey on display. As though what he did was wrong. They had no idea the service he provided. The good that came of his efforts. It wasn't only his clients who benefited. Certainly not, but you couldn't explain that.

It was an economy, and he played the role of the middleman. The producer reaped a huge harvest. And the client gained immeasurably. He was only doing his part to facilitate the process.

He downed the final mouthful of his drink. Time for another trip to his special closet. It was the only way he would get any peace.

Sam stepped out of his office and glanced at the small child nestled in the far corner of the recreation center. *Flora.* Somehow Ana Burns had gotten the little girl to speak. To give her name. How many times had Sam looked at the child, one of so many he couldn't reach? Across the room, her dark eyes studied him, pinned him.

Accused him.

Like a bullet fired from an assault rifle, the memory of another child's brown eyes shot into his mind and tore through his heart, wrenching and twisting it. Unable to shield himself from the onslaught, he saw the girl's thin fingers reaching for him. Smelled the dust on her soft skin as he lifted her in his arms.

He could hear own his breath, heated and heavy. He heard her cries as blood dripped from a bullet wound in her abdomen. The pain he had caused. The terrible, inconceivable, unthinkable thing he had done.

"Oh, God, help me!" The strangled words wrenched from his lips. Sweating, clenching his fists, he swallowed against the knot of pain in his throat. "Forgive me!"

Propelled by the agony in his chest, Sam strode toward the front door. He passed Duke and the dog's caretaker without a word. Bursting through the metal detector, he stepped out onto the searing pavement.

"Where is she?" he demanded of the youth at the door.

Raydell straightened. "Who?"

"The reporter? Which way did she go?"

"Down the street. Must have parked around the corner. You okay, Sam?"

He started in the direction Raydell had pointed. "Tell T-Rex I'll be back."

"What'd she say to you? What's she gonna do to Haven?"

Unable to explain, Sam broke into a run. As he

rounded the corner, her tan Chevy was pulling away from the curb. He leaped in front of it, slammed his palms on the hood, forced her to stop.

Ana braked, threw open her door and jumped out. "Hey, that's my car you're beating on, you jerk!"

"The little girl. Flora. She talked to you? Where's she from?"

"I don't know. She speaks Spanish."

"Spanish." He let out a breath. "Where does she live? What does she need?"

Ana frowned at him. "Why?"

"I have to know." He struggled to find a plausible reason. "Maybe I can help her."

She crossed her arms. "What's going on, Sam?"

He dropped his head, rubbed his eyebrows, fought the tide of emotion that threatened. "It's nothing," he managed.

"You chased me around the corner. I nearly ran over you, for pity's sake. It's not nothing."

He nodded. "Okay. All right." Filling his chest with air, he forced out the words. "Iraq, '03. The start of the war. I was there. The girl reminded me of someone." He paused. "Something happened there. In the desert."

Ana was silent. Her car engine hummed. People passed on the sidewalk. Staring.

Sam tried to make himself move. Return to his normal life. But he knew if he went back into the center, she would be there. Sitting. Looking at him. Gazing with her brown eyes as if she knew.

“Listen, do you want to get something to eat?” Ana asked. “It’s early for supper, but I’m hungry.”

He considered her offer. A kindness, because she saw his obvious struggle. He didn’t much like the woman, didn’t care for what she was doing, the threat she posed to his dream. But for now, she was better than the memory. Better than going back into the center and facing the demon that wouldn’t let him go—no matter how many hours he spent with a counselor, no matter how hard he prayed.

“Yeah,” he said. He rubbed his hand over the stubble of hair he kept short. “There’s a barbecue place down the street. We go there sometimes, Terell and I. We can walk.”

She nodded, stepped back into her car and eased it into its parking space again. Waiting, he pressed his hands on his thighs, drying the perspiration. Ana shut her door and locked it. She walked toward him. Pretty, kind, wary, concerned. Her eyes were brown, too, but older and wiser. Not so frightened. Not so innocent.

“Barbecue,” she said, joining him. “I hope they have onions.”

Ana tugged another napkin from the rectangular dispenser and blotted her chin. This was a mistake. In the first place, she looked like an idiot—dribbling barbecue sauce from the oversize shredded-beef sandwich. Not that she cared how she looked in front of Sam Hawke. But she did want to be as professional as possible at all times. Hard to do when the man kept staring at her with those faded-denim eyes, as though he could see straight into all the places she kept so well hidden. His gaze made her feel off balance, one minute the intrepid reporter and the next a silly schoolgirl oozing barbecue sauce.

She had hoped to talk with him about the incident on the sidewalk, the memory Flora had triggered. Her motive wasn't all charitable, Ana had to admit. Without taking up too much of her precious remaining time—she had to eat, after all—she hoped she could actually interview Sam. She wanted to find out more about his reasons for founding Haven, his interest in children, the strict military atmosphere he had created there. If she could dig out some information on Terell, even better. And she could always use more details about the lead paint.

But instead of some quiet neighborhood coffee bar where she could question him to the soothing strains of mood music, they had entered a hectic barbecue joint crowded with customers. The shouts of the kitchen workers, the clang of ladles on white ironstone plates, the whoosh of crushed ice falling into empty glasses and the hiss of soda dispensers filled the small room. On top of all that, rhythm-and-blues music blared from a jukebox.

"Pork, chicken or beef?" someone yelled at a customer. The questions from the cooks came rapid-fire, loud and impatient. "Shredded or sliced? Pickles on that? Onions? Potato salad, baked beans or coleslaw? Make up your mind, fella—there's ten people behind you! You gonna take all day, or what?" There was no way Ana's recorder would pick up any information she could use. Her hands were so sticky she couldn't hold her pen.

She had a sneaking suspicion Sam had planned it this way. Despite his obvious distress on the sidewalk earlier, he was too smart not to know she would try to interrogate him. He took a bite of his sliced brisket sandwich, chewed awhile and then licked a dollop of barbecue sauce from the corner of his mouth—the whole time staring at her with those blue eyes. Every time she asked him a question, he tilted his head as though he couldn't hear—which was probably true. Then he went back to chewing and staring.

As the crowd began to thin, the sound level decreased several decibels. "I've got to tell you, Haven feels like a military compound to me," Ana said. "The dress code, the dog, the guard at the front door. Do you really need so many rules?"

For the first time since they'd met, he smiled at her. "Rules keep people safe. You like that."

"How would you know what I like?"

"I know." He tipped up his Coke glass and drained the contents. "You like rules."

"You don't know anything about me. We've met exactly twice, and I'm the one who interviewed you."

"Tell me what you know about me, then."

"You played college basketball, you were in the Marines, you served in Iraq, you founded Haven—"

"That's not who I am. That's what I've done." He

leaned back. "I brought you here for a reason. Bet you didn't know that."

"*I* asked *you* to dinner."

"I chose the place. Thought I'd see how you like my favorite barbecue joint. You don't. Too messy."

"I do like it. The food tastes fine."

"Yeah, but the napkins. You've used seventeen."

"You counted my napkins?"

"No, but it's a good guess." He leaned across the table, his long arms on the red plastic tablecloth. Setting his index fingers on her plate, he gave it a quarter turn. "You don't like things out of order."

"How do you know?"

"When I brought your plate to you, I set it with the sandwich at the top. You turned it so the sandwich was at the bottom. When you looked away a minute ago, I turned your plate again. And you moved it back."

Now she was the one staring. "So I like the main item at the bottom. That doesn't tell you anything about me."

"You've folded every one of those seventeen used napkins. Used napkins. Folded them."

"So what?"

"The first time you came to Haven, you learned about our dress code. Today you have on a white shirt of your own. You're not wearing red or blue, because you know the rules, and you follow them. You follow them, because you like them."

"That is so lame."

"You hated the towel pile. You griped about Terell's

office, but you complimented mine. It's neat. Clean. That's because I like rules, too."

"Okay, I do appreciate a certain amount of order in life," she admitted. "That's not unusual. And it's not the most important thing about me."

"No?" He shrugged. "Then I surrender. What is the most important thing about you, Ana?"

Now he had backed her into a corner. Clever. But Ana had escaped from many corners.

"What's most important about me can't be the least bit important to you," she said. "I'm not the issue here. Haven is. Tell me why you and Terell are so interested in these kids. In two short visits, I've observed a child with a bruised cheek, another hiding like a scared rabbit in a corner and a third with cerebral palsy being coerced into playing basketball. That's enough to set off my alarm bells. What's going on over there, Sam? What's with all the rules? And why is Terell forever fawning over the little girls? What are you two men getting out of this?"

"Hold on now. Fawning over little girls?" His brow furrowed. "What are you insinuating, woman? I give you access to Haven, and this is what I get in return? You've seen what we do. Terell and I are helping the kids. Don't you dare write anything else."

Standing, she shouldered her bag. "And don't you tell me what I can or can't write."

She pushed in her chair, and started for the door. Halfway there, she swung around, stormed back to the table, grabbed the napkin and wadded it into a ball.

Then she tossed it at Sam, who caught it neatly in his hand.

She could hear him laughing as he followed her to the door.

Chapter Four

In three strides, Sam caught up with her. Ana kept walking, heading for her car, forcing him to move fast.

"You'd better explain yourself, Ms. Burns," he said. "You threw out a lot of loaded accusations back there."

"Kids with bruises? Defend that."

"Half our kids come in the door with bruises. They get slapped, punched, burned with cigarettes, and worse. From their bedroom windows, they see drug deals, murders, uncles shooting up, mothers prostituting themselves. Our kids are dirty, hungry and sleep-deprived. I could go on."

"But guard dogs and metal detectors?"

He stopped walking. "Fine. You want to find fault, go ahead. There's nothing I can do about it."

She swung around. "Show me the good, Sam. Open things up for me. Take me to your appointment with Jim Slater. I want to hear why he supports the center. Let me come back tomorrow and talk to your kids. Your volunteers. Give me more of your own time and Terell's. Show me Haven is a good place, a healthy environment. Prove what you're doing is valid. Give me reasons why the city shouldn't shut you down."

He let out a pent-up breath. “I don’t want you bothering our staff or our kids.”

“Afraid they might say something negative?”

“Absolutely not,” he barked. “They’re busy, that’s all. Besides, they don’t know anything about the lead paint. Jim . . . he’s on our board, and he’s a big supporter. He won’t want to talk to you about the paint problem, either. I’m visiting him today in the hope that he’ll give us a hefty pledge. If I can show the health department I’m closing in on the funding to fix the problem, they might allow me a few more weeks of grace. I need Jim’s support.”

“He’ll give it to you, Sam. I know the man—and he knows me. He won’t have a problem answering a few questions about his involvement with Haven. He’ll trust me to treat the situation fairly.”

“I don’t know.”

“Look, I have to turn in a good series. My editor is on my back, and I need this interview, Sam. Please.”

He frowned, then shrugged. “Okay, but if Jim doesn’t want to talk about Haven, you have to respect his wishes. I can’t jeopardize my relationship with him.”

“Agreed. We’ll ease into things—talk about his adoption agency, maybe take a look around the place, discuss Haven for a few minutes, and then you can ask for the money. It’s a good agenda, and he’ll be comfortable with it.” She pulled a personal digital assistant from her purse and pressed a few buttons. “Yep, Ladue. Just double-checking the address. Whew—

ritzy suburb. Must be a nice house. Jim was a building contractor before his wife died, you know. Colorado, I think."

"He told me he was in real estate."

"Could've done both."

"I don't think so."

They were heading toward her car, and Sam wondered about her change in attitude. She seemed at ease now, her accusations and suspicions no longer an issue. Had she conned him?

"If Jim got in early at Aspen or Vail," she said, "he probably made a mint."

"A real estate agent is different from a building contractor," Sam insisted. "Those are separate occupations."

"They both have to do with land and housing. You probably misheard Jim."

"I don't mishear people." He said it so forcefully that Ana flinched as she pressed the button to unlock her car. Still, the woman couldn't refrain from arguing back.

"What makes you so sure of yourself?" she challenged as she slid into the driver's seat. "You're not the reporter. You're not trained to investigate things."

"Yes, I am." He hunched into the seat beside her and immediately lifted the lever to slide it back. Even so, his knees touched the dashboard, and his head grazed the roof. "It was part of my work in the Marines. Reconnaissance. I was trained to watch people, to listen to what they say. I don't forget."

As he latched his seat belt, he realized that her baiting had caused him to let down his guard. He didn't want her to know him too well. Didn't intend to give away the private, tender places inside himself that should be known only to God. That relationship dominated his life, and Haven was the result.

He had to keep the center going, Sam mused as Ana pulled out of the parking space. Neither lead paint nor a pain-in-the-neck reporter could stop him from giving God his complete obedience. Though he had been forgiven and redeemed, he believed his work at the recreation center was a kind of penance. An earthly labor of love—not only for the children, but also for the One who had given him a reason to live.

"Reconnaissance," Ana observed, doggedly keeping to her one-track agenda. "A piece of the puzzle that is Sam Hawke. So that's why you noticed the way I set my plate and how many napkins I used."

"I see things," he said. "I'm trained to look carefully."

"You were a spy in the Marines?"

"Recon. We went in ahead of the main forces. We were there at the start of the conflict. Planning. Tracking. Scoping things out. Securing zones."

"I've always thought of reconnaissance as something to do with terrain and assessing the strength of enemy troops. Why were you trained to analyze people?"

"I'm trained. Let's leave it at that." Head turned

away, he stared out the side window. Remembering.

"So you went to Iraq in 2003? What was that like?"

"It varied. In the north, with the Kurds, it wasn't too bad. In the south it was sandy and dry. Hot."

"You traveled all over the country?"

"I got around."

"Why didn't you stay in the service? I hear the retirement plan is great."

"I needed to make a change. That's all." He rubbed his palms on his knees. "We were talking about Jim Slater. He told me he sold real estate in Colorado. Said that's how he made his money. He didn't mention he was a widower."

"I think that's what changed him." She was leaving the downtown area now, driving west toward Ladue. "Evidently he had been very focused on his construction business—"

"Real estate," he cut in.

"You interrupt a lot, you know."

"You bother me. You're irritating, and when people bug me, I let them know it."

She smiled. "Nothing I like better than irritating a smug man."

Smug. Sam shook his head, wishing he'd driven his own car. "So, Jim Slater lost his wife, and that led him to start an adoption agency in St. Louis. That's something you don't hear every day."

"Neither is a Marines recon man starting an inner-city recreation center. Why did you do it, Sam? What's the real reason?"

He was silent a moment, trying to give her an answer that would satisfy without revealing too much. "I told you already," he began. "It was Christ. He became real to me over there. It's hard to explain. You know, it was like I saw myself—who I really was. And I saw Him. I realized what He wanted."

"God wanted you to start Haven?"

"No, I mean I realized not only what He wanted from me . . . but what He wants from everyone."

She glanced at him. "What does He want?"

"Surrender."

Ana scrunched up her nose. "That's not how I see God. I think He wants our love. *Surrender* makes God sound cruel. Like He's a despot."

Sam's memory of the lines of Iraqi insurgents—trudging across the sand, hands on their heads, giving themselves up—sobered him again. "Surrender takes on new meaning to a soldier."

As Ana pulled onto the street where Jim Slater lived, she slowed the car. Sam was still gazing through the side window, oblivious to the rows of mansions with groomed lawns and expensive cars in their driveways. Seeing the windswept desert instead.

"Like turning yourself over to another commander?" she asked. "Is that what you mean by surrendering to God?"

"I mean dying. Giving up everything that you thought mattered. Letting it go. And the main thing to give up is yourself. Who you are and what you want. You have to die. Your dreams, your plans, your schedules, your family, your money, all of it. Give it away. It doesn't matter."

"How can you say that? Those things do matter."

"No. Not with real surrender. Jesus kept saying it over and over, like we were too stupid to understand—and we are. He said take up your cross and follow Me, remember? Your cross is where you die, Ana. It's the end of your life. He said whoever lays down his life for My sake will save it."

"He also said love Me more than you love your own father and mother, wife and children, brothers and sisters."

"Love is important, but surrender is the key. Jesus told a rich young ruler to give up everything and follow Him. He told His disciples that if they gave up their families and properties for His sake, they'd get a hundred times as much in return—plus they'd have eternal life."

She shrugged. "But Jesus couldn't have meant we're supposed to quit living, could He?"

"Once you get to that point," Sam explained, "to crawling-on-the-ground-naked-and-bleeding surrender — you'll do anything your Master tells you."

"And He told you to start Haven."

"Yeah." He kept his voice low, praying she would understand. "After I gave God everything, He gave most of it back. But it was all different. The same—but completely changed. He gave back my urge to dream and make plans. He gave back my scheduling and training and discipline, all those things I'd been taught. And then He told me what to do with them. They're for Him now. That's why I started Haven, and that's why I'll defend it with my life."

Ana stopped the car in the street next to Jim Slater's gated residence. Sam opened the door and stepped outside, unfolding his tall body into the sunlight. She followed, walking around to join him on the sidewalk.

"You sound sincere," she acknowledged. "But I've heard people talk that way who didn't really mean it. People can be deceptive. They may claim to honor God, but that's to cover a web of lies and dark motives. I know it, Sam. I've seen it firsthand."

"You don't trust me," he said. "I'm not asking you to."

"Thank you," she said in a low voice.

She looked up at him, her brown eyes lit with gold by the late-afternoon sun. Disturbed by this woman far more than he liked, Sam focused on the large black iron gate. He couldn't care about the pain in her eyes. Couldn't take her in his arms and rock away the hurt. Couldn't let the tenderness take over. Ana was pushy and irritating and nosy. Her writing could kill Haven. She couldn't be any part of his life, Sam realized. He had work to do, challenges to overcome, goals to accomplish.

Forcing himself to turn away, he shook the gate. Locked. He studied the two massive concrete pillars topped with decorative statues of cherubs—angelic-looking babies with wings. "Jim's expecting me this afternoon, but we hadn't set an exact time."

As he spoke, two Doberman pinschers bounded out of a wooded area to one side of the gate and began barking at the visitors. White teeth bared, they snarled and snapped and leaped at the gate, as if eager to lock their jaws on anyone who dared to invade their territory.

"I guess I won't be climbing over," Sam said.

"The intercom." Ana reached for a panel on one of the pillars. She pressed a small black button. "Someone will buzz us in."

When a voice came over the speaker, Sam gave their names. A piercing whistle drew the Dobermans away, back into the woods, as the gates swung open.

"Mind if we walk?" Sam asked.

"Not at all."

Jim Slater's long driveway was lined with wide bands of golden daylilies punctuated by pedestals on which sculpted marble children played and angels danced. Fancy place, he thought. Like a palace. Ana had known exactly what to do with the gate. He glanced at her, wondering about her background. Brownsville, Texas, she had told him. Had her father been wealthy?

"Yes, James Bond, I grew up in a gated community." She cut into his thoughts. "You don't have to analyze this one. We lived in a large house with a pool and servants and a fleet of nice cars."

"And dry cleaning."

She laughed. "Of course. Old habits die hard."

"You didn't want to hang on to that lifestyle?"

"That surrender you talked about . . . I understand some of it. I know I'm supposed to write. Money doesn't matter that much."

"Good thing. I hear journalism is no way to make a mint." He frowned as they passed a statue of a winged child playing a harp. "These are wrong, you know. Biblical angels are male adults."

Ana looked up. "What are you talking about?"

"The figurines. Remember Gabriel, Michael and all the angels who sang at Christ's birth? In Scripture, when people see angels, they're so frightened they fall on their faces, go blind or lose their ability to speak. Angels bring messages and visions. They carry swords. They rain fire on cities, destroying everyone. They're powerful, awesome beings who exist to serve God."

"There you go with your scary, military-style view of religion," she said. "I think these angels are cute. They're little cherubs."

"Cherubim guarded the Ark of the Covenant, Ana. In the Old Testament, that was God's holiest dwelling place. Cherubs are not fat babies with wings."

"Oh, there's Jim!" She lifted a hand to wave at the distinguished-looking home owner waiting at his front door. Sam thought he saw the trace of a frown cross their host's face, but it disappeared as he and Ana began talking.

"I hope you don't mind that I came with Sam," Ana said after the two had exchanged small talk about their church. "I'm writing an article on Haven's lead paint problem, and it occurred to me that this would be a great opportunity for both of us to talk to you."

"You want to interview me?" He glanced at Sam. "Ana, I don't think we should bring Haven's problems to light in the newspaper."

"Too late," Sam said, seeing his hopes of a pledge fading before his eyes. "She's been hounding us."

"You know me," Ana said with a laugh. "Come on, Jim, I only need a quote or two."

"I don't see that I could contribute anything. Sam can tell you about the paint issue."

"Wait a second." Ana held up a hand to stop the conversation. Her mouth fell open, as she studied the facade of the brick mansion. "Oh, my goodness, I can't believe this your home, Jim. It's just now sinking in. This is beautiful."

"Thank you," Jim said, his focus following hers. "I'm proud of the place myself. It's rather large, but I needed space for the children."

"So, your adoption agency is here, too?"

"I run the business out of my home. I have a network of outstanding foster parents who look after our children until the adoptions are finalized. But our little ones are in and out a lot, of course."

Ana stepped up onto the stone entryway just outside the front door, and Sam followed with grudging admiration. The woman was incredible. She could con her way into anything she wanted.

"Your marble floor is amazing," she was saying as she stepped toward the foyer. "When I was a teenager, we moved into a large house in Brownsville—did I tell you about it that Sunday when we worked in the church nursery together? I thought our place was wonderful, but it couldn't compare to this."

As Jim Slater moved back to allow Ana inside, Sam's deeply ingrained reconnaissance training led him to scan the man quickly, memorizing details. Today Jim wore the kind of polo shirt Sam had seen him in often—this one in peach and blue horizontal stripes. Creased gray slacks and leather sandals completed his outfit. Every hair had been carefully combed into place, his jaw clean-shaven, and his eyebrows trimmed.

As he followed the older man into the house, Sam spoke up. "Thanks, Jim. I appreciate your time."

Jim glanced at him in resignation. "I'd like to welcome you both to the headquarters of Young Blessings Adoption Services."

"It's great," Sam said, genuinely impressed.

"When I moved to St. Louis, this was the best house I could find for the money. It needed a lot of work when I bought it, but remodeling is a hobby of mine."

"You once owned a construction company, didn't you?" Ana asked.

"That's right. In Aspen."

She shot Sam a look of victory. "Thought so."

"Did you do your own decorating?" Sam asked, brushing past her to examine a wall lined with oil paintings.

"I brought most of the furnishings from Colorado."

"Sam thinks your cherubs ought to be holding flaming swords," Ana confided.

"A little frightening, don't you think?" Jim led them down a short hallway and into a large, carpeted sitting room. "My wife loved angels, God bless her. She couldn't get enough. We had glass display cases full of them. I brought the garden statues with me when I moved here. Couldn't bear to part with everything."

"Of course not. That must have been difficult for you. Losing your wife and then moving so far away."

Ana's voice was soft and sympathetic. Sam felt bad for criticizing the statues. Poor guy must be lonely in this huge house surrounded by reminders of his wife.

"Jim, would you be willing to give us a tour?" Ana was asking. "I've considered adopting a child someday. Even though research says kids do better with two parents, I think being a single mom would be all right. I'd love to see your offices."

"I would, too," Sam said. "You've been a great support to Haven, Jim, and I'd like to learn about your ministry."

"Well, I . . . I had planned to chat in the living room." He rubbed his hands together for a moment. "I actually have a couple of children here at the moment. They're in the playroom, which is next to my office. You see, Young Blessings provides respite care for our foster parents. Once a week or so, kids can come here for a couple of hours so their caregivers have time to tend to personal business—even see a movie or go out to eat. Looking after these children can be stressful. Most of our adoptees come from orphanages in South America, and they've been through a lot. I don't like to surprise them with unexpected visitors."

"Oh, but it would mean a lot to me, Jim." Ana's brown eyes pleaded. "We don't have to disturb the children."

"I suppose that's right."

"Great," Ana said, taking a notebook from her purse. "Before we take the tour, though—how did you get the idea to start an adoption agency?"

As Jim told her about a mission trip to the Caribbean and the orphans he had seen there, Sam studied a marble figurine on a table near the door—a sweet little girl seated on a tree stump, her hands on her knees and a flower stem threaded through her fingers.

"No wings," he commented, turning to face Jim.

The man shrugged. "Not all of them are angels."

"Let's see your offices." Ana had finished quizzing Jim for the moment, and she was eager to move on. "Where are the two in the playroom from? Somewhere in Latin America?"

"Honduras." Jim gestured toward a door at the far end of the parlor. As they walked down a hallway, Jim explained to Ana how hard it was to cut through the red tape in the foreign countries where he found children in need of adoption. His story would make a terrific feature article, Ana realized, scribbling notes as she walked. The drama alone was enough to draw readers, and the sympathy factor would be huge.

She sensed Jim Slater was a man of great integrity. It must take an enormous amount of determination and dedication to surmount the legal obstacles to local and international adoptions. The fact that he was willing to take on such a challenge on behalf of needy children bore testimony to the genuine quality of his Christian faith.

Sam was cut from a similar cloth. The type who put his words into action. No doubt he had climbed countless barriers in his effort to navigate the minefield of St. Louis city and county building ordinances. Though he annoyed her at every turn—even now he was lagging behind in the hall, examining pictures and peeking through doors—she couldn't deny that Haven appeared to be powerful evidence of Sam's commitment to obey God.

"Here's our playroom." Jim lowered his voice as they approached a pair of closed doors in the hallway. He ushered Ana and Sam into a small room furnished with four blue velvet-upholstered chairs. A large window on one wall, Ana realized, was actually a one-way mirror.

"This is where I bring clients seeking adoption," Jim murmured, motioning his guests to be seated. "I like to let them have a look at the children before the initial meeting, just in case."

"In case of what?" Ana asked, taking one of the chairs. "I'd think the parents would be dying to meet their new child."

Sam chose to stand, taking a position behind her left shoulder. Through the silvered glass, Ana could see two young girls watching television in the adjoining room. They appeared to be about eight and ten years old, with black hair and bronze skin. One wore bright pink shorts and a matching top. The other had on similar play clothes, only hers were purple. The outfits looked new. Both girls had on spotless white sneakers.

Around the room hung shelves lined with books and toys of every kind imaginable. Plastic slides, playhouses, dolls, trucks, and balls in all shades of the rainbow lay scattered across the soft gray carpet. Despite all this, the girls sat cross-legged with their backs to the window and stared at a large, flat TV screen where cartoon characters zipped around and bopped each other on the head.

"Our adoptive parents have been provided with photographs, of course," Jim informed Ana. "But we've learned—much to our dismay—that sometimes the child isn't exactly what they were wanting."

"Really?"

"It's something I take a lot of care with—making perfect matches. We want our clients to be happy."

"So the children will be happy."

"Well, of course." He leaned toward the mirror. "These two haven't been in the States long, and they don't understand English. Still, their foster parents have had little trouble communicating. We've found that cartoons seem to be a universal language."

"Ana knows Spanish," Sam spoke up.

"That's right," she confirmed. "Hey, Jim, I could talk to the girls for you. I'd be happy to interpret."

"Thank you, but as I said, I try not to disturb them." Jim turned to Sam. "This is my own version of Haven. It's a place where children can come and feel safe. These two will move in with their adoptive parents in a couple of days. In addition to life in an orphanage, they've been through quite an ordeal—departure from their country of origin, a long trip by airplane, adjustment to foster parents. When they're here for a visit, I keep things very quiet."

"Makes sense to me," Ana said.

Sam nodded. "But I'd think they might get attached to this playroom."

"It's certainly a wonderful area," Ana agreed. "I've never seen so many toys."

"Nothing but the best for our little ones." Jim smiled as he observed the girls. "I collect toys, you know, Ana. Sometime you'll have to come over for a longer visit, and I'll take you down to the basement where I keep my collection. The toy hobby started with my own kids—the wife and I bought baby dolls and such for our daughters. Linda said I enjoyed indulging the girls because I grew up with so few playthings of my own. Anyway, I continued to purchase toys even after our three were grown and gone."

"Do you collect anything in particular?" Ana asked.

"Dolls, as a matter of fact—and Sam, don't give me that look. It's not as odd as it sounds. It's quite a lucrative pastime, and there are a number of male collectors in the field. My focus is the Mattel company, and the Chatty Cathy in particular. I've got Chatty Cathy dolls from the 1959 unpatented original to versions produced throughout the sixties. And that's not to mention the Chatty Cathy games, dress patterns, accessories, outfits, shoes, the whole nine yards."

"I think my mother still has her old Chatty Cathy," Ana said, recalling the doll's matted blond hair and missing teeth. "I used to play with her sometimes. By then, though, you couldn't understand the words when she talked."

"That's the problem with Chatty Cathy. The voice box malfunctions too easily. But I own quite a few that still work—say the original phrases and all that. I can see Sam is skeptical of my hobby."

"I've heard of adults collecting Matchbox cars and Happy Meal toys." He paused. "You said you have three children?"

"Daughters, yes. We adopted them. Linda and I." He pulled out his wallet and flipped it open to photographs of the dark-haired children, each in pigtails, ribbons and lacy dresses. "Here they are. Michelle, Penny and Jill."

Ana craned to see. "So, that's another reason you became interested in adoption?"

"Another reason?"

"Other than that trip you went on. The one where you first saw the orphans."

"Oh, exactly. Yes, Linda and I had adopted these three, and then on my trip I learned there were many children available in the poorer countries, particularly Central and South America. I thought, well, why not facilitate the process for others?"

"It must have been hard to give up your real estate business," Sam said.

"To some degree."

"Jim was in construction," Ana spoke up, unable to disguise the annoyance in her voice. Why did Sam have to be so obstinate about this?

"Which was it again?" Sam laid his hand on her chair. "You once told me you'd sold land."

"Did I now?" Jim chuckled. "Well, actually I did a little of both. If I found a good lot for a fair price, I snapped it up, built a spec house on it and sold it. I even developed a small subdivision. We named it Loma Linda, after my wife."

"That's so sweet," Ana said.

"Your work in Colorado must have been profitable."

"Much of the time." Jim set his hands on his knees and stood. "Well, you two didn't come here to listen to my life story. Let's pop into my office for a quick look-see, and then we'll go back to the front room and talk business. I believe our agenda is Haven's lead paint problem."

As they left the room, Ana took a last look at the two little girls. They were watching Mickey Mouse now, and holding hands.

Chapter Five

The house gave Sam the creeps, and he wasn't sure why. A far cry from the run-down Wyoming mobile home where he had grown up with his father and younger brothers, Jim Slater's Ladue mansion nevertheless impressed him more as a hotel than as a home. Sam's own current living situation in a couple of rooms above Haven couldn't be further from this luxury and extravagance, but he preferred it.

Everything in Jim's place was perfect, no doubt about that. The man must have a household staff. The gray carpets had been vacuumed recently—Sam could tell by the absence of footprints marring the groomed surface. The ornate gilt picture frames were dust free. Every lightbulb in every chandelier worked. Curtains matched sofas and pillows. Books lined shelves. Candlewicks had never been lit. Pristine.

Maybe it was the smell that bothered him. Sam followed Ana and Jim around a corner and down another hall, lagging a little behind as was his custom in a new place. He often had trouble identifying scents, but this one was obvious. Roses. Some kind of potpourri, no doubt, or a plug-in room deodorizer. Sam never thought of things like that—as evidenced by the pile of mildewed towels in the front office at Haven.

He knew he had no right to find fault with Jim for the way his house smelled. The man obviously cared about children. After all, he had started an adoption agency, he regularly worked in the church nursery and his generous gifts had covered the entire cost of new bathroom tile at Haven. If Jim wanted to fill his house with the scent of roses, why should Sam begrudge him? Still, the fragrance made him a little queasy.

As they neared the sitting room, Ana asked Jim how he would feel about her writing a feature article on his adoption agency. "It would be great PR for you," she said. "Think how much attention it would draw to the wonderful things you're doing for children."

"I'm sorry, Ana, but it's against my policy to comment on the agency," he told her. "I don't promote my work in any public venue. It's all done through word of mouth."

"But you might find more local parents looking to adopt. It would make such a heartwarming story, Jim. The international aspect is fascinating, and the way your wife and three daughters inspired you would make great reading."

"Afraid not. I have more clients than I can handle. I'm not interested in any publicity." His voice softened. "Listen, Ana, I don't mean to be difficult. I simply try to follow biblical teaching about doing things for the glory of God and not for the honor of men."

Without waiting for her response, he brushed past her and headed for the living room. Ana hurried behind, her long legs eating up the carpet and her voice echoing along the cherrywood paneled corridor. She hadn't switched gears, Sam noted. Ana still pressed for a feature article, though now she suggested it could combine both the adoption agency and Jim's support of the recreation center. Sam dawdled, admiring both the woman's aggressive style and Jim's stubborn adherence to his rules. The three of them made quite a trio.

As Sam followed the other two, he reflected on the little girls in the playroom. Peering through a one-way mirror at the children had reminded Sam of gazing into an aquarium in a pet shop. He had always felt sorry for the fish as they swam in circles, taken from their natural habitat and oblivious to the future that awaited them. Personal experience told him fish usually lasted a few days and then ended their short lives floating belly-up at the top of their tank. Thank God, the children who were placed in adoptive homes by Young Blessings could look forward to a far better destiny.

Though he knew Jim meant well with the adoption agency's pristine, silent environment, Sam preferred messy, smelly, loud Haven. Even a child as withdrawn as Flora took some comfort in the bouncing balls and screeching whistles that resounded through the building. Or would she be happier watching cartoons in Jim Slater's fishbowl?

Ana had finally given up the fight to draw a lengthy interview out of Jim. Sam could see it in her posture as he entered the living room. He wasn't surprised that Jim had been reluctant to talk—only that Ana had actually accepted defeat. Nice try, Miss Burns, Sam thought. I just hope your pushiness hasn't jeopardized Haven's future.

She folded down onto a sofa now, looking like an umbrella closing up after a rain, useless and slightly bedraggled. He felt a little sorry for her, but it was time to focus on the business at hand.

"Lead paint," he began, taking the chair across from Jim. "Seems like that's all I'm hearing these days. I'm on the phone constantly, making visits, talking to everyone I can. Frankly, since I spoke to you the other day, Jim, I haven't been able to drum up much support."

"How much will it cost to take care of the problem?" Jim asked. "Do you have any figures for me?"

Ana began scribbling again, her face brightening a little.

"We're looking at twenty thousand, minimum."

Jim whistled. "That much would have built a nice fence and gotten you started on your outdoor recreation area, wouldn't it?"

"Sure would. Let me tell you, I'd love to spend the money that way. But we have no choice except to follow government regulations on the paint removal if we intend to let children under age six into the building—and we do. Running an adoption agency, you know how important it is to start kids off on the right foot as early as possible. In fact, Terell and I have already put some great activities in place for the preschool age group. Finger-painting, crocheting, dance and music, tools—my volunteers are outstanding."

"I've seen them at work," Jim said. "I couldn't agree more."

Sam nodded, heartened. "There are several areas in the building where we can legally paint over the old walls. But most of the original paint is crumbling and peeling. To scrape that off requires professionals with specialized equipment. We looked into covering it up—new wallboard, dropped ceilings, all that. Any direction we went, we came up with similar figures. Even with our volunteers providing labor, we can't bring down the cost."

"How much of the twenty thousand have you found, Sam?"

"A church gave us two. The owner of a dry cleaning business in the area came up with another thousand."

"Dry cleaning?" Ana put in.

Sam shot her a look. "Yes, dry cleaning. And Granny gave us a hundred dollars."

"Who's Granny?" Jim asked.

"She's an elderly woman who teaches the crochet class at Haven," he explained. "Evidently, she has a little something put away. She comes up with a donation for us every now and then. We've tried to encourage her to use it on herself—she needs a hearing aid and new glasses. But she says it's the Lord's money, and she won't touch it."

"So, thirty-one hundred dollars. And you need twenty thousand?"

"I have nearly two weeks left to work on it before the county steps in. I need to show them that I've got the money. Then they'll give us more time to clean the rooms and put in new walls. I'm not giving up."

"I didn't think so. Well, you can put me down for five thousand, Sam. It's the best I can do right now."

"Five thousand? That's great, Jim, thank you."

"You're still a long way off, my friend."

"Yeah, but that puts us over eight thousand—almost halfway. We're in firing range." He got to his feet and grabbed Jim's hand. "Thank you, sir. I promise you, that money will make an enormous difference in the lives of my kids."

"That's all the thanks I need. I'll bring you a check in a few days." Jim stood. "Ana, will I see you in church Sunday?"

"Sure. And I'd like to take a look at your toy collection someday."

"Of course. We'll schedule a lunch one day when there aren't any children visiting."

"Thanks again, Jim." Sam pumped his hand another time. "You've encouraged me."

As Jim shut the door behind them, Sam slung his arm around Ana's shoulders and gave her a squeeze. "Five thousand bucks! Did you hear that? Terell's gonna freak!"

Ana's back stiffened at his embrace, but she continued walking beside him down the deeply shadowed driveway. "You need a lot more."

"I'll get it."

"Always so optimistic?"

"God doesn't give you a job and then fail to deliver

the tools. One way or another, that lead paint is *gone.*"

"I'm happy for you."

He glanced at her. "What's wrong? Upset Jim wouldn't give you a good interview?"

"I got some quotes." She fell silent again, her head down. Then she shrugged his arm off her shoulders. "It's those poor little girls."

"What about them?"

"They looked so small. So alone."

"Alone? They had more toys than they could know what to do with."

She sighed as they stepped through the steel gate that guarded Slater's property. "Do you think the girls understand what's happening to them?" Ana pressed a button on her key ring, and the doors to her car unlocked. "I wish Jim would have let me talk to them in Spanish. I'd have told them everything is going to be okay, and that they're going to get new parents who will love them and take care of them. Are they sisters, do you suppose? And will they go to the same home? It bothers me."

"I'll tell you what gets me. Jim's secret window for adoptive parents. Like they're picking out a puppy."

"His heart is in the right place, though." Her voice was soft as she nursed the car through the evening traffic.

"True. Sounds like he runs a gauntlet every time he brings kids to the States."

"He's a wonderful man," she said.

"And how 'bout that Chatty Cathy collection?"

Ana laughed as she pulled into a parking space near Haven. "Give poor Jim a break. He's lonely. He lost his wife, and his daughters are grown and gone. Let him collect dolls if he wants to."

"I'd feel better if he collected Tonka trucks."

"Jim's obviously a shrewd businessman. You don't live in Ladue unless you know how to manage money. I have no doubt that dolls are a better investment than toy trucks."

Sam let his focus rest on Ana as she put the car in Park. He knew their time together was over, and he needed to get back and help Terell shut down the center. But he couldn't deny how good it felt to be near a woman again. And not just any woman.

Ana Burns made a great sparring partner. Sam found her ideas interesting and her personality more than a little intriguing. He hadn't had time for a relationship when he was in the Marines, nor had he made time for one since. Now—in the midst of his battle to keep Haven open—he couldn't let himself think in that direction.

"Sam, may I come back and interview the kids at Haven?" Ana asked. The streetlight bronzed her skin and lit her brown eyes with a golden glow. "I'd like to get some quotes from your volunteers, too. It would round out my series."

"I'm not comfortable with this, Ana. You know that. Neither was Jim."

"Please, Sam. Let me come back to the center.

Maybe I can get more information out of Flora. If she starts to feel comfortable, you might get her to join in the activities."

"Ana, I appreciate your concern for Flora and your interest in Haven," he said. "But I don't want the center by name in the newspaper. The less you say about us the better."

Her lips tightened. "You don't trust me to write a positive story. You're afraid you'll lose your donations, aren't you? For you, this is all about money."

"*Money?* What do you think Haven is, woman? It's nothing like Jim Slater's grand palace, that's for sure. You didn't have any problem praising him to high heaven, but you accuse me of money-grubbing?" Angry now, he opened the car door. "I don't have spare cash to spend on fat, winged babies and doll collections. I need to keep my donors happy if I want Haven's doors to stay open. And that means *no* newspaper articles."

"You don't even know what I'm going to write. Give me a little credit. I could slant this story in your favor. Trust me, Sam."

"Trust a woman who accuses me of being in this for the money?" He climbed out of the car and slammed the door. "You want to know what I'm all about, Ana? Open your eyes. I'm here for these kids."

As he strode down the sidewalk, Ana's car kept pace. "I can come back to Haven if I want," she called out to him. "I have the right to talk to anyone, Sam."

"No, you don't," he shouted back. "Not at Haven.

It's my operation, and you're not welcome."

As her tires squealed down the street, Sam stepped up to the metal detector.

"Hoo-wee," Raydell said, shaking his head as he eyed the vanishing car. "You got woman problems. Big-time."

"Rod Davidson . . . how are you this morning, my friend?"

"Well, what can I tell you? Murders, suicides, drive-by shootings—the usual."

He chuckled at the Post-Dispatch *publisher's greeting. "I don't know how you do it day in and day out."*

"It never gets old. Keeps the adrenaline pumping anyway." Davidson sounded cheerful. "Listen, I've got a meeting with my editorial board in a few minutes. What can I do for you today?"

"I won't keep you long. I'm calling in reference to Haven. One of your reporters, a young woman by the name of Ana Burns, is proposing to write a piece on the recreation center's lead paint problem. It's a serious issue, certainly, and I can understand why the newspaper considers it worthy of coverage."

"You've got that right. Lead levels in St. Louis's children are at an all-time high. We published some big stories on the defunct lead plant in Herculaneum—the contaminated dust that kids were breathing. Now we're learning the lead abatement crews here in the city aren't making more than a dent

in ridding houses and apartments of the old paint. And that's not to mention the public buildings that are still contaminated."

"I guess that's where Haven comes in. Obviously we're all doing our best to deal with the problem. But this reporter of yours isn't going to make things easier. If the paper publicizes the center's troubles, fund-raising is only going to get harder." He fell silent for a moment, letting his words sink in. "Why don't you call her off, Rod? Tell her to focus on the situation in a more generalized way. You don't need to go throwing names around."

The publisher considered the request. "I hear you, of course. But the public has the right to know what's happening in the city. I don't like to weigh in against an issue that one of my editors feels is important enough to investigate."

"But think of Haven. Think of the future of all those children if this story turns away potential donors. If you let this Burns woman print the problems, it could shut the center's doors forever."

"I certainly wouldn't want that to happen. I'm sure you know that. Tell you what. I'll talk to Carl Webster about the situation. He's the editor in charge here."

"Thanks, Rod. I admire your courage. I know you'll do the right thing."

As he said goodbye and pressed the button to shut down his phone, a breeze ruffled the curtain near his chair. Despite everything he had done to calm himself, the motion of the fabric startled him. He knew it was only wind, but he leaped to his feet and checked behind the drape anyway. Satisfying himself of his safety, he let out a breath as he pulled the window shut and locked it.

This couldn't go on much longer. Stu had failed to call back and was not returning his voice mails. No doubt the weasel had scampered off with his tail between his legs. Expected, of course.

As usual, he would face things on his own. He doubted Rod Davidson would help out, either. The publisher's own agenda came first. Printing scandals, selling papers, making money—never mind how it might harm others.

And that nosy Ana Burns. He couldn't believe how easily she had manipulated everything. If Davidson didn't put a stop to her, there would be no choice but to step in and take care of her himself. Fortunately, he had connections. Not friends, of course, but people—acquaintances—who could make things happen to a single young woman, working downtown, walking the city's streets.

From his earliest memories, he had known he was alone. The things he had suffered. The thoughts that plagued him. No one cared. Once he had told his best friend, Stevie, how he was feeling—shared his deepest emotions, his most troubling experiences, his inmost fantasies and fears. And from that moment on, Stevie had ignored him. Turned away. Abandoned him. Worse than putting him down or making fun of him, Stevie had simply pretended that his once-dearest friend no longer existed.

Though unbearably painful, the experience had been useful. Now he knew that no one could really understand him. They thought he was a deviant, a "sicko." Well, they were wrong. What he did wasn't perverse or strange—it was simply who he was. He was created this way, a unique and special human being—and how could anyone say that was wrong?

He never hurt anyone. His so-called "victims," as the prison therapists had put it, weren't bothered by what he did. They welcomed it. In a way, he was helping them, awakening them, and teaching them things they would need to know later in life. It wasn't as though he got that much out of his "crime" anyway. His own pleasure lasted just a short time, and then he was forced to spend weeks preparing for it all over again.

The trouble was that no one was as smart as he. People were fools. They imagined their sex offender lists would deter him. How naive. He had simply left the state and changed his identity. Easy enough. He had contacts everywhere. His clients were respectable businessmen who worked in high-level positions. They had made his transition flawless. The authorities had no idea how effortless it was to elude them. Just thinking of this, he felt his anger grow. Idiots! He grabbed the curtain and gave it a jerk. He had intended to close it, but the fabric tore loose from the pins that held the pleats to the rod.

There! he thought, staring up at the dangling drape.

That was exactly the kind of thing that infuriated him! Carelessness. Stupidity. People didn't do things the right way. Someone had failed to properly secure the curtain, just as Stu had failed to set up the safeguards.

Sinking down onto the floor, he held his head in his hands. He thought he was going to vomit.

"Why not, Carl?" Ana set her palms on the city editor's desk and leaned across it. She could hardly believe it was already Thursday, and she had only six workdays left to complete her assignment. Most of the previous afternoon had been eaten up with her fruitless visits to Haven and Jim Slater's house. Though she had interviewed health workers, day care supervisors, a variety of public agencies, church youth ministers and the operators of two city recreation centers, the series was not coming together well.

She had worked hard on the stories, trying one angle and then another. But as the hours passed, Ana only grew more convinced that the *children*—and not the lead paint—needed to be the focus of the series. More important, she felt certain that something was going on behind the scenes at Haven.

Her news nose was rarely wrong, and it was telling her that she was onto a very smelly trail. A frightened child hiding in a corner, a little girl with a fresh bruise on her cheek, guard dogs and a man too free with his affection—Terell Roberts stood out like a blinking beacon on a dark night.

How could Ana ignore an investigation with such

news value? Worse, how could she abandon the victims of a possible predator? Despite her trepidation about confronting and pushing Carl Webster—aware the editor could very well fire her and send her back to Brownsville—Ana knew she could not rest if she didn't at least try.

"It's the children," she told him. "They should be the center of attention in these articles."

Carl rubbed his eyes. "Lead paint, Ana," he said wearily. "That's your story. Contaminated paint."

"Who cares about paint? You said it yourself—*children* draw readers. This series has everything, don't you see? The potential for gripping photos. Sidebars on individual victims of lead paint poisoning—I have an interview set up at Barnes Hospital tomorrow morning. It'll be compelling, Carl. Just give me another week, and I'll write a package of stories guaranteed to tug on readers' hearts."

"Stories that would make strong contest entries. Isn't that what you mean, Ana? You're still trying to win awards when what I want is good, solid coverage of an issue affecting this city."

She straightened. "Fine, if all you want is paint, that's what I'll give you. But then no one will ever learn about Tenisha, who has cerebral palsy and is playing basketball for the first time in her life. Or Granny, the elderly deaf woman who teaches Gerald and the other little boys how to crochet. Or Flora, who came here from . . . from who knows where and can't speak English and hides in a corner. And that's just Haven."

She grabbed a pile of press releases from his desk and straightened them as she raced on. "I've got great leads on children in home-based day cares—kids whose dads were murdered in drive-by shootings, kids whose mothers are thirteen years old. And those church basements you mentioned? Carl, there's a group of grandmothers sitting day after day in a moldy basement with crumbling paint—and they're rocking babies, reading to babies, singing old hymns—"

"Okay, okay." He held up a hand. "You've made your point. But there's no time for that. Besides, it's out of the realm of what we're looking for. I've told you what I want, and I see no reason to change it."

"Carl, please. I'm all over this story. Just give me another week."

He sighed and rolled his chair back from the desk. "You drive me crazy, Ana. And quit organizing my desk every time you come into my office." He grabbed the papers from her hand and tossed them down.

"Yes, sir, but—"

"Goodbye, Ana." He stood. "We've both got work to do."

Her mouth dry, Ana swung back through the door and returned to her desk. Great. She had failed to win Carl to her point of view about the lead paint series. Now she would have no choice but to make the health department and its regulations the central theme of the series.

Sure, she could sprinkle in a few examples of local

agencies in trouble. But the real children would take a backseat to droning quotes by politicians and physicians. And any hope of uncovering a scandal behind the scenes at Haven must go right down the drain, along with the dream that her writing could ever make a difference in this world.

Dropping onto her chair, Ana once again reflected on Sam Hawke and his military-style activities center. His dedication to the place appeared genuine. His long-term friendship with Terell Roberts gave a seemingly healthy impetus to the program. But something nagged at her. What lay behind that relationship? Why had two bright young men forsaken careers and financial security for a group of needy children whose problems were mind-boggling?

Sam said his Christian faith had motivated him. But was that really it? She sat staring at her computer screen, trying to absorb what he'd said, wanting to believe Haven was all it seemed, aching to trust that Sam was telling her the truth—yet skeptical all the same.

Ana's experience with God had been different in so many ways. And yet, in essence, it was similar. She had wanted to die. And He had saved her. She trusted God and followed His guidance—at least she tried to. But was her passion for her life's work actually self-driven, while Sam's was God-driven?

Did they even believe in the same God? Why was her image of Him steeped in love while Sam's was angry, hostile, a commander of forces armed for battle? Suddenly she wasn't sure she knew God's true nature or was even following Him.

Ana thought of the volunteers she had met in the past week. Young Caleb—why had the teenager relinquished a carefree summer to try to repair an ancient computer? How did an old woman who could hardly hear benefit from teaching crochet to a bunch of rowdy kids? Those grandmothers in the church basement? What did they get out of rocking babies day after day? Was God behind all this? Or was something else motivating these people?

Ana felt certain that her articles needed to focus on more than the lead paint. Her writing had to capture the plight of the children who might accidentally ingest it. But she also sensed a need to write about the adults who chose to work in these run-down old buildings, helping youngsters who probably never would utter a word of thanks. Dare she defy Carl and tell the stories her way?

The thought of the consequences that would surely follow made Ana's stomach clench. As she absently cleaned up her desk, she reflected on the Texas home in which she had spent her teenage years and the latest phone call from her parents. They had sounded so forlorn, the sadness and blame echoing behind their words.

Ana took the letters and memos that had collected in her in-box and sorted through them quickly, tossing most into the trash. As she scanned the file of lead paint articles that the archives librarian had laid on her desk, tears sprang to her eyes. During that brief time as a reporter for the *Brownsville Herald*, she had made such huge errors. She had failed. Failed her parents . . . her sister . . . herself. Her brilliant series about drug traffic in the city won first place for investigative writing from the Texas Press Association. Despite what others thought, the award had been meaningless to Ana.

Swallowing the lump in her throat, she opened the desk drawer and lifted her file of current assignments. She picked up the small framed picture and gazed at her family. The smiled into the camera, so pleased with themselves and their two lovely little girls. And the children—missing teeth, countless freckles, gangly legs—forced hollow grins to cover the pain they could tell no one but each other.

As Ana gazed into the eyes of the child she had been, another child's eyes stared back at her. Flora. They shared the same silent, haunted terror. The dark secrets. The unspoken fear.

Do you know La Ceiba? The words bubbled up inside Ana's head, sounding like tiny echoes, barely audible.

La Ceiba. La Ceiba.

Propelled by a sudden need, Ana switched on her computer and clicked open an Internet search engine. She typed in the name of the silk-cotton tree that grew in Brownsville, then she chewed her thumbnail and waited for the screen to fill with information.

Hunching over, she scanned the entries. La Ceiba was a popular tag, it seemed. Ana found several hotels and spas in Mexico, a lodge in Costa Rica and a luxury resort on the Amazon, all named after the tropical tree. Had Flora's parents worked at one of these hotels before coming to the United States?

As Ana stared at the computer screen, her confusion only grew. Flora's mention of La Ceiba could mean any number of things. A hotel, a condominium, a town, a tree. It could mean a place in Mexico, Costa Rica, Puerto Rico, Honduras, or on the lengthy course of the Amazon River.

Frustrated, she turned over the information in her mind. Had little Flora, who hid in the dark corner of a downtown St. Louis activity center, come all the way to St. Louis from Central America? But that region was half a continent away.

Mexico seemed the most likely place the child might have lived. Ana found she could sympathize with those who crossed the border, as her own mother had done so many years ago. Young Guadalupe had been carried across the Rio Grande on the back of a *burro*—a man who helped people enter the United States illegally. Guadalupe's father had worked long hours in a pants factory in Brownsville, eventually earning U.S. citizenship for himself and his family. And his daughter had grown up to fall in love with the eventual CEO of that very company. Bob and Guadalupe Burns's marriage had created the perfect melting pot American family. And their daughter, Ana, felt profound gratitude for what they had provided. She deeply loved her parents, despite her reluctance to return home to them.

Why had Flora said the name La Ceiba? Or had Ana misunderstood the child's softly spoken words? Maybe Flora really had been speaking of the silk-cotton tree. What if Flora had asked Ana about the ceiba in hopes that she might find such a tree here in St. Louis?

Heart aching, Ana pushed away from her desk. How could she ignore the fear in Flora's brown eyes? How could she blindly turn away from her suspicions about Terell Roberts and his behavior at Haven? Even if her forebodings proved unfounded, could she write about lead paint without focusing on the children who would suffer its consequences?

Ana thought of Carl Webster's threat. Do it his way, or he had ten other reporters eager to take her place. Focus on the paint and ignore the children, or get out. Get out . . . go back to the home she had fled, the parents who blamed her, and the cottage . . . the cottage where she had failed to protect her sister. Go back to the reality of the emptiness in her life. Face the hopeless darkness.

Ana hovered on the cusp for a moment—craving escape, clinging to security, yet hearing the unspoken cries from the children who beckoned for her help. Then she understood, because her dead sister's voice cried loudest of all. *Save us, Ana, save us.* And she would.

Rising from her desk, she shouldered her purse and started for the door to the stairs. This evening's run would do her a world of good.

Chapter Six

Ethelou Childers crossed her arms and stared at Sam through half-lidded eyes. He realized this was not a good sign.

Lulu, as the kids called her, knew the city of St. Louis as well as she knew an aria from *La Bohème.* She could sing jazz and opera, and she could rap alongside the toughest of the boys. She taught tap and ballet, and she could back a sassy teenage girl into a corner and hammer her into shape with a few choice words. Lulu's straightened black hair was swept up into a tight dance mistress's chignon, while her dark, muscular biceps sported muted blue tattoos. No one messed with Lulu.

"What's this reporter really after?" she snapped, her full lips pursing into a sneer. "She sounds like trouble to me, honey."

At the regular Thursday night meeting of staff and volunteers, Sam had decided it was time to update everyone on the many uphill battles the center was facing. Bathroom repairs had fallen behind schedule. Someone had gotten a knife past the metal detector when another boy had substituted for Raydell Watson at the front door. A gang had sprayed graffiti on an outside wall that volunteers had just plastered. And then there was Ana Burns.

"Miss Burns says she wants to write about our lead paint situation," Sam replied. The meeting had not gone well thus far, and the matter of Haven's problems being splashed across the *Post-Dispatch* only added to the tension in the group. "I gave her a short interview, and she talked to one of our donors. So I'm hoping that'll take care of it. But I can't guarantee what she's going to write about us."

"She'll be back here before she writes anything," Raydell Watson predicted. Though paid only a token wage, the teen attended every meeting and participated as though he were a full-time staff member at the center. "She ain't gonna drop it. I know her kind."

"Yeah," Terell said. "She told me the editor assigned her a whole series of articles to write. Like a couple weeks' worth, or something. She'll be back."

Sam scowled down at his clipboard. "Well, nobody better talk to her without seeing me first. We've got to minimize the potential damage from this."

"Lead paint," Ethelou scoffed. "Who wants to read about that?"

"Head pain?" Granny looked up from the mound of pink crochet work on her lap and blinked behind her thick-lensed glasses. "I think I've got some aspirin here in my purse, Ethelou. Just you hold on a minute."

As she started to dig through an enormous macramé bag, Terell laid a hand on the old woman's arm. He leaned across to explain, but Ethelou stopped him.

"It's okay, honey, I've got myself a royal headache over all this nonsense anyhow." She turned on Sam. "Look here, honey. I need a private room to teach my dance classes. I cannot and I will not do them outside on that parking lot. The kids'll burn up out on that pavement, not to mention me. You just give us a bucket of paint, and we'll slop it on ourselves."

"That's the problem, Ethelou," Sam said. "Most of these walls are going to have to be repaired by a professional lead paint abatement company. And we don't have the money to pay for it."

"Well, if we had paint, we could do some of the rooms ourselves." A strapping young man spoke around the last bite of a doughnut he had found in the center's kitchen. "The ones that don't have to be scraped, anyhow."

Billy had come to Haven from New Mexico with his church youth group. The young people were the same age as many of the kids who used the center. Billy, his friend Caleb and the other volunteers worked many hours each day in the building. It pained Sam to think that if he couldn't resolve the lead paint issue soon, all their labor might be in vain.

"We've had a little money donated already," Sam assured the group, with a wink at Granny. "And the other day, Jim Slater pledged five thousand from his adoption agency."

"But you said we only got two weeks to take care of this problem," Raydell said. "Me, I got a bad feeling about it. I think we oughta do something."

"Do what, Raydell?" Sam asked. "What would you suggest?"

The teen shrugged, and gave his dreadlocks a shake.

"Just let her know not to mess with us. We ain't gotta take nothin' off of nobody."

"Yeah, we do. The health department, anyway. We can't get around them. The paint problem has to be fixed, or they'll shut us down. And if Miss Burns wants to write about us, we can't stop her. As she reminded me, it's a free press, and she can put anything she wants in her article."

"That stinks," Raydell snapped. "Who does she think she is anyhow? She ain't nothin'. I'll show her."

Sam heard this kind of bluster at the center so often, he had learned to turn a deaf ear to it. Instead, he focused on the determined woman who sat across from him. "Lulu, you've fought some battles in the past. How did you manage?"

"Hard work and lots of prayer. My husband ran off and left me to bring up our three children before the youngest was a year old. I raised them by working at the IHOP by day and singing in jazz clubs at night. When the kids got old enough, I took dance lessons at the YMCA. I taught myself to sing opera by listening to cassette tapes I checked out of the library. It wasn't easy, but I did it, and my kids turned out all right."

"There you go, then," Sam said. "Hard work and prayer. That's what we'll do."

Terell stood and stretched. "Just a sec, Sam. I need to check on something."

Sam struggled to refrain from growling in frustration as his friend ambled away. It was just like Terell to take a lackadaisical attitude about the possible closing of the center. He had frittered away his NBA career and most of his money—and he didn't even care. Would he also let Haven slide out of his grasp without a fight?

Sam certainly wouldn't. He had invested his life in this place. His heart was here, and he wasn't about to give up on it.

"Are there any more questions before we wrap up the meeting?" he asked.

Heads shook.

"Then I'd like to say a special thank-you to Caleb for the great work he's done on the computer system. The screen lit up today, and I think I saw some words appear."

Caleb looked glum. "It's a piece of trash."

"A rash?" Granny said. "Well, I believe I've got something for that, too, sweetie pie. Just hold on."

As she rummaged in her purse again, Sam continued. "Ethelou, thank you for insisting that boys participate in the tap dance classes as well as the girls. I think we need to stick with that as long as we can."

"Gregory Hines. He was a good man, God rest his soul. Just keep telling those boys about Gregory Hines."

"Right." Sam nodded. "And the construction crews are doing a great job with the main floor bathrooms and the wiring upstairs. Billy and all of you young people, thanks for that. And the crochet—"

“Excuse me for interrupting,” Terell said, returning to his chair at Sam’s side. “I’ve got a presentation to make. We’re up against this lead paint problem, as we all know. But I’d like to remind everyone—especially our leader—of something important.”

He pulled a small object from behind his back and gave it a shake. Sam recognized it at once.

“Why do you keep this in your desk drawer, Sam?” Terell asked.

A wave of emotions surged through Sam as he stared at his military beret. “You know why,” he said in a low voice.

“I know why you *say* you keep it there. But that’s not what it means to me. This cap is a symbol of who you are, Sam. You’re a leader. You’re *our* leader. God told you to find me after all those years. He told you to buy this building. And then He put you in charge of what we’re doing with these kids. Sam, you led your men through the desert of Iraq, and you’ll lead us through this problem with the paint.”

The volunteers began to clap as Terell set the beret on his best friend’s head. Unable to bring himself to speak again, Sam motioned Terell to close the meeting. After a round of sentence prayers and final words of mutual encouragement, the others filed out of the building. Terell wandered over to the main switchbox to begin turning out the lights.

As he watched his friend walk away, Sam reached up and tugged the beret from his head. Pressing it against his chest, he fought the rage that flamed like a wildfire through him. Against his will, he saw the face . . . the small face, dark hair, pale lips, large brown eyes.

Clenching his jaw, he fought the tears that welled. But this was one battle Sam Hawke could not win.

Friday morning, Ana parked near the entrance to Haven, opened her car door and stepped out onto the street. As though whisked beneath the open pores of a steam iron, she winced and drew in a fortifying breath. Humidity instantly plastered her white blouse to her skin. Heat pressed down on her head and radiated up from the pavement through her sandals and onto her bare legs. Her mouth dried out, and her normally straight hair began to curl.

As Ana crossed the street, she prayed that her determination wouldn't waver. Defying Carl Webster, digging into Haven's private business, investigating Terell Roberts and trying to uncover Flora's secrets were bad enough. But walking down these inner city streets didn't help her nerves, either. She tapped the side of her purse, taking some comfort in the can of pepper spray it held.

Nearing Haven's entrance, she noticed two teenage boys sitting in the shade of the tattered green canvas awning. Shirtless, they wore baggy blue jean cutoffs that displayed their multicolored boxer shorts, muscled legs and enormous athletic shoes. Red bandannas capped their heads, while heavy gold chains and large pendants stuck to their sweaty chests. The boys watched Ana approach, and she was conscious of their eyes following her movement—staring at her legs, the hem of her cotton skirt as it grazed her knees, the heels of her sandals tapping the sidewalk. When a third boy emerged through the doorway, she tensed, paused and caught her breath. Recognizing him, she exhaled and stepped forward again.

"Hello, Raydell," she said. Though the job was intended to rotate among the Haven helpers, the muscular, gold-toothed Raydell Watson had been on guard each time she visited. "I'm Ana Burns with the *Post-Dispatch*."

"The reporter, yes, ma'am. I know who you are." He eyed her from behind a forest of dreadlocks. "So, how you doin' today?"

"Fine." She signed the clipboard. "It's awfully hot out here. Why don't your friends go inside the building?"

He regarded the two on the sidewalk. "I can't let 'em in. We don't allow no gang colors, you know. They won't give up their do-rags."

It was her turn to stare at the two. They stared back. "What you lookin' at, lady?" the bigger one asked, a sneer curling his lip.

"Just wondering why you'd rather sit out here in the heat than take off those scarves and go inside."

"Scarves." The teen snickered. "Don't nobody tell me what to wear. Nobody mess with me—'less it be a pretty lady like you."

"Yeah," the smaller one said. "Want some, pretty lady?" Both laughed.

Ana shrugged off the prickle that ran down her

spine. "I believe I'll go on inside, Raydell," she said. "There's nothing in my bag that will set off the alarm."

"That's good, Miss Burns, but I can't let you in." The dark eyes narrowed. "Mr. Hawke. He don't want to talk to you no more."

She stiffened. "He told you to keep me out?"

"He said he don't want to talk to you."

"Well, I don't want to talk to him, either. I want to ask him a question."

Raydell glanced at the two boys, who were observing the conversation with interest. "Asking a question is the same as talking."

"No, it's not." Ana searched her memory banks. "Talking involves conversational discourse in simple declarative sentences. But asking is interrogative. They're two completely different things."

"Still—"

"I'm going in." She took an old conference badge from her purse, a favorite ploy. "I'm with the press, see? I have the right."

Before he could stop her, Ana slipped through the metal detector. Her least favorite part of the entry process bounded forward as she stepped into the building. The German shepherd sniffed her up and down, his tail wagging as the current child on "Duke duty" led him around by a leash.

The building was cooler inside—but not by much. Ana wondered if the air conditioner was working. Did Haven even have a cooling system? As her eyes adjusted to the light, she noted the usual basketball game in progress. Through the broken window in the front office, Ana could see Caleb laboring on the archaic computer. Several children watched over his shoulder—evidently a new class that had formed to learn from the young man. She noted his obvious patience with the group of wiggly youngsters.

Down the row of classrooms, the doors stood ajar, presumably to help with air circulation. Jazz music and the pounding of hammers drifted out. A teenager rounded up a child whose hands were covered in blue paint. A ball of yellow yarn rolled across the floor. Granny's crochet group, Ana thought with a smile.

A short distance away, Ana recognized a familiar figure watching the action on the basketball court. Surprised at first, she then remembered the conversation from the day before. Of course. Jim Slater had brought Sam his check for five thousand dollars.

"Jim, hey!" she called, striding toward him.

He swung around, and she noted that his face was pale and oddly gaunt. Unlike his usual affable demeanor, the man appeared stiff, as though he had been stricken with a sudden bout of illness. He gaped at Ana as though he didn't recognize her.

"Jim? It's Ana Burns." She paused before him, fears of a heart attack or stroke racing through her mind. "Are you feeling all right? You're white as a sheet."

He swallowed and stared, as if listening to words in a foreign language. "Ana? Oh, hello."

"Hello, yourself." She smiled at him. "I guess you're here to talk to Sam, too."

He rotated, his focus swiveling to the far corner of the room. "That girl . . ." he muttered.

Ana followed his eyes. "Her name is Flora. She's sad-looking, isn't she? I've tried to talk to her, but she won't communicate much. She speaks Spanish."

Flora was huddled into the corner, her green skirt pulled to her knees, her legs tucked carefully to one side. But today the child's brown eyes studied only the wall. Forehead against the peeling paint, she stared vacantly.

A pang turning Ana's heart, she forced herself to look away. This is why I've come, she thought. For Flora and Raydell. For Granny and Tenisha. Maybe even for the two gang members sitting out there in the sun—too proud and angry to take off their do-rags and play some basketball.

"She breaks my heart," Ana said, focusing on Jim. "The way she sits—it's like she's shell-shocked."

"What's the last name?" Jim asked.

"Flora's?" That was an odd question. Ana studied him more closely, her concerns about his health growing again. "I have no idea. Listen, Jim, would you like to sit down? They've got an old bench in the office—

"No." He shook his head. "I need to go."

"Uh-oh, here comes Uncle Sam," she said, spotting the tall man leaving the office and heading toward them. "He'll be eager to talk to you, I'm sure. He may throw me out on my ear."

As Sam approached, Ana tried to fortify herself. Too bad if he didn't want to talk to her. She would talk to him instead. "Ana?" As he recognized her, Sam's brow furrowed. "What are you doing here? I thought I told you not to come back to Haven."

"I realize you need to talk to Jim, and I'm sorry to interrupt, but I have a quick question for you."

"Jim, good morning." Sam turned to his other visitor, ignoring Ana. "I didn't realize you were coming by today. Welcome. You've brought the pledge check, I guess?"

Jim glanced at Ana. "Actually, I came here to discuss the lead paint article."

"What about it?" she asked.

"Maybe we should step into the office," Sam said. "It's clear for the moment."

As she and Jim followed him across the floor, Ana noted that the older man seemed better. Maybe the heat outside had gotten to him, and now he'd had a chance to cool down. It was easy to see why a bevy of churchwomen usually fluttered around Jim like butterflies drawn to a solitary red rose. A handsome man, he was trim and fit, with silver at the temples of a full head of hair. He rarely wore ties, preferring polo shirts in the summer and turtlenecks with geometric patterns in cooler weather.

They entered the front office and took seats on the old vinyl booth and a couple of splintered chairs. Jim let out a deep breath. "Well, I see you didn't give much heed to the concerns Sam and I expressed about the article, Ana."

"I'm on assignment," she reminded him. "The press

has a responsibility to keep the public informed."

"Surely you have enough information by now," Jim said. "I'm not surprised Sam is reluctant to continue meeting with you. Your presence here is a distraction from his work, and we've both made it clear we don't want Haven's problems to receive exposure in the newspaper."

"But I've decided to go with a more anecdotal slant to the series." Ana was slightly taken aback at the man's strong defense of Sam. "I want to show what Haven means to the children, and how if the lead paint problem shut it down—"

"Nothing's shutting us down," Sam cut in.

"—children like that little girl, Flora, for example," Ana continued, "would have no place to go. She comes here every day, and even though she doesn't participate in the activities, she's clearly getting something out of being at Haven. I want to interview her."

"No," Jim said firmly. "Absolutely not. It's a big mistake. In fact, I think the whole idea of putting the children at Haven in the article at all is just plain wrong. I must tell you, Ana, you caught me off guard yesterday. I had expected the meeting with Sam, but when you arrived, too, I was unprepared."

"She's the type who just shows up," Sam said.

"I've found that setting appointments rarely works," Ana explained. "One interview can run too long and throw off the next. Besides, I prefer to catch people by surprise. I find they're often more open and honest when they haven't had time to think about what they want to say."

"That's exactly the problem," Jim said. "Now that I've had time to think about it, I've decided I don't want to be included in your article after all."

"Why not?" She fought the rising panic in her chest. "You're a great source, Jim. Support of the center from a well-respected member of the community will speak volumes."

"But my name will naturally be associated with the adoption service, and I simply cannot allow the organization to receive publicity. It's against policy."

"I don't understand. You're helping children."

"Ana, I mentioned the Bible verse that talks about doing good deeds in silence. That's why so many donors prefer to remain anonymous. Including me."

"But you're not anonymous. Your name is on Sam's list."

"What list?" He turned to Sam.

"My donor list." Sam was glaring at Ana. "It's not for public use."

"Yet you showed it to a reporter?"

"That was obviously a mistake. I'm sorry, Jim. I had no idea she was going to cause this much trouble."

"I'm not causing trouble," Ana protested. "I'm gathering information for my series. And if I don't have a variety of interesting quotes—including some from donors—then my articles will suffer. In the long run, Haven will be the worse for it."

Sam crossed his arms over his chest. "Your series is

not going to make or break Haven, Ana. And I won't mince words with you, either, Jim. If I'd known bringing a reporter with me yesterday would be a problem for you, I never would have done it. Time is running out for us, and I need your donation. Can I still count on you?"

"This is difficult." Jim shook his head. "Money is tight, and I can't afford to give it away unless my own requirements are met. I've got a group of three children—siblings, actually—waiting in El Salvador, plus two boys in Costa Rica. It takes a lot of cash to cut through the bureaucratic red tape in foreign countries, and I can't always find good homes right away. Many times, I end up fronting the costs out of my own pocket. I'm sure you understand."

"Jim, are you telling me that you won't honor your pledge if your name appears in the newspaper?" Sam asked.

"I'm sorry," Jim said. "I really can't allow the publicity."

"You're costing Haven five thousand dollars, lady." Sam faced Ana, his jaw tight. "That means you're endangering the welfare of all my kids. You'd better promise to keep Jim's name out of the paper, understand?"

"Or what?"

"Or nothing." His blue eyes snapped. "You want to do some good with your article? This is how—leave Jim Slater out."

"Fine. I'll agree to omit Jim's name when you

promise to let me interview—"

"No, no, no." He jabbed a finger at her. "No deals, Ana. You agree to this, and that's it. Promise me now."

She focused on Jim, then on Sam again. "All right. You win. I won't include any mention of Jim or the adoption agency."

"Thank you, Ana," Jim said. "Haven does great work, and I'm sure you wouldn't want to threaten that. You certainly shouldn't draw attention to individual children in your article. It could appear as though you were holding them up for public exhibition as the outcasts of our society."

"That's right," Sam spoke up. "I cringe when I see articles about women's clubs donating school supplies or corporations throwing Christmas parties for inner-city children. It's humiliating enough for parents to have to use programs like that to provide for their kids. Then to see their names and faces plastered across the newspaper is downright degrading."

"Think about it, Ana," Jim said. "Leave Haven alone."

For some reason, his words sounded less like a plea than a threat, Ana mused. Was Jim warning her? Did Sam's argument have validity, or was it a ploy to get rid of her?

"I'll call you in a few days and touch base," Jim was telling Sam as he stood to leave. "Don't lose heart, young man. You're doing important work, and I'm sure God will bless you for it."

As Sam accompanied the older man to the recreation center's door, Ana flipped open her reporter's notebook. She might as well use the moment alone to write a description of the director's lair. As much as she had to admire Sam for his lion-like dedication to the center, Ana couldn't make herself like the man. He was single-minded. Driven. Totally one-track.

"Still stalking that story," Sam said as he stepped back into the office. "Don't you ever think about anything else? You're like a bloodhound on a convict's trail."

She rolled her eyes. "*You're* the one who never wavers from his agenda. Did you even hear what Jim was saying? He's got bunches of needy children waiting for good homes, and very little money coming in."

"Of course I heard him." Sam moved around the desk, flipped open a file and traced down the names on a list inside it. "Haven has needy children, too. They're my priority. In order to keep this place open for our kids, we've got to have money, plain and simple. Jim Slater has money—more than he lets on, if you want the truth. I appreciate your agreeing not to use him as a source. Now, if you'll recall our last conversation, I have nothing more to say."

Ana went cold inside. His words had exactly the opposite effect from what he intended. Instead of backing down, she flexed her claws and readied herself for battle. No matter what it took, she intended to investigate Haven's secrets. She would uncover the truth about Terell Roberts. She would find out why toddlers clung to him, who had slapped that blond-haired girl, where Flora had come from and why she hid in the shadows.

That meant talking to the children.

Ana cleared her throat. "Sam, may I have permission to interview some of the kids here? My article won't be complete if I don't include several perspectives."

"You talked to me and Terell." Sam didn't look up. "That's two."

"Why won't you let me interview the children? Sam, are you hiding something?"

His blue eyes narrowed as they focused on her. "No. Are you?"

"Of course not." She leaned toward him. "Listen, you and Terell are college-educated, military-trained, young, healthy. Men like you don't give up their future in order to rehab a run-down building in the inner city just because they're Christians. Hard to believe you're both that noble. You've got some other motive, and I want to know what it is."

"What's your motive, Miss Nosy? You're not coming here day after day, bothering me and everyone else just to please your editor. There are plenty of other contaminated buildings in St. Louis. Why Haven all the time? And don't tell me you're trying to be a do-gooder and help me get donations. Reporters aren't known for being noble, either."

"I never said I was noble."

"Neither did I. I'm just trying to do what needs to be done. And if you'd go bother somebody else, I could get it done a lot faster."

She crossed her arms, glaring at him in frustration. "All right," she said finally. "You win again. I do have a purpose beyond completing my assignment, earning my salary and keeping my job—although those are worthy goals, you have to admit. I'm aiming for the peak, Sam. One day I plan to write a story that will win a Pulitzer. Who knows? Maybe this is it."

"Your life's goal is to win an award?" He laughed. "How shallow can you get?"

"It's not shallow to want to do your best. In Texas, I earned a top writing honor. My newspaper expects the same quality here, and I intend to deliver. I want to write good stories. Great stories. I want to be the best."

The blue eyes deepened. "Why?"

"Because. That's who I am."

"Sorry, Ana, but I'm not going to be able to cater to your little fantasies. You'll have to be perfect somewhere else."

She thrust her pen in his direction. "You won't give me access to your people because you're hiding something, Sam Hawke. I haven't been a journalist this many years without learning a few things. I told you my hidden agenda. What's yours?"

"Helping kids. That's all there is to it. No big secret."

"I don't believe you."

His face hardened. "Miss Burns, I need to make some phone calls. Would you mind stepping out of my office?"

"I thought so." She flipped her notebook shut. "Good day, Mr. Hawke."

Fury boiled up inside Ana as she stormed out of the front office. Why had she even mentioned the award? He had made it sound so paltry. Like a cheap trinket. Like a sin.

It wasn't wrong. Awards were human measures of success—and she wanted to succeed. Not just for herself, but she believed God intended her to be the best she could be. All her life, she had strived for perfection. The cleanest desk. The neatest penmanship. The best book reports. The tidiest room. The highest GPA. The best job. The latest fashions. The most disciplined runner. The top awards.

In everything—everything—she had to succeed. She couldn't do less. Couldn't let down for a moment or . . . or what? What would happen if she weren't the best, the brightest, the most perfect . . . if she failed?

Recalling her greatest failure—not hearing her sister's pleas for help—Ana glanced toward Flora's corner. The dark shadows were empty. The thin huddled figure who had stared glumly at the wall was gone.

Where was the child?

Fear prickled through Ana, almost as though she had carelessly mislaid part of herself. Flora was *supposed* to be there . . . right in that corner wearing her green skirt and plastic sandals. It was her place.

The afternoon wasn't half over. Had Flora actually

joined one of the activity groups? It seemed unlikely.

Ana glanced into the front office and saw that Sam, too, had disappeared. She quickly crossed to the row of classrooms and moved down it, checking at each open doorway. No sign of Flora.

Stepping toward the shadowed corner, she studied the empty space, imagining the huddled figure wedged as far as possible into the corner. Did Flora always wear a green skirt? Or were there other clothes? And her long black hair, was it always in one braid—or sometimes two? Such questions suddenly became important, and Ana needed answers.

Crouching, she thought how it might be to sit in this corner for hours and hours each day. Did Flora nap here sometimes? Or sing to herself, little Spanish songs she had learned from her mama or her grandmother—her *abuela*? Did she think about La Ceiba—the town, the hotel, the tree, the place of witchcraft, or whatever it was? Or did she just hide here, her heart trembling as she tried to stay undiscovered, unseen, secreted away like a mouse?

Tempted to try to fit herself into Flora's corner, Ana gazed down at the floor. Such a dark, cold place. Concrete, bare and gray, and two dark spots near the wall. Ana reached out and touched her finger to the spots, smeared them, lifted her hand to the light . . . and saw that it was blood.

The color frightens me. The red is like the fingernails of the woman who walked with my father on the sidewalk the night that everything came apart. The red is like the ruffle on my mama's blouse when she ran out of our house in tears. The red is like the woman's high-heel shoes, and my father's eyes when he drinks . . .

. . . and oh, I am afraid. Afraid of the pain and the evil smell of sweat and the color red. And I stare up at the lightbulb, forcing my eyes to burn, commanding them to come out of my head, wishing to be blind so that I may never again see that color. The bright white ceiling turns to black as my eyes float upward into the light . . .

. . . and it is the sun glistening down on my sister's hair as I comb it. My fingers fall through the strands of her black hair, her blue-black hair, like a raven's wings. Aurelia laughs at me for combing and combing her hair, but I cannot stop. Today, we found the comb on the beach, a red plastic comb with large teeth, and we sat together under the shade of a silk-cotton tree to comb our hair.

Ouch! Aurelia cried out at first, because her hair was all in tangles and sticky with juice from the mango we ate at breakfast. She turned around and slapped my face, and a tear rolled from her brown eyes down onto her cheek, making a pale track through the dust there.

But I whispered to her. Softly, softly, Aurelia. All is well. I will comb your hair, and you will be beautiful, like a queen, like a woman in a magazine, like a movie star.

So she sits for me now, drawing pictures in the sand, catching the tufts of cotton that float down from the tree, and letting me comb her hair. All the tangles fall away. The dirt sifts out of her hair, and the oil slides in, and Aurelia's hair grows soft and shiny.

When, at last, it glows like the black coal in the bottom of a fire pit, I start to braid. Oh, my fingers are nimble as they divide my sister's hair into three thick strands.

Evenly sorted, none thicker than the others. And I set one over the other. Tuck another behind. My fingers twist and curl like my mama's when she braids the hair of her two daughters. But my mama is quick, always in a hurry, uncaring because too soon these braids will fly loose, and her children's hair will hang over their faces like a frayed curtain.

I am not quick. I braid Aurelia's hair slowly, weaving the strands perfectly, creating a rope of black pearls that falls down my sister's back. At the end, I tie a red ribbon—it is a strip of plastic torn from a packet of bologna and discarded on the beach—but I tell her it is a ribbon. A ribbon for a queen. For a lady in a magazine. For a movie star.

You are beautiful, Aurelia.

And she smiles at me, her teeth so white and her arms so warm around my neck.

I will take care of you always, Aurelia, and I will braid your hair and put red ribbons in it, and I will make you beautiful.

She nods, because she believes what I tell her. I believe it, too. We sit together under the silk-cotton tree with our combed hair and Aurelia's long braid. And we look at the water, at the glow on the water as the sun sets, the orange and pink sun, the red sun . . .

. . . and it is the lightbulb. But the pain is gone now. I can breathe. Thank you, God!

Chapter Seven

Ana staggered to her feet, unsteady as she searched her purse for a tissue. Moving out into the light, she could see the scarlet color, the sticky consistency. No doubt about it. This was blood.

Alarm surging through her, she heard a chorus of echoes in her head. *Tell someone! Wait—don't tell! Get help! No, hide, hide!* Swallowing against the fear that lodged like a bone in her throat, she focused on the office in the distance. Sam Hawke had wandered out now and was patting Duke. His large hand covered the dog's head, and his fingers stroked around and behind the large furry ears.

Should Ana tell Sam? No, he would sneer at her the way he had laughed at her desire to win a Pulitzer. *How shallow can you get?*

How dumb can you be? That's not blood. That's nothing. Strawberry jelly, maybe, from lunch. You're blowing things out of proportion. What are you doing here, anyway? I told you to leave.

No, Ana would not leave, not without finding Flora first. What if another child had hurt her? What if someone had scratched her or cut her with a knife that had been sneaked past the metal detector? Or what if Flora had suddenly begun her menstrual flow? That would be terribly frightening to a young girl all alone. Who could explain it all to her—the important information about her maturing body and its natural cycles?

No one but me, Ana concluded. I have to help her. Making for the restroom, she prayed that Sam wouldn't see her. She slipped into the hall and hurried down the steep steps. Was Flora old enough to have a monthly period? She seemed so small. But Ana had been young, too, and surprised. Her loving mother had talked to her about so many things. But not the unspoken privacies of women. Ana's own body had been an uncharted realm, mysterious and frightening. She had felt as though her secret places must be too unpleasant and innately disgraceful to be mentioned.

Worried that Flora might be just as innocent, Ana pushed open the door to the girls' bathroom and bent to look under the row of stalls. There—the pink plastic sandals.

"Flora?" She tried to make her voice light, to hide her concern as she spoke in Spanish. "Are you all right?"

Nothing.

Ana stepped up to the stall's metal door and tapped gently. "Flora, it's me, Ana Burns. I talked to you the other day, remember? You asked me about La Ceiba. Do you remember me?"

Nothing.

The door swung open. Flora stood against the tiled wall beside the toilet, her brown eyes focused on Ana, her green skirt spotted with dark blood.

"I saw you when I came in," Ana went on, feigning calm. "But just now, I noticed you were gone. Is everything all right?"

Flora nodded, then whispered in Spanish, "Excuse me."

Turning, she edged past Ana and hurried toward the door.

"Wait! Flora—I see the blood on your skirt." Ana caught the girl's shoulder. "Please tell me if you're hurt."

"I'm all right." She faced Ana again. Her face was calm, but her eyes were bright with tears. "I'm fine now."

"The blood on your skirt—what happened?"

"My arm. It's nothing, see?" Flora showed Ana that she had wrapped a strip of toilet tissue around her thin arm just below the elbow.

"Who did this?" Ana caught the child's hand before she could hide it behind her back again. "Who hurt you, Flora?"

"I'm not hurt. It doesn't hurt." She squirmed. "Let me go."

"I want to look at it—please."

"No, it's mine. It's my arm." She jerked loose and ran out of the restroom, her legs as gangly as a foal's beneath the short green skirt.

Ana leaned against a sink and tried to still her heartbeat. How had Flora been injured? Who had hurt the child?

"What's going on?" The deep voice startled Ana. She turned to find Terell Roberts standing inside the bathroom near the door. "What are *you* doing here? Did you sign in with Raydell?"

"That little girl—did you see her? The one who just ran out of here? She's hurt."

"Hurt? What happened to her?" He scowled down his nose as he strode toward Ana, his large white sneakers eating up the floor. "Who else is in here?"

"No one. It's just me."

"You're that reporter from the other day. Sam said he didn't want you to bother us anymore. Why are you sneaking around down here?"

"I'm not sneaking." She felt small beneath his stare. "I came to check on Flora."

"How'd she get hurt?"

"I don't know. I saw blood on the floor."

"Blood?" He took a step closer, intense. "Where?"

"Upstairs. In her corner."

His face went hard. "You better leave now, ma'am. I need to find that girl."

"I want to find Flora, too. She's been injured."

"Hey, what's going on down here?" Sam's voice echoed down the hall. "The kids are freaking out about T-Rex and some lady in the restroom."

"It's nothing," Terell called back.

Sam appeared in the doorway and his blue eyes focused on Ana. *"You."*

Sam could not believe it. Instead of leaving, as he'd told her to do, Ana Burns had stayed in the building, gone down to the restroom and caused a scene with Terell.

"Someone start explaining," he demanded.

"There's blood," Terell growled, poking a thumb at

Ana. "She chased that little girl out of the restroom. Flora—the one in the corner, you know? I didn't see the whole thing, but I don't trust this lady any farther than I could throw her."

"Where's the blood?"

"Upstairs," Ana said. "And I didn't chase Flora."

"Where upstairs?" Sam demanded.

"Wherever it is, it's blood," Terell said, "and that's not good. Blood is *never* a good thing."

At the sound of children whispering behind him, Sam turned to find a cluster of preschoolers staring wide-eyed at the two men inside the girls' restroom. Murmuring, elbowing each other, the kids pointed to the reporter. A little boy burst into tears.

Wonderful. Just what they needed. Hysteria.

"Where are you kids supposed to be?" he asked.

The boy sobbed. "Somebody's gonna kill us!"

"Nobody's going to hurt you, Andre. You'd better get back to your activities. Aren't you supposed to be with Granny right now?"

"But what about the blood? I'm scared of blood!"

"There are only two drops," Ana said.

"Two drops?" Sam raked a hand back through his hair. All this hullabaloo for a couple of drops of blood? He couldn't believe Ana was still here—and still causing him trouble.

"Listen, Terell," Sam said, "would you take these kids back where they belong? And see if you can find Flora."

Terell snapped to attention. "Come on, you ragamuffins. Stop your boohooing, Andre. Get up those stairs right now, you hear?"

"Talk to me, woman." Sam took Ana's hand to prevent her following the group. Her fingers were cold and trembling. "Tell me what you were doing in the restroom after I told you to leave the building."

She jerked her hand away and crossed her arms. "When I left your office, I noticed she wasn't in her corner. Flora. I went looking for her."

"Why? What is Flora to you? We've got more than a hundred children inside Haven at one time. Why are you after her?"

"I'm not *after* her. She just . . . troubles me."

He nodded, aware that the haunting child had affected him deeply, too. "What about the others? They don't trouble you?"

"Of course they do. But Flora is different, Sam. She's so alone. Did you know she talked to me the other day? She speaks Spanish. I wanted to see her before I left—to make sure she was all right. I went to her corner, and that's when I saw the drops of blood. They were still wet."

Sam studied the young woman. As much as he wanted to bite her head off for disobeying him, he responded to the tone of concern in her voice. After her comment about winning a Pulitzer, he had figured Ana Burns to be like he once had been—totally focused on himself and his own goals. Other people had meant little to him beyond what they might do to him or for him. He never thought of connecting.

Not until Terell. And Christ. And then people came to him in waves—the men in his command, the civilians at the base and those in Iraq, and finally that one child . . . that girl with the brown eyes. Now he had all these children and so much responsibility.

But Ana Burns had just one. Flora. Her humanizing connection.

"Tell me about the blood," he said gently. "Start at the top."

"I was afraid another child had hurt Flora." Ana's shoulders relaxed an inch. "She's so vulnerable, you know. I went looking, and I found her in one of the stalls down here. When she came out, I saw that she had a strip of toilet paper wrapped around her arm. Here, below the elbow. I saw the blood—enough to seep through the tissue. It was on her skirt, too. I tried to get her to tell me what had happened, but she ran out. I was headed after her when Terell stopped me."

"Do you think the injury was serious?"

"I'm not sure. A bad scratch, I guess." Ana shook her head in frustration. "Sam, something's wrong in that little girl's life. I just know it. She wears the same clothes, sits in the same corner, and today when Jim Slater and I were talking, she was staring at the wall. She had put her forehead against the concrete, Sam. Her eyes were open, and she was just staring at that blank wall."

Unable to resist the anguish in her voice, Sam reached out. Her shoulder was warm and tanned against the sleeveless white blouse. "Ana, it's going to be okay. This is what Haven is all about. Flora is like most of the children who come here. She lives in substandard housing, doesn't have many clothes, rarely gets enough to eat and has little parental contact. She may be depressed. I wouldn't be surprised."

"Sam." Ana's eyes filled with tears. "I think Flora cut herself."

The unexpected pronouncement startled him. "What? Why would she do that? Are you saying you think she was trying to take her own life . . . to commit suicide? A child that young?"

"I don't know. But people do cut themselves sometimes. I've read about it. It's a cry for help, I think. The cutting relieves stress."

"That can't be right. An injury *causes* stress to the body—not relief. In Iraq . . ." He paused as memories surged up once again, things he didn't like to recall. Sand, heat, wind, death. Stifling his thoughts, he forced himself to continue. "That's something you watch for in your men. A bullet wound or shrapnel can put a soldier into shock. The body's signals get scrambled, adrenaline pours in, things go into hyperdrive."

"I know, but I'm telling you, Sam, this cutting can happen. Someone did a study. I read it."

"But a child? Why would a little girl do that to herself?"

"If you're in a terrible situation, sometimes you do terrible things."

He shook his head. "I'll bet some other kid went into

her corner and tried to mess with her. They tangled, and Flora came out the loser."

"That might have been it." Ana's big brown eyes were soft now, filled with sadness. "Sorry I caused a scene."

"Forget it. I'm sure Terell got the kids back into their activities. Listen, Ana, I'll keep an eye out for Flora, okay? If I find out anything, I'll give you a call at your office."

"This sounds like a dismissal."

"Second one today. Here." He reached over and peeled a strip of paint from the bathroom wall. "My gift to you. Lead paint from Haven."

As he set it in her hand, she raised one eyebrow. "Why was Terell down here by the girls' restroom? The boys' is at the other end of the hall."

"Restroom duty." His hackles rose again. Did she never get tired of irking him? "Terell and I patrol this building. Keep it safe from unauthorized visitors."

"Enough, Sam. Authorize me, okay? I've told you I'll write a favorable article. Let me talk to your children."

"You want to talk to kids? Become a Haven volunteer. We talk to kids all day long."

"I can't wire a building or repair a computer. I don't have time to supervise basketball games or patrol your building."

"So teach a writing class."

She frowned. "I'm a reporter, Sam."

"I'll bet these children have lots of things to write about." The mortification on her face gratified him, so he pressed on. "You could start tomorrow. Granny spends Saturdays with her son and his family, so I'll let you have the crochet room. It's near the end of the row of classes where Flora sits. Maybe she'll even become part of your group. How's that sound? Shall I sign you up?"

She looked away, her lips tight. "You're the most stubborn human being I've ever met."

"Likewise."

Shouldering her purse, she gave him a shrug. "Adios, Mr. Hawke."

He followed her to the restroom door, then watched as she vanished up the stairs. Flora might have touched her, but not deeply enough. It would take more than a single lonely child to penetrate the hard shell around the heart of Ana Burns.

"It's about time!" he hissed into the phone. "I told you to call me right back. Where've you been?"

"Listen, things aren't good here," Stu said. "I think they may have found something in one of our clients' computers. The dead guy."

"What makes you say that?"

"A man came to my office today. He told me he worked for the company that services our computers. He was there to upgrade our system. That's what he said, but I don't think so. He wanted to see my files. He was in there for hours, fiddling with my computer and going through my stuff. I didn't have anything at the office, of course. But I don't know what he might have found. I mean, I've . . . well, once or twice maybe I've

accessed some of my home files—"

"Are you nuts? You used your office computer to pull up files from your house?"

"Just a couple of times. But I didn't save anything to the hard drive. It was only a quick—"

"You're dead meat, Stu." He tried to breathe. To think. To reason. The point was not Stu's fate. The man had cooked his own goose. The issue now was his own safety. "Listen, did you talk to your client? Does he still want to do this deal?"

"No way." Stu's voice quavered, as though he was holding back tears. "He says things are too hot right now. And look, you've got to help me. If they take me in—"

"You deserve it. I never should have trusted you." Trying to clear his brain, he found himself wishing for the blissful escape of alcohol. Lately, his martini consumption had increased to the point that he was concerned about driving. Not at all sure he could go out. Or talk to people. And yet, what choice did he have? Things had to be done. Situations resolved.

"Maybe I can help you, Stu." He was relieved at how easily the lie slid from his tongue. "I have connections here. I'll send someone your way, and we can try to cover your tracks."

"Really? Thanks. That would be great."

"First and foremost, I want you to take your computer and all your hard copy files to the dump. The city dump. Don't save anything."

"Okay." He was sniffling now. "Or maybe I could

just hide my things somewhere, you know. Rent a storage shed or something. I mean, I've been working on this for a lot of years now, and I'd hate to—"

"If you want to keep your sorry hide out of prison, you'll take everything to the dump. Call me back once you've done that. In the meantime, I'm going to need your help disposing of the problems I've got here."

"Disposing?"

"You know what I mean, Stu."

"Let's not get into that again. Please. It's one thing to go down for having files, trafficking, possession—maybe six years at the most. But you're talking serious stuff now."

"Of course I am. I've got to clear my property."

"What have you got?"

"Two here and a girl I sent to Jefferson City. Don't know how it happened, but she ended up back here. I have to deal with her. She can give them too much information. Information about me. About us. Blow the whole thing sky-high."

"You're talking about three. That's a lot."

"There's one more—a reporter. She's nosing around, asking questions, won't quit. I need to put a stop to her."

Stu was breathing hard, clearly in a panic. "Four?"

"Can you find someone for me? I need it done quickly and quietly. Nothing splashy, you understand. And no evidence."

"Right." He swallowed audibly. "I think I know someone who could help us. But it'll cost plenty."

"I can pay. How soon?"

"I'll talk to him today. Maybe he can get right on it. But it may take a couple of days." He sniffled again. "So, you'll send someone to help me out, too?"

"Sure, Stu. I know who to call. We'll be okay."

As he hung up the phone, he let out a shaky breath. What an idiot. Stu would bring down the whole organization. Everything he'd worked so hard to build would be gone in a flash, and he'd be on his way back to the slammer. He ought to get out his gun and drive to Illinois and blow the fool's brains out. The thought of leaving St. Louis set his heart racing. Maybe he would head for Texas, instead. And then Mexico.

But how could he leave the house this way? There was too much evidence. Too much . . . and they would come after him even if he left the country. It would be a federal case, no doubt about that. The authorities would hunt him down and extradite him. He would rot in some stinking prison somewhere.

He sat gripping the arms of his chair. If he drank only one martini, he could still concentrate. An anxiety pill would calm him. The two together couldn't do much harm, he reasoned. Maybe he could actually get some sleep. And perhaps his head would stop pounding.

Yes, he thought as he headed for his special cabinet. That was exactly what he needed to do to take care of himself.

Flora slipped through the metal detector at noon the

next day. As usual, she wore pink plastic sandals and a green skirt. Another female accompanied her, Sam noted in surprise, this one older and taller. With her dyed black hair, pink satin blouse and denim shorts cut far too high in the leg and low on the hips, the older girl had the world-weary appearance of a young streetwalker. Pointing to the oversized man's watch on her wrist, she made several exaggerated gestures, clearly attempting to communicate with Flora, who nodded and gave the first smile Sam had seen from her. Turning on her spiked heel, the friend strutted out of the center.

Sam watched with interest as Flora donned the white T-shirt given to her by the boy on Duke duty. The girl who had brought Flora to Haven was not Hispanic—a *Latina*, as Ana put it. How had she found the silent child, and what bonded the two?

Flora edged down the side of the basketball court—as far away as possible from the office and the row of classrooms. Her skeletal legs barely shadowed the wall. Her luminous brown eyes glanced at the ballplayers, then focused on the floor as she hurried to her corner.

Sam chewed on a bologna sandwich, all the while watching Flora through the broken front window of his office. She slid down into the darkness of that small triangular space and tucked her legs primly to one side. Once settled, she leaned back into the corner and watched the basketball game. Sam had seen many frightened, withdrawn children at Haven, but Flora's utter silence intrigued him. Only Ana had been able to break through to the child, and that bothered him.

"Hey, Caleb, you're from New Mexico, right?" Sam asked the young volunteer. Though it was a Saturday, and his friends had taken the day off to explore the St. Louis Science Center, Caleb had chosen to come to Haven and work. He was muttering to himself as he peered into the innards of another computer someone had donated to the center. "Do you speak Spanish?"

"Some. We have a housekeeper, Josefina. She taught me a few words. Why?"

"How do you say, 'Are you hungry?' "

"*Àtiene hambre?* Who're you planning to talk to?"

"That girl over in the corner near the classrooms. She sits there every day."

Caleb joined him at the window. "Hmm. I never noticed her before."

"Name's Flora. Ana Burns told me Flora speaks only Spanish."

"Ana Burns—is she that reporter who was in the girls' restroom with you and T-Rex?" Caleb chuckled. "That was weird. Dude, you wouldn't catch me in the girls' room no matter what. The kids were freaking, saying there was blood everywhere."

"It was Flora. She got cut somehow."

"Cut bad?"

"No." Sam swallowed the last of his sandwich, forcing down the bite as he recalled Ana's face. "You ever heard of people cutting themselves on purpose?"

Caleb peered out at the game. "We had this one girl at my school. She wore black eye makeup and black lipstick and stuff like that. Nobody talked to her. One day she cut her wrists, but she didn't die. They put her in a hospital in Albuquerque, and she never came back to school."

"It was a suicide attempt?"

"That's what I heard." Caleb grimaced. "I don't know though. Some of the girls said they had seen cuts and scars all over her arms."

"Wow. How can a place like Haven even begin to help someone like that?" Sam mused. This sort of thing was far beyond his knowledge or ability to handle.

"When you try to make a difference, you can run into all kinds of trouble." Caleb regarded Flora for a moment before speaking again. "But I don't think that means we should stop doing all we can. Jesus told His disciples in Matthew 25, 'I was hungry and you fed me, I was naked and you clothed me, I was in prison and you visited me.' Remember all that? I believe He really meant those things."

Sam nodded. "That's exactly what we're trying to do at Haven."

"Be obedient—it's all Jesus asked of us."

Sam studied the little girl in the corner. She hadn't moved an inch. Still wedged against the wall, she stared with dark eyes at the ball game. His heart felt tight, aching, each time he focused on her.

"When our youth group heard about Haven," Caleb continued, "we wanted to come. We're trying to really do Matthew 25. But we aren't responsible for changing people. God is the only One who can do that."

Sam shifted his focus from Flora to the teenager at his side. At Caleb's age, Sam had been angry and rebellious, bridled only by his drive to make the varsity basketball team. He had stayed in high school in hopes of getting to play college ball. Sports were at the center of a world focused on himself. He was motivated by what he could get—admiration, girls, beer, fast cars, the works. Everything revolved around him. He never would have considered giving up a summer to help disadvantaged children. Not in a million years.

"You're doing a lot at Haven, Caleb," he told the young man. "More than you realize. It's not just the computers—though they're going to make a big difference. But your presence here shows the kids that you care about them. That's something many have never known."

"Yeah, like that little girl in the corner. She looks as if she could use a friend." Caleb stared at her for a moment. "I'm not that good at Spanish, though, and I'd feel kind of weird befriending a little girl."

"It's awkward. Ana Burns did it, though."

"Hey, maybe you could get her to help you. She's hot."

"Hot?" Sam followed the boy with his eyes as Caleb returned to his computer.

"You know—good-looking. I mean, better than that. Pretty. Beautiful." He shrugged. "Hot."

Sam turned back to Flora and tried to remember the sentence Caleb had taught him in Spanish. Frustrated by how quickly it had slipped away, he reflected on Ana and how bright her eyes had been when she told him of her concern for the little girl. Ana had said that without God she wouldn't exist. There had been a desperation in her voice—and a conviction that had made him believe her.

Had Flora tried to end her young life? Was that why she had cut herself?

And could Ana Burns help to heal the child's pain—Ana, who somehow had detoured from her own self-focused drive to take an interest in a child? She wanted to win a Pulitzer, she had told him. Fame and glory. He had heard that one before, Sam thought, remembering his mother and the way she had abandoned her family in pursuit of shallow dreams. Contempt churned in his stomach.

Yet he had just admitted to himself that not so long ago, his world had revolved around Sam Hawke. Was it possible that little Flora could be changing Ana? He didn't want to believe it. People like Ana ran over those who got in their way. Ambition turned them inward. They didn't reach out. They didn't help.

Despite her claim to be a Christian, Ana Burns seemed destined to continue down the dead-end road toward self-absorption. Or did she need Flora as much as the little girl needed her?

Caleb, still a teenager, was so focused on following Christ that he had left the security of his home to come to these gang-infested streets. In the same way, Sam had given up his life for the children of Haven. Was this what Christ wanted? Did He demand such service of everyone? Or could "hot" Ana Burns continue gliding through life like Cleopatra, queen of the Nile, and still be serving God?

Sam began pulling off his T-shirt as he headed for the row of lockers. "Hey, Caleb, tell T-Rex I had to run an errand. I should be back before the next activity change, but if I'm not, help him out."

"Where are you going?"

"I think there's only one way to help that girl."

"Which girl?"

Sam thought about it—who needed help the most? Flora or Ana? "The one in the corner," he said finally. "I'll be back."

Caleb smirked as Sam rolled on some deodorant and pulled a dry T-shirt over his head. "You'd better take a shower if you want a hot chick to like you, sir."

Sam chuckled. "The only hot chick I'll ever want is one fried by Colonel Sanders. Believe me, I'm not interested in Ana that way. This is a mercy mission."

"Yeah, right." Caleb returned to the computer keyboard. He spoke in Granny's quavering voice. "Mercy me, that Ana Burns is one pretty lady."

"Get to work, punk." Sam rumpled Caleb's dark curls as he strode past him to the door.

He had no desire for a relationship of any kind with

a woman as hardheaded and pushy as that reporter. She disobeyed his orders. Refused to back down when he told her no. Argued with him. Distrusted him and his motives. Made disparaging remarks about the building, the wet towels, the office. And besides all that, she was proud.

The way she held her head so high annoyed him. And she didn't walk—she prowled. Just because she was tall and had big brown eyes and thick hair, he didn't have to acknowledge the slightest bit of attraction to her. None at all.

Chapter Eight

Ana typed the final period on her story and pushed the rolling chair back from her desk. She had come into the office on Saturday to try to get some more work done on the lead paint series. This particular article in the collection still had a long way to go. Why did her stories always hold such potential—and then turn out so bland?

She blamed space constrictions. Carl was forever telling her to cut, cut, cut. She blamed people she interviewed. Why couldn't they dish out the juicy information she was seeking? Aware they might be quoted, most people clammed up and spoke in the stilted sentences of a freshman in speech class. But most of all, she blamed herself.

If only she could ratchet her writing a notch higher. She wanted every verb to show action. She ached for sensory detail. Her leads needed to hook people and reel them to the very end of the article—no matter if they had to turn through five pages of other text just to reach her fascinating conclusion. Her stories ought to shine and sparkle like little diamonds, so brilliant that no one could ignore them. Perfection, that's what she sought. Perfection.

"Hey." A large hand waved before her eyes. "You there anywhere?"

Tearing her attention from the computer screen, Ana focused on a tall man standing in front of her desk. The surprise of seeing him sent a crash of conflicting emotions through her.

"Sam Hawke," she managed. "Welcome to the land of multicolored clothing and the freedom to walk through a door without being charged by a German shepherd."

He smiled, a flash of white teeth that charmed her in spite of herself. "I've come to suggest a meeting in neutral territory. The demilitarized zone."

"Aha," she said. "Well, that would certainly be where I live."

"How about a cup of coffee?"

"With you?"

He straightened and held out his hands. "See anyone else here?"

"Hmm. This sounds suspicious. A preemptive strike, perhaps."

He laughed. "Nope. Just a coffee."

"Hang on, I'll let my editor know I'm stepping out.

We were planning to meet about my series, but you're a good excuse to put that off until I've got more to give him."

Willing away the unexpected quickening of her heart, Ana stepped across to Carl's office. What on earth could Sam want with her? Had something happened to Flora? Had he learned something important about the little girl?

"Carl, can you and I find another time to meet?" she called as she simultaneously knocked on his door and swung it wide open. "I'm going out for coffee with the director of Haven."

Carl looked up from his desk. "Out for coffee? You?"

"Just to talk with the guy." She jabbed a thumb behind her.

The city editor's focus swung to the man who stood at her desk. Ana's followed. Away from Haven, she saw Sam with new eyes. Tall, broad-shouldered, appearing totally at ease in the newsroom, he leaned against a support post and studied his surroundings. The Marine Corps recon man back in action. The athlete ready to spring. Ana couldn't deny that the total package was impressive—the way he fit into those blue jeans, the shirt hugging his biceps . . .

"Ana?" Carl's voice brought her back. "You're doing an interview?"

She swung around, heat flushing her cheeks. "Yeah, an interview. He's a . . . a source."

"Ah." Carl grinned. "Have fun."

Turning away before he could embarrass her further, she hurried back to her desk. Certainly she'd never had trouble dealing with good-looking guys. Though she had dated a variety of interesting men through the years, love was out of the question. Intimacy was impossible. And marriage—no way. She had far too much on her plate to think in that direction.

So, Sam was handsome. What of it?

Ana scooped up her purse and surveyed her desk. The urge to take out her antibacterial cleansers and give the gleaming surface a wipe nearly overcame her. But she resisted. No need to be obsessive. Well, no more than she already was.

"Come on," she called, stepping past him toward the door that led to the stairs. "We'll walk down."

"Sounds good to me. That's how I came up."

"You took the stairs?" She stopped in her tracks.

"I always walk when I can. Good exercise." His brows lifted over those incredibly blue eyes. "Got a problem with that?"

"No, it's just . . . well, I walk, too."

"Hey, we have something in common. Whaddaya know?"

"You wish. We're as different as two people can be—and what's more, I can beat you to the ground floor."

"Not a chance."

She opened the door to the stairwell and took off. He let out a whoop and came after her, his sneakers pounding the metal steps. She flew down, her hand sliding along the rail and her toes barely touching the stairs.

"Ha!" she cried as she burst out into the parking garage. "I win!"

"You cheated," he said, nearly running into her.

"I did not."

"You didn't run. You flew."

She laughed. "Come on. There's a coffee shop on the corner."

Swinging away from him, she beckoned with one hand. A breeze danced the hem of her skirt around her knees, and her sandals skimmed the pavement.

"Caleb was right about you," Sam said, moving up to walk beside her.

"Right about what?"

He smiled, dimples curving into the corners of his mouth. "Oh, it's just a guy thing."

"So, have you seen her lately?" Ana asked across the small round table in the coffee shop.

"Who?" Sam feigned ignorance, hoping to draw her out, force her to feel her own connection to the child.

"Flora. The little girl who cut her arm."

"She's there today."

"Is she okay?"

"I don't know. Not sure. I can't talk to her, remember?"

She stirred her coffee, staring as the liquid swirled around in the paper cup. "Doesn't anyone at Haven speak Spanish?"

"Caleb does—the computer genius from New Mexico—but he's not fluent." He watched Ana's face. "Flora came in with another girl today. She's not much older, but I'm afraid she may be trouble. Has that look, anyway. They talked for a minute, mostly gesturing, and then the older one left."

"Oh, Sam." Her brown eyes glistened. "You don't suppose that Flora is—"

"No, no." He held up a hand. "I doubt it. She looks too young. The cops would grab her in a second if they saw her walking the streets. But, as I drove over here, it occurred to me that the older girl may have taken Flora under her wing. When she's working, she brings the kid to Haven. Then when she's through, she comes back and picks Flora up. They must be staying someplace together. A motel room maybe. That would be typical. I just hope she's not grooming Flora. There has to be a pimp lurking around those girls."

"This is horrible." Ana threaded her fingers through her hair and propped her elbows on the table. Looking down into her coffee, she shook her head. "If Flora's living with a prostitute, her future is hopeless. We've got to do something, Sam."

His heart softened at her obvious concern. "Any ideas?"

"I wonder if Jim Slater would know of a family who might take Flora. If he could help out in any way, I'm sure he would. Have you heard from him today? Did he bring you his check?"

"Not yet." Sam didn't like to think about the fact

that he was still so far from his financial goal. "I'm trusting he'll come back in the next few days. I'm not having much luck drumming up any other support. But if I can tell people that Jim came through and we're a lot closer, maybe they'll kick in a few bucks."

"He'll be back. Jim was upset with me yesterday, but I know him too well to think he'd cop out on you. I wonder if those two little girls we saw at his house are out of foster care and with their new parents by now."

"I hope so." As he savored his coffee, Sam studied the woman across the table. Each time she spoke of those children or mentioned Flora, her mood altered. Sadness filtered across her face, and her eyes darkened. She seemed to go away somewhere for a moment, as if she had lost herself.

"I wish I could have explained why they left their home country," she murmured. "Where did Jim say it was?"

"Honduras."

She looked up. "Are you sure?"

"Positive."

Sam fiddled with the little box that held packets of sugar and artificial sweetener, lining up the corners. The coffee tasted good despite the intense, muggy heat outside the shop. With the air conditioner on full blast inside the quaint shop and a lulling tune playing, he could almost imagine himself in France or Germany—places he had visited on military leaves.

"So," he said, "have you given any more thought to the idea we talked about yesterday?"

"Which idea?"

"That you teach a writing class at Haven this evening. So you can talk to the kids, you know."

She frowned. "Sam, are you certain Jim Slater said those two girls came from Honduras?"

"Absolutely." He saw she was back to the children, and her sad expression had returned. "Why?"

"La Ceiba . . . the name Flora mentioned to me the time we spoke in her corner. There's a town named La Ceiba in Honduras."

"Hmm. Maybe the girl would have heard of the place, but that can't be Flora's home. Honduras is a long way from St. Louis. Her family would have needed money to travel so far. If they had that much money, why does Flora spend her days crouching alone in a corner at Haven?"

"I can't imagine."

"She's probably Mexican. I suspect her parents brought her across the border illegally. Somehow they must have gotten separated on the way to St. Louis."

"Maybe she got lost," Ana suggested. "I've heard that sometimes the Immigration Service deports adult aliens without knowing children have been left behind."

Sam shook his head. "That's bad. On the other hand, what if Flora ran away?"

"No. I don't want to think about what a child would have to do to survive."

"Happens all the time."

"Did I tell you that La Ceiba is the name of a tropical tree?" Ana changed the subject as swiftly as she had run down that flight of stairs. "The tree makes a silky fiber that comes floating down out of the seedpods. Kind of like snow, only better, because it's not cold."

As she spoke, she lifted her hands, her graceful fingers moving back and forth as if she were playing an imaginary piano. "We used to have a silk-cotton tree near our house in Brownsville. It might still be there."

She seemed lost for a moment, then she continued. "Anyway, after Flora mentioned La Ceiba, I looked it up on the Internet. Followers of the Santeria and Palo Mayombe religions revere the tree."

"Santeria? Isn't that voodoo or something? I've never heard of the other one."

"Palo Mayombe is similar to Santeria. Both originated with slaves in the Caribbean islands. They combine African beliefs with Catholicism—and sometimes witchcraft. The *ceiba* tree is supposed to be the seat of witches."

A prickle raced down his spine. "Okay, that's weird."

"Worshippers pray to the tree. They put things under it, too—offerings, sacrifices, curses. And they leave cauldrons filled with human remains."

"This is not good, Ana. Are you sure you heard Flora right?"

"Positive. But there's more. All kinds of hotels and

condos in Mexico, Costa Rica and along the Amazon River have the name La Ceiba. In addition to the city in Honduras, there's one in Puerto Rico. It's known as La Ciudad del Marlin, the city of the marlin, and it's a little over an hour east of the capital, San Juan."

"Still too far, in my opinion," Sam said. "Mexico is my bet, although the Santeria thing is interesting. Do you think Flora cut herself for religious reasons?"

"I'm not sure." She paused. "I've heard of sects that practice penitence. They do whip themselves until they bleed. Sometimes they even reenact the crucifixion. People have died."

"I read about that, but it was in the Philippines."

"It's here, too. New Mexico. Texas. Sam, do you know of any Santeria practitioners living in St. Louis?"

"No, but we have a growing immigrant population. It's possible that some of them come from the Caribbean."

"In Santeria and Mayombe, they believe the leaves of the *ceiba* tree help them see into the past and future. Witches use the branches as the main ingredient in the broth they make in their cauldrons."

"Great. I thought I had my kids on guard against every possible evil—guns, knives, drugs, AIDS, unplanned pregnancies. Now you tell me Haven has to be on the lookout for witches."

"Well, Flora's certainly not a witch. When she mentioned La Ceiba, she might have been talking about a town. Or the tree."

"But Ana, she cut herself. Rational, healthy people don't do that." Sam pondered the child who sat in a corner of the recreation center each day. She seemed harmless. So frightened and withdrawn. "The thing is, I can't have her hurting herself again. I think I'm going to have to put her on the list."

"What list?"

"Raydell writes down the names of kids who've caused trouble. He won't let them into Haven. It's for the good of everyone."

"Flora isn't a danger!" Ana cried, her brown eyes sending sparks across the table. "You can't kick her out. She has nowhere to go—except to some motel with a prostitute!"

"How can I be sure she's not a threat? She cut herself—that means she got a weapon into the building."

"She probably picked up a piece of glass or a broken tile. You've got potential weapons scattered all over the place, Sam. Screwdrivers, razor blades, wire. If someone wants to hurt a child, your metal detector isn't going to prevent it. Flora's act wasn't intended to harm anyone else—it was a cry of desperation, a plea for help."

"If that's what you believe, then help her, Ana. You're the only one who can speak her language. You've made headway with her. Now come teach that class, and see what you can do to save Flora."

She looked away, her lips tight. "You have no idea what kind of pressure I'm under. The lead paint series is due next Friday, Sam. I can't even get the first article right. No way can I teach writing class or anything else for you. I don't have time."

"You have time to give our kids one hour. You're single. No children. No pets."

"How do you know I don't have a pet?"

"No hair on your skirt."

She stared at him. "I might have a bird."

"So how much time does that take up? Besides, you don't have a bird."

"Are you spying on me?"

"I spy on everyone. I told you that—it was part of my training."

She leaned forward in her chair and pointed a finger at him. "Do not know too much about me, Sam Hawke. I won't like it."

"Why not? What might I learn?"

"Just stick to your own agenda, okay? Help kids. Save their lives, or whatever it is God told you to do."

"You can help."

"With a writing class? Please. How many of those children will finish high school, much less go to college? How many have the slightest hope of publishing something?"

"Is that the only reason to write? To get published? To win a Pulitzer prize?"

She clenched her teeth. "Go on and say it. How shallow can I get, right?"

"That's not the only reason you write, or you wouldn't keep coming back to Flora. You nosed around in her corner when she wasn't even there. You found the blood, and you went after the kid like a rocket. You care about her. You want to make a difference in her life. And you can do that by volunteering at Haven."

"Flora won't come to a writing class. She doesn't speak English, Sam."

"But you speak Spanish. So draw her into your group. Talk to her about what's going on. Find out why she wears that green skirt every day. Why she sits in that corner. Maybe even why she cut her arm."

Ana's fingers tightened on her coffee cup. "You would let me interview the kids?"

"How could I stop you?"

Moistening her lips, she assessed him. "What time?"

"Come this evening—say six? That's when we have the biggest crowd. They all want to play basketball, and we don't have enough room. We end up with a lot of kids loitering. It'll be good to have another place to put them."

"Basically, I'm there to babysit until the basketball court frees up. Is that what you're saying?"

He leaned back in his chair and shrugged. "You're a little overqualified to babysit, but if that'll get you there, so be it."

"Why are you doing this, Sam? Jim Slater doesn't even want Haven mentioned in my series. Yesterday, you did your best to throw me out of the building. But today you came all the way over to my office. Why the change? What's in this for you?"

"It's not for me. It's her. Flora." A familiar knot formed in his throat. "She needs you."

"I don't buy that. Why do you suddenly care about her so much?"

Sam cleared his throat, looking away and hoping she couldn't read his face. "Some kids . . . some are just special, you know?"

She sat up and leaned forward, her face suddenly intense. "Sam, what is it about Flora that you're not telling me? You know something. It's Terell, isn't it? Tell me the truth. He's been abusing kids, hasn't he? He molested Flora that day in the restroom. That's why he came in so fast. That's why she was bleeding."

"What?" Sam couldn't believe what he was hearing. "Terell? Molesting kids? Absolutely not. Are you nuts? Terell is the kindest, most compassionate man I've ever met."

"I saw the way he was holding that little blond girl on his lap. The one who'd been slapped. Sam, be honest with me. Terell did that, didn't he?"

"You cannot be serious about this, Ana. Terell would never touch a child inappropriately. The man has never hit anyone in his life. He's a teddy bear. You've seen how the kids hang on him."

"Yes, and how he hugs them and rubs their backs."

"Of course he does. Most of those children have no male figure in their lives. Terell is not—" He pushed back from the table. "I'm not going to participate in this conversation. Terell and I've been friends since we were eighteen. I lived in the same dorm room with him for four years. Terell Roberts is no child abuser."

"Then who hurt Flora?"

"You said she cut herself."

"Before that. Why does she hide in the corner, Sam? And why are you so determined to get me over there to help her?"

He let out a breath. "Because . . ." He shook his head, fighting to clear his scrambled thoughts. "It's just that Flora . . . okay, she reminds me of someone."

"Who?"

"It doesn't matter, Ana. Let it go, will you?" He wiped his mouth on a paper napkin and fought to keep the memories at bay—the whiteness of the napkin taking him to the glaring desert sand and the white van rolling toward him and the white robes of the men beside him and the blinding glint of afternoon sunlight on the barrel of his gun.

"Do you have a daughter?" Ana asked. "Does Flora remind you of her?"

"No." Sam slammed his palm down on the table. "And I told you to drop it." He stood, knocking the chair over backward, startling the other customers.

Yanking the chair upright, he turned and strode out of the coffee shop. He didn't have to talk about it. The post-trauma psychologist he'd been sent to had tried to make him talk, and he had said all there was to say. The past was gone, he told them. The past had nothing to do with the future, and that was where he was headed. Moving forward. Going on down the road. His mother had taught him the hard way, and he would never forget that lesson.

This reporter—this Ana Burns who believed Terell could molest a child—thought she could force Sam's past out into the open. She was crazy. And now she wanted him to go back there, to take out the memory and look at it and discuss it like some trite tidbit she could put in her little article. He didn't have to do that, and he didn't have to remember any of it.

"Sam!" She was behind him now, running to catch up, her hand touching his arm. "I just want to ask you one thing."

He turned on her, fists balled at his chest. "I told you. I don't want to talk about it. It's in the past."

"Stop," she said, covering his hands with her soft palms, pulling them toward her and holding them against her stomach. She lowered her head and stared down at his fists and cradled them even more closely. "Sam, I'm not trying to force you to talk. I only wanted to ask you what time I should be at Haven for my class."

He blinked back a droplet of sweat. "Six."

"Okay." She rubbed her thumbs over his knotted fingers. "I know about painful memories. About not wanting to talk. It's all right, Sam. I won't ask."

He nodded. "I'm sorry."

"I shouldn't have accused your friend. Things are tense right now. I should have kept my concerns to myself." Her voice was soft, barely audible above the sounds of traffic on the street. "Flora reminds me of someone, too, Sam. I knew a girl like her once—

scared, alone, hurt. My sister. I tried to protect her, but I failed. I failed her, and now she's gone. That's why I keep going to Flora's corner. It's why I followed her to the restroom, and it's why I researched that name she gave me. Flora is why I'll come tonight."

Despite the broiling heat and the gawking passersby and the call of his duties at the center, Sam thought he could probably stand just this way with neurotic, tightly wound, beautiful Ana Burns the rest of his life. For this one moment, he felt understood. Connected. Accepted. In some mysterious way, she knew him, and he could put his anger and guilt and regret into her hands . . . and for this single instant, he could let them go.

But she stepped back. "All right, then. I'll see you."

"Yeah."

She started away, walking down the sidewalk toward her building, but she turned back once and looked at him. He lifted a hand, tried to smile. Her brown eyes were sad and deep, and he knew where he had seen eyes just like that, and he understood now why Ana would visit Haven and go to Flora's corner even when the little girl wasn't there.

Chapter Nine

As she got out of her car, Ana tugged down the hem of her new white blouse. She hadn't intended to buy it. White wasn't her best color. But two days before, she had passed a boutique on her morning run, and there it was on a mannequin in the window, looking so perfect with its cap sleeves and scooped neckline and row of tiny pearl buttons. On her way back by, she had jogged into the boutique just to have a closer look. And somehow, without meaning to, she had bought it. Now, wearing the new blouse with a skirt and slip-on sandals, she stepped onto the sidewalk down the street from Haven.

Okay, she admitted to herself as she locked her car and set off toward the recreation center, she did look good. But she hadn't bought that blouse just to wear to Haven. A white blouse was versatile, and this one didn't even need to be dry-cleaned. Which was of little consequence, because she had no intention of mentioning that fact to Sam Hawke. Or even talking to him at all, for that matter. This evening, after teaching her writing class, she would speak to some of the younger children—those most likely to be affected by the lead paint. After getting what she needed for her series of articles, she wouldn't need to return to the center at all.

One writing class—an hour at the most—ought to do it. Reflecting on memories of favorite teachers in school, Ana had written out a lesson plan she thought the children might enjoy. They would do a little writing, and then the time would be over. She had promised Sam only this one Saturday.

Ana couldn't imagine that Flora would leave her corner to attend a class taught in a foreign language. As much as she cared about the child, Ana was under no illusions. A girl might get some help and encouragement along the way, but that was about it. Flora would have to make her own way through this world just as everyone else did. No matter what Sam had said about Ana, one fallible human being could not truly change another's life for good. Ana had learned that lesson the hard way. Only God knew what the future held.

Absorbed in memories of her sister's painful last months, Ana crossed the street toward Haven. She was passing a boarded-up storefront when two young men stepped out onto the sidewalk, blocking her path. The early-evening sunlight slanted across their glistening skin and gleamed on the gold chains around their necks. From one teen's chain dangled the hippie symbol for peace outlined in large fake diamonds. A large gold cross adorned the other. They wore their shirts unbuttoned, their shorts slung low on their hips, and their sneaker laces looped loosely through the eyeholes. A silver blade glimmered, the weapon held low but angled so the point faced Ana.

"Hey, lady," the taller one growled, his voice husky. He gestured with the knife blade toward the shadows of the nearby door. "Get in there."

At the command, Ana went rigid. Her breath vanished as her brain was jolted by an adrenaline rush of fear. "What did you say?"

"Into that store. Go inside. Do what we tell you, or else."

"No." She said the word slowly, evenly, remembering

the can of pepper spray in her purse, assessing the deserted sidewalks and the knife.

"Do it," the tall one barked, taking a step toward her, brandishing the blade at her belly. "Do what I say!"

"Yeah," the other one echoed.

Blustering. Teenagers. Ana's mind reeled. She had to think her way through this, outwit them. They had no advantage except the knife.

"What do you want?" she asked. "Money? I have a ten-dollar bill in my wallet."

"We gonna teach you a lesson." The tall one smirked, revealing a chipped front tooth. "You gonna learn you're in the wrong hood."

"Listen, I'm a volunteer at Haven. I teach a class . . . a writing class." She took a step back, stalling, hoping someone would appear. How could the street be so empty? "This is our hood, and we don't like no reporter ladies stickin' they noses in our bidness, you know what I mean? Now get in there."

He gave Anna a shove. She tried to push out from between the two of them, but the shorter one caught her. He slung his arm around her neck and slapped his hand over her mouth. The tall one, panting, swearing under his breath, jammed the fist holding the knife against her side.

"Get in! Get inside!"

"No!" she tried to scream. Panic swirled around Ana's eyes like a black curtain as she fought them, fingernails scratching and knees slamming into their bare legs. *Dear God, please help me!*

They wrestled her through the narrow door, partially boarded with plywood. *Help me, God!* She stumbled forward into the darkness, dropped to her knees and made them drag her.

"Now we gonna teach you! Get her down!"

Terror like the fangs of a snake stared her in the face. A snake—mouth open wide, jaws unlocked, venom oozing from white needles as slanted yellow eyes focused on her. Ana had seen this snake before. She recognized it. Knew it well. And this time, the fangs would fail to find their mark.

Grasping the smaller youth's wrist, she jerked his hand from her mouth and shouted for help. Her cries echoed through the empty building, louder and louder as her voice gained strength. She lashed out with her teeth, her elbows, her knees as they tried to pin her.

"Shut her up!"

"I'm trying!"

Again and again she yelled, screaming for help, deafening even herself. Pain skittered up her arm, but she barely noticed as her kick found its mark in the taller boy's groin. He let out a surprised grunt and fell to the floor. Ana heard him coughing and gagging. The second youth stayed with her, his sweaty hands pressing and pushing, trying to keep her down.

"What? Jamal, what happened?" he called into the darkness.

"You boys better get on outta here now!" A new voice called out—husky and threatening. "Go on! Get!"

And then the boy was gone.

Ana rolled up onto her knees and found the rectangle of light eking in from around the boarded-up doorway. Screaming in silence now, she ran toward it, her hands out and her fingers stretched wide. Her palms met the plywood full force, and she burst through. She staggered out onto the sidewalk, the sun too bright even at this late hour.

And then she ran, all her years of jogging poured into a headlong sprint toward the familiar square of concrete with its tattered green awning and small white sign, *Haven.* She blew past the child at the entrance and dashed through the metal detector, which let out a hiccup and began to beep. Duke charged at her, barking, barely contained by the startled boy who gripped his leash. And she kept running with the dog at her heels and the children crying out all around her and the metal detector whooping.

"Ana?"

Sam met her halfway across the gym floor, caught her in his arms and pulled her close. "Ana, what happened? You're bleeding! Who did this?"

Then he was talking to the children, calling off the dog, giving orders, all the while holding her against him in a cocoon of warmth. Ana trembled, shuddered, tried to breathe as she hugged her own arms and let Sam lead her away from the crowd. She kept her face buried in his shoulder, grateful for its solidity and strength. She didn't want to see the children or let them see her looking so fragile and imperfect.

No one should see her this way. She hated it. Hated

herself for her weakness. How had she let it happen? Why hadn't she anticipated an attack? How could she have been so naive as to stroll thoughtlessly down a street in this neighborhood? She should have known. She did know. Stupid. *Stupid.*

"Ana." Sam's voice was low, almost a whisper. "I want you to sit down."

He lowered her onto a chair. They were in his office with the door shut, and she folded over, put her face in her hands, fought the urge to scream again.

"Talk to me, Ana," he said, crouching beside her on the tile floor. His hand was on her arm, stroking gently, his fingers strong and firm. "Tell me what happened."

She shook her head, squeezing back the tears, fighting the revulsion. "I'm all right," she managed, hearing her hoarse voice.

"You're bleeding," he said. "There's a long slash down your right arm. Terell will be here in a minute with the first aid kit. You've got glass in your hair, Ana. Your skirt is torn."

"Okay," she whispered.

"Did you recognize anyone?"

"Two boys. Teenagers. One with a chipped front tooth and a peace sign on his necklace, and another one, smaller but strong. They had a knife. They forced me into the store."

Sam's hand stopped stroking her arm. "Ana, did they . . . did they violate you? It's important that you tell me."

Yes! she wanted to shout! They took away everything I've worked so hard to rebuild! They stripped away my security and my comfort and my peace, they tore through the barrier that is the knowledge of who I am, and they defiled my fragile confidence, the tender certainty that I can survive in this world.

But she knew what he meant, and she shook her head. "I got away."

"Thank God."

The words stirred another memory. "Sam, someone else was there. He came at the end and threatened them. He helped me break free."

"Did you see him?"

"I couldn't see anything in there."

He let out a breath. "Here's Terell."

"Aw, man, this is bad." The man stepped up to her, his sneakers even bigger than Sam's, which seemed impossible. "No one saw it happen, of course. Raydell is gonna ask around. The cops won't find anything. It was a deal that went down. I'm sure of it."

"Any idea who set it up?" Sam asked.

"Not a clue."

"She says there were two of them. One had a chipped front tooth and a peace sign on a chain."

"Now how many kids in the hood does that describe?" he scoffed as he knelt on the floor beside Ana. "I reckon we've got about fifteen or twenty busted teeth right here in the building, and at least that many peace signs."

"But not all on the same kid. And this boy was outside."

"Outside, inside. It doesn't matter. It was a setup, Sam, and nobody talks if it's a setup. That's the deal." He shook his head. "Miss Burns, let me have a look at that arm."

"T-Rex is our blood man," Sam explained. "I take care of vomit and excrement."

Despite her pain, Ana managed a grin. "Thanks for the information."

Terell pulled on a pair of latex gloves and washed her arm with an iodine solution. The knife had slashed her, but not deeply, and both men agreed it would not need stitches.

"Think we should shut down the center for the night?" Sam asked. "Give the kids a talking-to and send them home to think about it?"

"I reckon." The other man sighed.

"They got her purse, Terell. She lost her shoes, too. Things will show up. When the police get here, she can give them a list of what was in the bag."

"No," Ana said. "Please don't call the police."

"They're already on the way, ma'am," Terell said. "A lady gets attacked in this neighborhood, you can bet the police will be over here like a shot."

"Haven doesn't need this in the newspaper," she said, trying to make sense of her rambling thoughts. "It would be worse than the lead paint."

"Yeah, but there's no way to stop the cops."

"I'll tell them I'm fine," she insisted. "I'm not going to file a report. And don't shut down the building, either. I have a class to teach."

"Ana, you can't be serious."

"I made my lesson plan, Sam," she said, meeting his eyes for the first time. They were blue and clear and filled with concern. "I'm going to teach. And then I'm going to get my interviews. Nothing has changed, okay? Nothing."

He swallowed. "Whatever you say."

"I won't let it be different. I won't let them win." She lifted her head and squared her shoulders. The phrase that had been her defiant anthem for so many years found its way to her lips. "I'm not a victim," she said firmly. "I'm a survivor."

I see him coming from a distance, the man with the blue eyes. I know this is not the good time now. This is the time of evil. Fear rises from its slumbering place in my stomach and steps into my heart. There it begins to hit my chest with its fists, pounding hard, as though it wants to crack open my ribs. When fear has filled my chest to the point of breaking, it forms a ball and crawls up into my throat. There it sits, laughing at me and trying to choke me. I swallow and swallow as the man comes closer, but fear grows larger in my throat, and it dries my tongue and glues it to the roof of my mouth.

"Come," the man says, the goodbad man, the love-hate man. I look up at the lightbulb, which is my hiding place. It is where I am safe, where I can find the sunshine again. But the man takes my arm and pulls me away from the lightbulb, from my safety.

I follow him, and fear slides down into the very bottom

of my stomach. There it rolls and turns, doing its dance, first this way and then the other. My hips ache, and my intestines twist into knots, and my legs go weak from the dance of fear.

The man takes me into the room, and that is when I see her. The girl who looks like me. Her brown eyes blink. Her black hair shines. Her mouth sits tightly on her face like a small pink rosebud that has not opened.

Is this girl me? Am I seeing myself or someone else? Who is this child? Why is she here? Where has she come from?

The rose of her mouth does not open, and I stare at her. She knows nothing. She is like me, but she is not me, for I know everything. I know it all. I am filled to the brim with knowledge. She is empty. Empty of the evil and the pain. And she has not yet met fear.

The man walks across the room to her, and I see how it will be. I look at this girl with the rosebud mouth and the brown eyes. Then I stare up into the light. Fear quiets inside me. Fear knows my power over it. Fear understands that God has given me the light. And soon it must go back to its hiding place.

"We're going to start with poetry."

The chorus of groans confirmed Ana's misgivings. Only three youngsters had shown up for her writers' group—two of them boys. Tenisha, the little girl with cerebral palsy, sat across the small round table from her archnemesis, Gerald, whose buckteeth gleamed in his thin brown face. Between them sat the hulking

Raydell Watson. He normally guarded the entrance to Haven, but he told Ana that on hearing about her writing class, he had signed up.

"I like poetry," Raydell announced. "I write poems, Miss Burns. Rap, you know? That's my thing."

"Great." She pasted a smile on her face, wishing she were anywhere but here. And yet she was determined to go on. The children had asked why she ran into Haven in such a frightening way with her hair hanging down and her arm bleeding. They wondered if someone had attacked her. But Ana refused to cater to their curiosity. She would show strength, control. Her assailants had not won.

As Ana stood before the little group, she reflected for a moment on the world outside Haven, the world beyond the hood. Things had been normal there. She had made sure of it. And she had decided to return to that world unchanged by this evening's incident.

A couple of loads of laundry waited by her apartment door for her weekly trip to the dry cleaner. The plants on her balcony needed water, and she would see to that when she got home. A basket of vegetables she'd bought at the farmers' market on Laclede's Landing yesterday sat on her counter. She would steam them and stir them into pasta mixed with olive oil. Today, a man from work—someone in the advertising department—had invited her to take a stroll through the Botanical Gardens on Sunday afternoon. His name was Bill, and he was nice looking. Ana liked him well enough, and maybe she would take him up on his offer. Why not? Nothing had changed.

"You wanna hear one of my raps?" Raydell's gold tooth gleamed. "I got it mesmerized."

"Memorized." Ana nodded. "Okay, but no obscenities. No cussing."

"Here goes." He stood and began to rock back and forth making deep drum-like sounds in his throat. His deep-set eyes fastened on her.

"I am cool
Ain't nobody's fool
You think you are the best
But it's you that I detest . . ."

Raydell stumbled on, swaying, gesturing, rumbling out the words until he came to an abrupt halt. He paused and inhaled. "That's all I got so far. How do you like it, Miss Burns?"

It's you that I detest . . . The words penetrated Ana's brain. The folding chair was cool as she sat down suddenly, and she realized her legs ached. "It's interesting," she heard herself say, as though speaking through a tunnel. "I think you have good rhythm."

"I got another one I was making up this morning when I was out at the front door." Raydell began to swagger as he pumped out lyrics Ana couldn't understand. The slang. The dialect. The pain in her arm.

"That's all I got of that one, too," he announced, dropping down into a chair. "What you think?"

"I think it's good," Tenisha piped up. "It's about crack, like what the boys smoke in the alley down the street."

"It's about cocaine," Raydell said.

"Crank," Gerald put in. "That's what it is."

"Not crank," Raydell snapped. "That's speed."

"I don't like those boys," Tenisha said. "They tease me when I go through the detector."

"That's 'cause you walk like a dork," Gerald said. "You look like Frankenstein with your legs all stiff and jerky."

"Gerald!" Ana cut in. Outrage forced her mind into gear again. "That's enough. You have to be polite, or you can't stay in the group."

"I don't wanna be in the group. Uncle Sam made me. I wanna play basketball, not write dumb poems."

Ana's sigh trembled as she glanced at her watch. Only ten minutes into the hour. The class was a waste of her time and everyone else's, but she had made Sam a promise—and she would get her interviews. As for Flora, Ana had seen the girl sitting in her corner. She hadn't looked up as Ana went into the classroom nearby.

"All right, let's talk about poetry." Ana had lost her lesson plan along with her purse, but she thought she could remember it. She brushed aside a strand of yarn left over from the crochet class and set her folded hands on the card table. Sam had found her a pair of large flip-flops in the lost-and-found box, and she studied her painted toenails as she began.

"Raydell recited a type of poetry known as rap," she said. "There are many different kinds of poems. The one I want to talk about today is called a limerick. It's kind of tricky, but it's a lot of fun to write."

"I want to write rap," Raydell declared.

"You can, but tonight we're going to learn about limericks."

"Is that a kind of rap?"

She thought for a moment. "It could be, I guess. You could use the same themes anyway. Let's talk about your first rap—the one where the guy thinks he's cool, but he's really a fool."

"That's not how it goes. Man!" He shook his head, obviously disgusted. "He's cool, nobody's fool."

"Okay, let's rewrite it as a limerick." She passed out sheets of paper and pencils. And then she realized she could not remember the rules for limericks. She was blank. Empty.

The children stared at her, waiting for her to continue the instructions. And she had nothing to say. Her arm began to throb under the white bandage Terell had wrapped around it. Her mouth went dry. Her stomach churned.

"Give me a second, okay?"

While her little class waited, Ana stepped outside the room to try to collect herself. As she drank down a deep breath, she spotted a huddled shape next to the classroom door. *Flora.* The girl had left her corner and crept closer. She had come to the writing class after all.

Ana put her palms behind her against the wall, hoping for support. She could feel the child's brown eyes on her.

"He did this thing," Flora said in a low voice, her Spanish almost inaudible. "He did this thing to you."

"I'm all right," Ana said, and then she knew she couldn't lie to those eyes. She shook her head. "It hurts."

"Yes." Flora got to her feet, opening up slowly like a cat. "I saw you come into this place. You were running."

"I was afraid."

"Did he catch you?"

"Yes, but I escaped."

"What bad thing did he do?"

"He cut me on the arm with a knife."

Ana could hear Gerald arguing with Tenisha in the classroom. Tenisha was on the verge of tears, and now Raydell spoke up in his deep voice. Ana knew she should go back in, but she couldn't remember limerick rules or anything else.

"He is bad," Flora said. "A very bad man."

Ana wondered at the child's matter-of-fact tone. Did Flora know about the attack?

"There were two of them," Ana told her.

"Two?" Flora looked up, startled. "The one with yellow hair also did this? Segundo? The Second Man? He is here, also, in this city?"

Ana frowned, wondering what she could mean. "Neither one had yellow hair. They both had black hair. They were boys, street boys, you understand?"

"I thought it was Primero, the First Man, who hurt you." Flora's face grew solemn. "Anyway, you shouldn't come to this place. He's here. You won't be safe."

Confused at the child's rapidly whispered words, Ana gazed into the luminous eyes. "Then why do you come?"

"She tells me I must. Today, she brings me here, that one. Hipsy."

"Hipsy? Is she your sister?"

"She's my friend. Hipsy feeds me. We have a room and a bed." Reaching out, Flora touched Ana's arm with her small hand. "I like you, but you must not come here again. This place isn't safe. He can catch you here, if he sees you. He'll hurt you more the next time."

"Who?" Ana's heart hammered. "Who will hurt me?"

"Him. Primero—the First Man." Flora moistened her lips. "I'm telling you the truth, and it's for your own good. Do you understand? I cannot protect you from him. It's impossible, even though I would try. You must not come back."

Flora's dark eyes glanced from side to side as though she expected someone to pounce from the shadows. Ana regarded the child, amazed that this young girl seemed so determined to protect her. But from whom? Who was this Primero? Did Flora know the boys who had attacked Ana? Or was it someone else?

"I must go now," Flora whispered. "*Cuidado!* Take care!"

"Wait!" Ana caught her hand. She gave the child a sheet of paper and a pencil. "Why not come into my class, Flora? I want you to sit with the others. We're writing poems."

"Poems?" Flora's face transformed for an instant. Light shone from her dark eyes. "Like school!"

"Yes," Ana said. "A little bit like that. Please come."

But clouds quickly covered the sunshine. "I cannot. They're not like me. They don't know La Ceiba."

"What is La Ceiba? A tree?"

"No, it's my home. My city. It's far away. There, they speak another way."

"Yes, but I'm like you, Flora. I can talk to you. Let me be your teacher. And your friend."

The hesitation was palpable, as if the girl teetered on a narrow fence. And then she leaped away. "No. I must go."

Before Ana could stop her, Flora hurried back to her corner and curled into the dark shadows. She leaned her forehead against the wall. Eyes fixed forward, she stared at the blank white plaster.

Ana hovered, listening to the three in the classroom and hearing words that meant nothing to her. An argument. Defiance. Swearing. Then she looked at Flora in her corner. A knot of green skirt and brown legs. Hipsy. La Ceiba. Primero. Segundo.

None of it made sense, and suddenly into Ana's brain came a limerick by Ogden Nash, the silliest poet who ever lived. The rhyme scheme bounded out, and the rhythm began to patter with the beat of her heart. Limericks made sense. And above all else Ana's lost lesson plan made sense. So she stepped back into her classroom to begin.

Chapter Ten

"A limerick is a poem," Ana began as she sat down again. "It has a pattern of rhythm and rhyme, usually in iambic meter."

"I don't get it," Gerald announced, wadding his blank paper and tossing it to the floor.

Determined to get through this next hour with as little emotion as possible, Ana didn't glance up. She felt sick inside, confused and off balance. In defying her editor and trying to refocus her series around children affected by lead paint, she had walked into a booby trap. But her urge to flee Haven ran up against her determination not to let her attackers know victory. So here she sat, numb and frightened, worried about Flora but certain she could do nothing to help, and trying to teach poetry to three children who didn't give a rip about it.

She cleared her throat. "Iambic is the name for a kind of beat, like on a drum. It goes duh-*duh.*" She tapped the table in time to her voice. "Can you hear that?"

"I can hear the ref's whistle." Gerald's chair screeched as he pushed it back across the concrete floor. “Let’s go see if the game is over.”

“Gerald, sit down.” She slapped her hand on the table again. “Did you hear the iambic beat? Sit-*down*.”

Tenisha giggled and whapped the table. “Sit-*down*, you-*fool*.”

Ana felt an urge to smile, but she kept the small triumph to herself. “Right, Tenisha. So limericks tend to have an iambic beat, although we’re not going to be picky about it. And they’re five lines long.”

“That’s all?” Raydell scowled. “I like my raps to be longer. Five lines ain’t nothin’.”

“Five lines is all you get with a limerick. I’ll draw you a diagram.” She sketched the meter and rhyme scheme on a sheet of blank paper. “It’s like a map, and if we follow it, we’ll be able to turn your rap into a limerick. Shall we try? I’ll do the first line, Raydell, and then you do the second.”

She thought for a moment. “You know I am really too cool.”

Raydell closed his eyes and worked his chin in and out for a moment. “Because I ain’t nobody’s fool.”

The grin felt awkward on Ana’s face, as though her mouth hadn’t expected it. “That’s it, Raydell. Now the next two lines are going to rhyme with each other. And they only have two beats each. Tenisha, want to try?”

“I can’t do it,” she whispered.

“Sure you can. I’ll do the first line of this pair, and you do the second. Here goes.” She paused. “You think you’re the best.”

“But it’s you I detest!” Raydell called out. “That’s it.

That's my rhyme, only with the limbrick."

"It was my turn!" Tenisha wailed. "You already had your turn. You cut in! Miss Burns, Raydell took my turn!"

"Let Raydell have his rhyme," Ana said. "You make up your own. Here's my line: You think you're the best."

Tenisha wrung her hands, twisting her small brown fingers around each other. Finally, she burst out, "The best in the West!"

"Okay, that works great! Gerald, you get to do the ending. Here's our limerick so far.

'You know I am really too cool
Because I ain't nobody's fool
You think you're the best
The best in the West'

"And your line has to rhyme with cool and fool."

Gerald frowned. "I don't wanna write no stupid poems. And I don't hafta. Uncle Sam made me come in here. I wanna play basketball."

"Just try, Gerald," Tenisha urged.

"Shut up, you idiot!"

"Miss Burns!"

"Hey, you!" Raydell grabbed Gerald by the neck of his white T-shirt and yanked him out of his seat. "Be nice to the girl, or I'll wrench them ugly buckteeth right outta your face."

He launched into a stream of profanities that caught

at the back of Ana's throat, as though she had suddenly swallowed an ice cube. Before she could react, a large form materialized in the classroom.

"That's enough," Sam commanded. "Raydell, you know that kind of talk is not allowed at Haven."

The teenager flung Sam a look of defiance. "Gerald was messin' with Tenisha. I was just defendin' her."

"By attacking Gerald? That's not how I taught you to defend somebody, is it?" Sam sat down at the table, his long legs folding and his knees poking out like a frog's on the low chair. "Raydell, you're my main man. I set you up at the door because I trust you to know the rules and do things the right way. I expect you to be an example to the others."

"Yes, sir." Raydell hung his head.

"Who's in charge in this room?"

The young man's eyes darted to Ana, hostility burning in their dark depths. "Miss Burns is in charge, sir. But you told me you didn't want her here. You said she was messin' with Haven, tryin' to shut us down. How come you let her teach a class?"

"I decided maybe she could help us out. And here you are, Raydell, learning about poems."

"Huh. I don't care about that. I came in here to keep a watch on *her.*"

"If there's a problem, Terell or I will handle it. Have you ever seen me grab a boy by the throat and threaten him and cuss at him?" Sam paused, studying the youth. "That's because we don't do things that way at Haven."

"Yes, sir."

"And that goes for you, too, Gerald." Sam's voice deepened as he turned to the child. "I've had it with you pestering Tenisha. You do it again, and I'm going to put you on the list at the front door."

Gerald's thin pale face crumpled around his protruding teeth. "And I won't get to come to Haven no more?"

"That's right." Sam put a hand on the boy's scrawny shoulder. "Be nice to Tenisha."

"Okay." He sniffled as a drop of moisture appeared under his nose. "But I don't wanna write poems, Uncle Sam."

Ana sat watching the interaction as though she were in another place—Jim Slater's observation room, perhaps—looking through the glass mirror at those on the other side. How had Sam calmed the children so easily? What was his hold over them?

Raydell . . . who was this boy with the ropy muscles and gold tooth? Gerald . . . why hadn't someone given him braces? He needed to go to an orthodontist. His appearance could hold him back his whole life. And Tenisha . . . with her crooked gait and timid manner, what could she ever become? What would any of them grow into, and why must they sit in this room and try to write limericks?

When Ana snapped back to the present, she realized that Sam had gone and the three in the room were bent over their paper scribbling furiously. Had Sam spoken to her before he went away? Had she answered?

The sense of disconnectedness felt all too familiar.

She had been behind that glass window before, looking on things from a distance and not sure who she was or where. How many years had it taken to put away that hiding place? Ten . . . or was it twelve?

"Miss Burns?" Tenisha's face wore a frown. "Miss Burns, I been tryin' to tell you it's time for activity change. Can me and Raydell and Gerald go now?"

Ana looked at her watch in surprise. Had an hour passed? Surely not. Where had she been all that time? "Of course. Yes, go on to basketball or whatever it is. Sure."

"Do you want our limbricks?" Raydell asked. "I followed them 'structions you wrote out."

She glanced at their outstretched hands, the pages covered with pencil scratches and erasures. But she wasn't coming back to Haven. She would have no way to return their writings.

"No, I don't think so." She shrugged. "You can keep them. Show them to your parents."

"You don't wanna see what we wrote?" Gerald asked. "I wrote one. I did a poem."

As he held it out to her, Ana comprehended the significance of the gesture. "Oh, yes, Gerald, that's great. Of course, I'd love to see it. And yours, too, Tenisha. Raydell?"

"I wrote rap limbricks."

"That's fine." She collected the poetry. "Thanks for coming."

As the three left the room, Tenisha turned back. "So, you gonna be here again next Saturday, Miss Burns?

Because I might write you some other limericks at home. I live with my grandma, and she don't know how to read or even write her name, because she just puts down a big X instead, so I could bring them back here for you. And you could read them and tell me what you think."

Ana nodded. "Maybe. If I'm not here, Uncle Sam could give them to me."

"You shouldn't let those boys scare you off," Tenisha confided. "They try that stuff on me, like pushin' me and sayin' what they'll do to me, but I don't let myself get scared. If I was to get scared, I'd hide in the corner like that girl out there with the green skirt. Even though I got the palsy, I look at those boys like 'Ha, don't mess with me.' T-Rex taught me that—to be brave and not scared—and he always tells me to keep on going. Just keep on going, Tenisha."

"Terell says that?" Ana tried to focus.

"Yeah, 'cause he loves me. He gives me rides on his back when my legs get too tired. He lifts me up high so I can put the ball into the basket. Uncle Sam fixes the rules to keep everything safe here, and he cares about me. I know that. But T-Rex loves me."

"Loves you . . . how?"

"Like a daddy." She grinned. "Like God."

Ana sat in silence, absorbing the child's message. "You're not scared of T-Rex? He's so big. And maybe . . . maybe he touches you."

"He hugs me. And I give him big kisses right on his cheek."

"But does he touch you in other places? Like your private parts?"

Tenisha's face looked stricken for a moment. "No!" she gasped. "T-Rex would never do nothing like that. That's bad! Nobody supposed to touch you there!"

"That's right," Ana said. "But I—"

"Miss Burns, don't you know better than to talk like that about T-Rex? He's my friend. He tells me not to let anybody mess with me. T-Rex is the one who says I got to keep on going no matter what. You know?"

Ana did know. She knew how to keep on going. She smiled at the child. "Write some limericks, Tenisha. Write as many as you can. I'll look forward to reading them."

With a wave and a smile, Tenisha worked her way out of the classroom. Ana sat in silence for a moment, taking in the large flip-flops on her feet, the white bandage on her arm, the rip in her skirt. Her new white blouse had lost three buttons near the hem. And she had bled on the sleeve. She touched her hair and felt a chunk of glass in a tangle near her neck. The two boys had tried to defeat her. Tried and failed. But who were they, and would they try again?

And who had come to help her? Had it been one of those mighty male angels that Sam had told her about?

How should she interpret what Tenisha had said about Terell? Clearly, he had been only kind and loving to the child. Was Ana completely off base in her suspicions about the man?

Pushing up out of her chair, she gathered the poems

and the pencils. As she stepped out into the main room where a new basketball game was already in full swing, she heard a voice call her name.

"Señorita Ana!" Flora had left her corner and was standing beside the door. She held out a sheet of paper folded into a tight square. In Spanish, she whispered, "It's a poem. I wrote it for you."

Ana took the paper. As she opened it, her eyes took in the carefully penciled Spanish words.

It comes.
Like moonlight.
Like wind before rain.
Like a green bud on a dead tree.
Esperanza. Hope.

By the time Ana had digested each line, the meaning in each word, Flora was starting back to her corner. Ana reached out for her, caught her arm. "Wait," she called. "Please! Tell me where you came from, Flora. Where is La Ceiba?"

The child hesitated only a moment. "Honduras," she whispered, then she put her finger to her lips.

"Flora, wait," Ana called, but Sam was striding toward her. He laid his hand firmly on her shoulder.

"I'll walk you to your car," he announced. "Are you parked nearby? Do you have your keys?"

She looked up, trying to think beyond the small gift in her hand. *Hope*, Flora had told her. *Keep on going*, Tenisha had urged. They knew, these children who had endured so much. They saw her pain, and they understood it, and they knew the secret to victory.

"My purse," she whispered. "The keys were in my purse."

"Then I'll drive you home."

He was leading her toward the door, and she heard her flip-flops slapping the floor. "But my interviews. I didn't get to talk to the kids."

"Come back tomorrow. I'll bring you. Do you have a set of spare car keys at home? Can you get into your house?"

"Apartment. I keep a key hidden in my mailbox. It has a combination lock."

"Good. Let's get you home, and then you can rest."

"But wait." She stopped and folded her arms around herself. "I don't know you, Sam. Not really. I don't want you to see where I live, because I . . . because . . ."

He was staring at her. "Ana, I'm not going to hurt you."

"I don't know that. I thought I could trust . . . thought I had gotten to the place where it was okay . . . with people, you know? But I feel vulnerable again. I can't lose my privacy."

His brow furrowed over his blue eyes. "Ana, do you see me? Samuel Nathan Hawke. Have you listened to who I am? Do you remember the name of this building? Haven. Protection is what I do. It's my mission. My life is built around providing protection and healing and hope."

"Hope . . ." She spotted Flora in the corner, head

against the wall. "Hope is fragile, Sam. It's hard to catch. It's even harder to keep."

"Let me help you, Ana. At least let me protect you. Please trust me that far."

She closed her eyes for a moment, grateful for the darkness that eased the buzzing in her head. "All right." She sighed in surrender. "Take me home."

"Hold my hand."

She stiffened. "No, I don't—"

"Hold my hand, Ana. I'll keep you safe. I promise."

Swallowing hard against the knot of fear in her throat, she took his hand. His large, warm fingers wrapped around hers. Protection. Or control? Safety. Or danger?

Breathing hard, she followed him through the metal detector and out onto the sidewalk. Night had descended over the street, the stars invisible above the haze that blanketed the city. Music pulsed from open car windows. Where had those cars been when the boys attacked her? Now the low-slung vehicles slid by, teenagers sunk down in the seats, black lights flashing across the dashboard. Someone yelled out a foul name, and Ana jerked.

"He's not talking to us," Sam said, moving against her down the sidewalk. "There's a girl in a car up ahead."

As he spoke, the girl stuck her head out of her own car window and shouted back at the boy. Then she honked and sped off, tires squealing. A truck rumbled by, another car, a boy on a bicycle.

"There it is," Ana said, instinctively squeezing Sam's hand. "The store. That's where it happened."

He slowed his pace. "They came out from the alley?"

"No, from the overhang there." She shuddered at the memory of the two teenagers who had accosted her. "The taller one had a knife. They told me to go inside the store. Said they wanted to teach me a lesson."

Sam was silent, staring at the plywood board bolted across the door and the broken glass on the sidewalk. Someone had spray painted graffiti on the wall beneath the window—gang signs, Ana supposed. She wondered if Sam had ever noticed this place, even though it was just down the street from Haven.

She let out a trembling breath. "They told me not to come back to their hood. They wrestled me inside the building. I fought and screamed, but they pushed me down. Then I kicked one of them, and he let go."

"The bigger one?"

"With the peace sign, yes. And then the stranger came and told them to leave me alone. That's when I realized I was free. So I ran to the door."

"Did they come after you?"

She thought for a moment. "I don't think so."

"I wonder if your purse is still inside."

"They would have taken it."

"Maybe not. It's dark, and they weren't out to rob you. You know that, don't you, Ana? Rape is not about physical desire or attraction." He spoke in a low voice, serious but gentle. "It's about control. Power. Soldiers—the victors—it's what they do, especially in guerrilla warfare. Paramilitary troops in the Third World. It's why women suffer so much during wartime—civilians and female POWs. Men want to prove their dominance. That's what those two were doing this evening with you, Ana."

She nodded. "I know. I understand it."

"It's because you're different. You're a woman, educated, white, wealthy—and you've come into their territory. They're frightened of you in some way. You represent a lifestyle they'll never know."

"Terell said it was a setup."

"Maybe, but I don't think so. I suspect it was a crime of opportunity. You walked by, and they acted out of instinct."

"But there were no cars. No people. The street was suddenly deserted." She swallowed. "Sam, those two guys knew who I was. The taller one told me he didn't want reporter ladies sticking their noses in his business. *Reporter*—he said that."

"Are you sure?" Sam was frowning, his face a pale yellow and his eyes green in the streetlight. "He used that exact word?"

"Oh, maybe not." She shook her head. "It's fuzzy now. But it seemed like that was his focus. He didn't like it that I was a reporter nosing around where I didn't belong."

Sam fell silent again.

"I need to go home," she said. "My arm hurts."

"Listen, I'd like to talk to the man who helped you out. See if he knows who attacked you. Maybe I can get your purse back. Would you mind waiting outside a minute while I go in there?"

"What? You're insane. Those guys could be in there now, looking at us through the window."

"Ana, I'm not afraid of two teenage boys."

"With a knife?"

"Always bet on the Marine. I can handle them. Trust me."

"You tell me that a lot, you know."

"Get used to it. I'm one person who won't let you down. Ever."

He was studying her, and she looked away quickly, uncomfortable at the significance of his words. She ran her eyes over the door and the broken windows, remembering the attack and wondering if she would ever feel truly at peace with anyone. Then she thought of Flora's poem.

Esperanza. Hope.

Just keep on going, Tenisha had urged her. *Don't be scared.*

"You can start proving it now," she said. "Take me in with you. I want to meet that angel."

"And you called me insane?" Sam's grin carved dimples in his cheeks as he switched on a small, powerful flashlight that he had slipped out of his pocket.

"Stick with me," he murmured. He pulled open the heavy door. Ana stepped into the cavernous room beside him and clutched his hand as he moved the beam methodically across the darkness. During her attack, the place had seemed empty. But she discerned several objects now. A chair and a table with one broken leg, a shelf leaning against a wall, a heap of crumpled fabric, old newspapers. But no humans. Maybe it had been an angel, after all.

"They took the purse," she said. "It happened there—where the dust is disturbed on the floor."

He shone the flashlight on the bare spot. "You weren't far from the front door."

"I fought them. Made them drag me every inch of the way."

As she took a step toward the place, a hand grabbed her wrist and a deep voice growled, "It was *you.*"

With a gasp and a cry, Ana swung around. A shroud in gray rags stood next to her, a breath away.

"You was the one them boys drug in here."

Before the words were out, Sam had set Ana behind him. Arms extended, he crouched, shining the flashlight beam on the figure. "Who are you? What are you doing?"

"Watch it, now! Watch it!" The creature blinked and threw up an arm to block the light. Long, graying hair. A toothless hole of a mouth. Charcoal skin with black moles scattered under the eyes. An odor so foul it could hardly be endured. And Ana's purse over one arm. "You the police?"

"Tell me your name," Sam demanded.

Ana looked around his shoulder. Layers of old clothing hung on the skeletal frame—a pink sweater, a man's blue-and-white-pinstriped shirt, a sweat-stained green bow tie hanging loose at the collar. Khaki shorts held up with a length of yellow nylon rope. Knobby knees, gray from kneeling on the dusty floor. A pair of purple socks. And Ana's sandals.

"You tell first." A wrinkled tongue darted out to moisten the lips. "Who're you? And the lady."

"I'm Sam Hawke. I'm a director at Haven, the recreation center down the street. This is Ana."

"I'm Glen."

"Do you live in here?" she asked. "Did you help me?"

The dark eyes studied her, up and down, squinting in the light. "You the one they drug in here, them two boys, ain't you? I seen what they was up to. I figured you was gonna get it, sugar. I didn't do nothin' but yell. Scared 'em is all."

"I appreciate it. Very much." Ana stepped out from behind Sam. "You . . . uh . . . you realize you're wearing my sandals?"

Glen tipped up one foot and studied the shoe with its thin straps. "Well, what do you know about that?"

"That's my purse, too."

"Ain't nothin' in it."

"I don't care about the money. You can have that. And the purse. But I would like my keys. They're on a beaded keychain."

"I don't got your keys."

Ana noticed Glen's furtive glance, and she spotted a long cord around his neck. A necklace of sorts. It was strung with keys of all shapes and sizes—old iron house keys, tiny padlock keys, and a row of gold and silver car keys. Ana's hung on the far end of the necklace, still attached to her beaded key chain.

"There they are." She pointed.

"Them are my keys. I need keys, because you never know. You might come up to a door someplace and be tryin' to get in, and there you'd be without a key to unlock it."

"Like my car door," Ana said. "I can't open it without those keys you have around your neck."

"Them are my keys. Mine."

Sam gave her a look that indicated it was a hopeless case. "What about her wallet? She'd like that back, Glen."

"Yes," Ana concurred. "It has pictures."

"I seen 'em. You a real pretty gal." Glen dug around in the pocket of the pink sweater and brought out a stack of treasures—Ana's driver's license and credit cards. "Look at you in this picture, smilin' so nice. I want to keep it. Put it on a shelf. I don't have pictures of nobody."

"But I need the license in order to drive."

"You have to give her the cards, Glen," Sam said.

The bedraggled man studied the small plastic rectangles one by one, and then solemnly handed each to Ana. "I felt real bad about what them boys was doin' to you. Them kids, they come in here and smoke their crack an' all. And shoot up. They's needles all over the place. Lucky you didn't get stuck with one them needles. You'd get sick like me, and wither up, and all you'd have left is settin' in the dark and wishin' you was dead. You can't eat, you can't sleep, you all broke out in sores and coughin' all the time and feelin' like a old dried-up turnip. Them boys has probably all got it and don't even know and is gonna wind up in here settin' day after day and wishin' they was dead. And they will be, too, just like me."

Despite the foul odor emanating from the ragged figure and her instinctive revulsion to the hollow mouth and scrabbly fingers, Ana's heart softened. "If you're sick, you could get help, Glen. The health department runs clinics. They have medications. You could get food and blankets, too."

"I don't like to go out, sugar. I can't leave my place here. All my stuff. Somebody'd steal it."

Glen gestured toward a far wall, and Sam shone the flashlight on a little arrangement of sagging cardboard boxes, old lightbulbs, empty food cartons, a pile of tattered clothing and a couple of tin cans. Ana reflected on her own tidy apartment. She had worked hard to decorate it, with entire weekends dedicated to shopping for just the right light fixtures, pillows, sofas and solid wood shelving systems.

Recently, she had bought a new comforter, goose down, with a duvet cover that featured hand-crocheted lace around the edges and a coordinating dust ruffle. Perfect on her queen-size bed. But she was annoyed when her stoneware pattern had been discontinued before she'd had a chance to buy the complete set.

Lacking the matching teapot, creamer and sugar bowl, she had felt bereft, as though life had conspired against her.

"I'm gonna put your picture up," Glen said, studying Ana's driver's license. "I like how you got your hair done so pretty. I wish I could do something with my hair, but you know how it is. Things just get the better of you sometimes."

Ana examined the matted locks, stuck with bits of dried grass and reeking with the need for a shampoo. "What would you like to do to your hair, Glen?"

"A nice cut, that's all." The tongue darted over the thin lips. "Well, you all go on home now. And stay away from them boys on the street, sugar. They gonna get you again, you know. Yeah, I heard what they said. They gonna try it, too."

Ana reached for Sam's hand. "What did they say?"

"They got to get you. Got to."

"Why?"

Glen squinted. "Because."

"Because why?"

"How should I know? I was just settin' there mindin' my own business. I ain't nosy like some people."

With that, Glen whirled around and headed off, Ana's sandals going clickety-click on the bare concrete floor. Ana's eyes met Sam's. He regarded the ragged figure a moment longer. Then he slipped an arm around her shoulders.

"Terell was right," he said, turning her toward the door. "It was a setup."

Chapter Eleven

As Sam raised his hand to press the buzzer on Ana's apartment door, he realized he was sweating. He paused a moment to analyze that fact. In the course of a normal day, he perspired a lot. Haven's air-conditioning system functioned poorly or not at all, and overseeing a basketball game, sorting out a spat, even racing up and down the stairs to check on groups of volunteers could call for a T-shirt change. Missouri summers, with their intense heat and cloying humidity, always made staying cool a challenge.

Sam tried to tell himself this was the root of the problem. He had parked some distance from the old brick house that had been converted into efficiency apartments, and strolling down the Sunday morning sidewalk had heated him. But the excuse wouldn't hold water. It was the prospect of seeing Ana that dampened his palms and sent a rivulet of perspiration down his spine.

Crazy to stress out over it, he admonished himself. She was merely a woman without a car. She would need a ride to church, that's all. And he had decided to show up at her door.

That was the problem. You didn't just show up at Ana Burns's door. She didn't like surprises. She liked plans. Routines. Schedules. She wanted control and order in her life. She did not want a man she hardly trusted appearing out of the blue and butting into her life. He ought to head back downtown and go to his own church as he always did on Sundays. If Ana wanted to attend a worship service, she would phone a friend.

He should have given her a call earlier and set it up. He would have. But he knew what she would say. No. No, I don't need a ride. No, I don't need your help. No, I don't want you.

So, he pressed the buzzer and waited. Her voice came on the intercom.

"Who is it?"

He rubbed a hand behind his neck. "Uh, Sam. Sam Hawke."

Silence.

"What are you doing here?"

"I thought you might need a ride to church." He studied the rows of windows overhead, wondering which ones were hers. "After that I could take you to pick up your car. You could talk to some of the kids at the center."

"I'm not dressed for church. I wasn't planning to go."

"Is your arm too sore?"

"I don't have a car, remember?"

Sarcasm—Ana Burns's favorite dialect. The barred door hummed to indicate that he could enter.

"Come upstairs," her voice said. "I'm in 2A."

Sam stepped into the foyer of the old house, recalling that she hadn't let him inside when he had dropped her off the night before. Now, the scent of lemon oil greeted him—freshly polished woodwork, gleaming oak floors, a shiny banister anchored by a large, carved newel post. A hallway lined with closed doors featured brass numbers neatly nailed to the wall. Each door had a knocker. He climbed the staircase, his shoes silent on the thick burgundy carpet. The first door to the left was hers. He knocked.

"You can sit over there." She spoke as she opened the door and pointed to a couch slip-covered in creamy cotton fabric. Wearing a pair of gray running shorts and a pink tank top, she padded away in her bare feet. "I'm changing. Don't move."

"So, good morning," he called after her.

"Not really," she replied.

He sat gingerly, concerned that a wrinkle on her perfect couch would irk her. The living area had a softer feel than Ana herself conveyed. Lace curtains, downy pillows on the sofa, a tablecloth edged with thick twisted fringe. Everything in shades of white, cream, ivory and soft butter brought a cocoon to mind. This was Ana's sanctuary, the quiet center of her world. Her haven.

On the table beside the couch sat three framed black-and-white photographs. In one, he recognized Ana as a little girl. Her large brown eyes gazed solemnly. She wasn't smiling. In the second, her parents' wedding portrait, the couple stood together inside an ornate chapel. Her mother, clearly Hispanic with the same brown eyes and angular figure as her daughter, carried a bouquet of white lilies. The father had broad shoulders and the radiant smile that Sam had seen only rarely on Ana's face. The third picture featured two little girls, arms draped across each other's shoulders, hair in pigtails, grinning at the camera. They must have been nearly the same age—about five or six, he guessed—and both were missing front teeth. One was Ana. The other must be the sister she had mentioned.

Sam could see the small round oak table where Ana ate her meals. Not big enough to entertain guests. Only two chairs. And the kitchen area beyond. Tidy, of course. Spotless white marble countertops. Large glass jars filled with flour, sugar and rice stood in a perfect row. Like the hallway outside, her apartment smelled of lemons and bleach and maybe a trace of ammonia. No floral potpourris or scented candles for Ana. She stepped out of her bedroom wearing a sleeveless beige dress and low pumps. She carried a matching purse on her uninjured arm. Her brown hair hung long and loose, softer than Sam had seen it.

She paused, one hip thrust out and her bare leg angled toward him, lean, tanned and perfectly muscled. "Man, you're hot," Sam said, coming to his feet.

"What?" Straightening, she crossed her arms over her chest and glared at him. "Hot?"

"Sorry, but it's true. Caleb said it. Billy confirmed it. And you're stuck with it. You are one hot chick."

A grin twitched the corners of her mouth. "Well, for once, Samuel Nathan Hawke, you've left me speechless."

He gestured toward the door. “Mind if I accompany you to your service this morning?”

“Do I have any choice?”

“You always have a choice.”

“Not always.” Her brown gaze touched his, then swept away as she stepped out into the hall. “Don’t make it sound so easy, Sam. Fixing the world. It’s hard, and you will never succeed.”

She continued speaking as they descended the stairs. “People don’t always have choices, especially children. Even if they might have a choice, sometimes they don’t realize it.”

“That’s why I’m there. To show them a different way.”

“You’re teaching them to play basketball and crochet hot pads.”

“That’s harsh.”

“Sorry, but kids like Tenisha and Gerald—and certainly Flora—need a lot more than that.”

“What do you suggest?” He followed her out of the old house and down the sidewalk toward his car. “You must have some ideas.”

“I know what might help, but it’s beyond what you could offer at Haven. The children need physical, psychological and spiritual healing. Even if they get that, it still might not be enough to alter the course of their lives.”

“Are you always this optimistic, Ana?” he asked, opening her car door.

“Just on the mornings after I’ve been attacked with a knife.”

Well, Sam observed as he rounded the car toward the driver's side, this was going to be a fun little outing. He wondered if Ana ever really enjoyed herself. She took life so seriously—her job, her running, even her housekeeping. Though Sam knew he had the same obsessive perfectionist tendencies, the identical need for order and control, he also enjoyed each day he spent at Haven. He loved the kids, he admired and appreciated the volunteers, and he had a longstanding friendship with Terell. Peace flowed through him, and with it came a sense of hope and joy.

As he stepped into the car, Sam saw that Ana had leaned against the headrest and closed her eyes. Like a lean lioness, the woman radiated physical beauty. But something inside her was raw and painful, and he suspected that it arose from more than just the incident the night before. Ana needed to be healed in the same way the children at Haven did. Only she didn't seem to realize it.

"You can't truly change these kids' lives, Sam," she repeated softly. "But you're trying to do some good things for them. If I can get my interviews and put the series together in time, I'll show St. Louis what Haven is all about."

"The power of the pen." He started the engine and pulled the car out into the street.

"You'd be surprised what it can accomplish," she said. "Last night, Gerald wrote a limerick."

"No kidding?"

"It's actually pretty good. And Sam, I spoke to Flora

again. I found out something about her. That name she said—La Ceiba—it didn't have anything to do with witchcraft. It's her hometown. In Honduras."

"Honduras?" His amazement that the child could have traveled such a distance was followed by the realization of an unsettling coincidence. "Jim Slater brought those two little orphan girls from Honduras."

"I know. Odd, isn't it? If I see him today at church, I think I'll ask about the country's immigration laws. Flora must have become separated from her parents. I imagine Jim could help us look for them."

"Us?"

"You know you want to help her as much as I do, Sam." Her focus slid across to meet his glance. "Flora gave me a poem."

"You got a lot out of those kids despite all your protests. What did she write about?"

"*Esperanza.* Hope." Ana raked her hair back from her face, unaware of the effect her striking profile and long neck had on Sam. "Flora saw me run into the building last night, and she asked what had happened. She had strange questions. She kept warning me—told me I shouldn't come back to the center because it wasn't safe."

"No way," Sam said, his ire rising. "The kid sits there every day, and nobody bothers her. Haven is a lot safer than the streets."

"Flora thought she knew who had attacked me. She spoke of two men. One named Segundo had blond hair. She called the other man Primero."

"But you said a couple of kids did it."

"That's right, two teenagers in do-rags and—" She caught her breath and then grabbed Sam's wrist. "I know who attacked me! I remember them now. The do-rags. One afternoon on my way into Haven, I saw them sitting outside under the awning with Raydell."

"Raydell doesn't hang with thugs."

"They weren't *with* him. Not like friends. They were sitting out there because he wouldn't let them inside. They had refused to take off their headgear."

"We've got a gang problem," Sam said.

"They razzed me—'Hey, pretty lady'—that kind of thing. I didn't like it, but it wasn't menacing. They were coming on to me the way men do sometimes. I didn't think much of it at the time. Sam, I'm sure they were the same two guys who attacked me."

"Then Raydell will know their names. He'll be able to tell us who they are and where they live." Sam gripped the steering wheel, hoping the thought that had just popped into his head was wrong. "I'll talk to him this afternoon. Could be he knows more about the attack than he's letting on."

Ana glanced at him. "Do you think Raydell might have played a part in it? He wasn't there, Sam. He was guarding the door. He even came to my writing class."

"Yeah, to keep an eye on you. That's what he told me, remember? He knew I was unhappy that you'd been coming to Haven and poking around in our business."

"Raydell has always been polite to me. Last night he

even wrote a rap." She twisted the handle of her purse. "Although . . . the lyrics were pretty hostile, now that I think about it."

"Ever heard a rap that wasn't hostile?"

She smiled. "You've got a point there. But I don't think Raydell would do something like that. You know he wants nothing more than to please you."

"Exactly." He frowned as he pulled into the church parking lot. "The first time Raydell stepped through the doors of Haven, he had just gotten out of juvie—juvenile detention—doing shock time for misdemeanor drug possession. He was tough and street-smart, and his mouth was filthy. But something clicked between us, and he's been stuck like glue to me ever since. He's the one who told me about the metal detector they were replacing at the city workhouse, and he helped us negotiate to buy the thing and install it at Haven. He loves his job guarding the door, but sometimes I worry about letting him stay there all day."

"Door duty allows him to keep walking the line," Ana said. "He can keep one foot in Haven's world of regulations, discipline and security, and the other foot out in the old hood."

Sam nodded in agreement as he climbed out of the car. "Right on target. I trust Raydell, and we rarely have an incident that he could have prevented. No guns and only one knife have made it past him. No drugs ever come in, as far as I've been able to tell. But he hangs out on the street most of the day, and people talk to him. Kids do sit under that awning sometimes. For all I know, Raydell could be keeping Haven clean with one hand and doing dirty deals with the other. If he wanted to scare you away, he'd have no trouble setting that up."

Ana accompanied Sam in silence as they climbed the steps to the church sanctuary. He had always admired the old structure, home to one of the earliest denominations to settle and build in St. Louis. With its long stained-glass windows and quaint wooden pews, it reminded him of churches he had seen in Europe.

Ana greeted several people as she made her way down the aisle, and they knew her by name. It seemed like a friendly enough place, yet it was nothing like the bustle and noise that filled his own church every Sunday morning—people setting up microphones, eating doughnuts, drinking coffee, banging on a drum set, tuning guitars, herding children off to Sunday school. Many different racial groups populated the early service Sam attended. Later in the day, a Korean group met to worship, followed by a Spanish-speaking congregation. During the worship hour, a praise band led singing, drama groups acted out skits, the pastor gave a sermon. It was a veritable three-ring circus.

Sam enjoyed it immensely, and his spiritual life had deepened in the months he'd been there. But he was eager to partake of the more solemn and reverent atmosphere in Ana's church. He believed God accepted worship in many forms, as long as it was sincere.

They took a pew, and Sam tried to arrange his long legs in the cramped space. Ana folded her hands and stared down at her purse. He wondered if she was praying. In a moment, the service began, and he was gratified to hear the soaring old hymns he had learned as a boy.

When their mother abandoned them, Sam and his younger brothers had turned to their paternal grandmother for affection. She didn't have much love to give the scrappy little fellows, but she did haul them to church every Sunday. Afterward they always stopped at the local mom-and-pop diner for lunch. Sam could hardly sing the familiar hymns without envisioning a plate of steaming fried chicken, a mound of creamy mashed potatoes drowning in brown gravy, gleaming ears of corn on the cob, green beans swimming in bacon grease and hot rolls dripping butter.

His stomach growling, Sam tried to concentrate on the message. He dug a pen out of his pocket and jotted a few notes on the back of the bulletin, but he was grateful when the pastor closed his sermon notes and stepped away from the pulpit. Ana rubbed her bandaged arm while the choir sang a chorus. Someone went to the pulpit and led in a final prayer, then Ana accompanied Sam down the aisle.

"Oh, look," she said, hurrying forward. "There's Jim Slater."

Jim smiled as he greeted Ana. At the sight of Sam, his eyebrows rose, but he said nothing. "May I introduce a friend of mine?" he asked.

A stocky man with a dark crew cut stepped up and stuck out a hand. He wore a pair of khaki trousers and a blue oxford shirt with a small brown stain near the pocket.

"Jack Smith works with me," Jim explained. "He's visiting from our Arkansas office. Jack, this is Ana Burns and Sam Hawke."

"Ana, Sam," the man repeated. "Good to know you."

"Arkansas?" Ana appeared surprised. "I didn't realize your agency had offices in more than one state."

As was Sam's custom, he assessed Jim while the man gave Ana a brief answer. Though dressed in a gray suit, black shoes, starched white shirt and blue-striped tie, Jim clearly had been ill over the weekend. His skin wore an ashen cast, and dark circles weighed under his eyes. His grin appeared artificial, like the smiling mouth of a doll. But here he was, shaking Ana's hand, and asking after her well-being. He mentioned the bandage on her arm, and she gave a detailed account of the incident.

"I must say I'm surprised to see you here, Sam." Jim turned his focus from the woman. "When did you start attending our church?"

"Today," Sam answered.

"Listen, Jim, there's something I've been wanting to

ask you." Ana cut in before Sam could continue. "Maybe you would have some thoughts on this, too, Mr. Smith. It's about a little girl who's been coming to Haven. We'd like to help her."

And she was off to the races, Sam realized, amazed at how doggedly Ana pursued everything. He had seen her frustrated, angry and sad, but never tired enough to quit. Discouraged but never defeated.

"Honduras?" Jim asked, cocking his head to one side as his smile faded. "My goodness, I can't imagine that. Are you sure that's what she said?"

"Yes. The town is called La Ceiba." Ana accompanied the two men outside the church into the bright noonday sun. Sam lagged behind, listening and watching. "It's on the coast. Have you been there?"

"Actually, I always fly into the capital. The government offices are there, and that's where I do most of our business. Filling out forms and such."

"Then you would know about Honduran immigration law?" she asked. "And you, too, Mr. Smith?"

"I don't know anything about that," the stocky man said.

"I know a good deal about immigration law," Jim spoke up. "Unfortunately, there are loopholes and small details in each country. Her parents must have found a way to get to the States. I'm sure they leave her at Haven while they work. I've seen many children in the same situation. Right, Sam?"

"Only not from Honduras." Sam leaned against the handrail that led down the church steps. No telling how long Ana would interrogate Jim and his colleague. Sam had been hoping she might agree to go to lunch. Maybe some fried chicken.

"I'm afraid I wouldn't be comfortable talking to the girl," Jim was saying as he shook his head. "My Spanish is not good, for one thing. The family probably moved here—maybe it was a refugee thing."

"What do you mean by that?" Ana asked. "I thought refugees came from war-torn countries. Honduras is politically calm, isn't it? So, how could a family enter the U.S. as refugees? Wouldn't they need a sponsor?"

Jim's eyes flashed toward the parking lot. "You know, Ana, I'd love to talk with you about this, but some friends are expecting Jack and me for lunch. We really need to be on our way."

"Oh, sure. Sorry to keep you." She started down the steps with them, Sam following. Despite her apology, Ana kept talking. "In Brownsville, I interviewed a family who had fled Romania during Ceausescu's dictatorship. In order to get to the States, someone had to sponsor them—to make sure they found a place to live, learned how to buy groceries, kept their green cards up to date and got decent jobs. If Flora's family had a sponsor, maybe we could find that person by contacting some kind of agency. From there, we could track down her parents. What do you think, Jim? Would we call Immigration or—"

"I'm not sure about that sort of thing, Ana." Perspiring in the intense heat, Jim tugged a white handkerchief from his pocket and began blotting his forehead. “I work with adoptions. Refugees are not my area. I’m not up to speed on immigration.”

“But don’t you have to work with INS when you bring children here?”

“Not in that sense.” He headed for his car, speaking over his shoulder as he and Jack Smith walked away. “Listen, I’m sorry to run out on you like this, Ana, but we really have to go. See you next Sunday.”

“Hey, Jim!” Sam called out. “Could I drop by your house to pick up the pledge? I could swing by tomorrow morning.”

“I’ll call you, Sam. Soon.”

As the man ducked into a car, Sam jammed his hands into his pockets. “Great. Soon, he tells me. How many days is that?”

“He’ll come through for you,” Ana predicted as they headed for Sam’s vehicle. “Did you get the feeling Jim was trying to evade my questions?”

“Who wouldn’t? You go after people like a pit bull.”

“I’m trying to help Flora.”

“You hit the poor guy with everything from immigration laws to refugees and Romanians. He’s been sick. I’m surprised he didn’t toss his cookies right here in the parking lot.”

“How do you know Jim was sick? Did you talk to him over the weekend?”

“He had bags under his eyes.” Sam opened the passenger door for Ana, then slid into the driver’s seat. “And his breath . . . might have been cough syrup. Whatever he’d been drinking—it had alcohol in it.”

"Are you accusing Jim Slater of drinking before the Sunday-morning worship service?"

Sam looked into her brown eyes. A grin tickled the corner of his mouth. Then he leaned over, tipped up her chin with his forefinger and lightly kissed her lips.

"Do you ever let up?" he asked as she gaped in astonishment. "Don't answer that. I already know. And by the way—you and I are going to have a fried-chicken-and-mashed-potatoes picnic in the park."

"Bering is here, and he's got the reporter in his sights. But he thinks she'll be hard to do."

"Why's that?"

He sighed as he clutched the cell phone. Things were looking a little better now. Bering had arrived late last night, and seemed eager to get to work. Still, the situation in Springfield grew hotter by the day, and he hadn't been able to throw up enough roadblocks to stop it. Step by step, inch by inch, the Feds were getting closer.

"The lady's got a boyfriend, Stu. They're together all the time. He's at her place, she's at his. And she's on our trail. Asked me a bunch of questions about the kid."

"Which kid?"

"The one who belonged to our client."

"So, get Bering to do her first."

"I'm sending him after her today. I'll take him down there this afternoon and point her out." The thought gave him some satisfaction. He would enjoy seeing the

girl's face when she realized he was back—with Bering at his side. She would know they had her, and she couldn't get away. She'd feel the same terror she had made him feel these past few days.

Many months ago, before he had handed her over to the Springfield client, he had warned her. He warned all of them. They were not to talk. They had to obey, or they wouldn't eat or have a bed to sleep in. They wouldn't get any more toys to play with. And if they ever told anyone about him, he would personally come after them and kill them. Simple. Straightforward. And true.

Now this kid would find out he was a man of his word. He had the power to do whatever he wanted. Let this be a lesson to anyone who would cross him.

"So, what's happening on your end?" he asked Stu.

"I think I've been hacked." The breathless voice, so weak and filled with trepidation, defined Stu's character. "My computer keeps rebooting all by itself. The screen goes black, the power shuts off and then the thing starts up again. Like it's possessed. Last night I noticed some of my files were gone. Deleted, just like that. I don't know how it happened. I think someone may have gotten in."

"Did you do what I said? I told you to take the computer and your hard files to the dump. Did you do that, Stu?"

"Look, I don't really know, okay? I'm so confused, I can't remember what I've done and what I haven't. I got Bering for you, didn't I? Why don't you just leave

me alone? Stop calling me, okay? My wife keeps asking who I'm talking to. She wants to see what's on my computer. She's gotten all suspicious now. It's coming at me from every side."

"Well, get rid of everything, you idiot! Erase the data on your computer. Take the thing to the dump along with all your other—"

"But I've been collecting these photos for years. This is my life's work. It used to be all I needed . . . until I met you. You're the cause of my problems, you know. This is your fault for roping me into your schemes! I had a wife and kids and a happy life before you came along. Before your name popped up on my computer screen, I never did anything. It was all taken care of. I had my collection, and that was it. And then you started me with the real stuff."

"You did that yourself. I didn't make you do anything."

"A fishing trip to Costa Rica!"

"You wanted to go on that trip. You paid your money, and you got what you were after. I provided you with a service. I'm just the dealer, Stu. You're the user."

"You used me! You got me into this trouble."

He jammed his finger on the off button and slammed down the phone. That's it, Stu, blame me. Just like everyone else. Blame me for giving you exactly what you wanted. What you had craved from the time you were a kid yourself.

"Stu's a loser," he told Bering, who had been sitting across the room eating a sandwich. "He's going down."

"Yeah, well, I'm keepin' my nose outta that stuff. You guys are all a bunch of sickos, if you ask me."

"Nobody asked you," he snarled. "You just do your job, and keep your opinions to yourself."

"Look, I'll do the lady, no problem. But three kids? C'mon, man. You can't be serious."

"Am I paying you, Bering? Am I paying you thousands of dollars to do what I ask?"

"Yeah, but—"

"Then you'll do it. Don't get sentimental. These kids aren't the way you think. They ask for what they get. They come begging at my door. They want this life, and they love it."

"Sure, that's why one of 'em ran away from that freak who had her."

"My client was not a freak! Stop denigrating us. You're just like all the rest. No one understands. You think we're creeps, sickos, nuts. You're wrong. My clients are good men. Honorable, upstanding citizens who work hard for the money they spend on my services."

"If they're not sick, how come they mess with children? That's disgusting."

"I'm defending my morality to a hired killer? Please!" He leaned back in the chair and rubbed his eyebrows. His headache came and went now, but he hadn't been able to back off on the alcohol. That bothered him. Made him feel out of control, and he didn't like that.

"The clients I serve," he explained calmly, "are

unique. Special. Different from the run-of-the-mill crowd. My clients are doing these kids a huge favor. They provide a home, food, companionship. The children come from places where they don't stand a chance anyway. My clients educate them about life."

"Sure they do."

"Listen, the product I import is nameless, faceless and hopeless."

"Product," Bering scoffed. "I got three little products of my own. You think I ain't got no morals, but at least I pay child support. I see 'em, too, when I can. I got a boy, and I'm gonna see that he don't grow up like his daddy. He's goin' to college, my boy is. And if anyone like you tries to mess with him, let me tell ya—"

"Shut up! Just shut up!" He stood and clutched his hair, tugging so hard it felt as though his scalp might peel off. "You don't understand, and you never will, so just shut up! Get your things, and come with me."

"Where we goin'? I'm doin' this my way, y'know. The lady goes down first. The kids, I do later."

"You'll do what I say when I say it." He gave his shoulders a shake to try and relieve the tension that had knotted his muscles. "I'm taking you to the club. I want to show you the kid who could inform on me. You'll do her first and the woman second. And you'll take care of these two here at the house by midnight. In the meantime, I'll be packing my suitcases. I'm taking a well-deserved vacation."

Chapter Twelve

"So, Jim Slater says Jack Smith is from Arkansas," Sam commented. He peered into the red-and-white box and selected a large piece of crispy fried chicken. Placing it next to the mound of mashed potatoes, heap of slaw and buttered roll on his plate, he nodded as if finally satisfied with the arrangement. "I'd bet my bottom dollar he's from Boston."

Ana had observed Sam's elaborate lunch preparations with interest. Though initially she had objected to a picnic with him in Forest Park, she finally relented. For some reason she couldn't quite understand, she liked Sam's company. He was good-looking, of course, but that had never been a priority for her. Maybe his military bearing attracted her—the staunch adherence to his moral code, the determined enforcement of rules and regulations, the firm devotion to his goals. She certainly admired those things about the man.

But maybe more than anything, she felt safe with Sam Hawke. Not just physically safe, though that mattered a great deal. But she instinctively believed he could be trusted with every private, hidden thing she chose to share. She knew he would never tease, hurt, or manipulate her. He would never use her.

These qualities were good, Ana acknowledged to herself. But they disturbed her, too. She didn't want to admire or enjoy or desire any man. Not now. Not ever.

Long ago, she had made up her mind on that. Watching her sister flit from one affair to another—desperately seeking some kind of fulfillment from the promiscuity to which she had become addicted—made Ana even more determined to steer clear of the relationship minefield.

And yet, she had liked Sam's kiss. More than liked it, she had responded to it with a deep, warm, unfolding welcome. As though it had been a rain shower after drought. Or a homecoming after long years in prison.

"I knew a guy from Boston," he was saying as he tore open his fork, napkin and condiment packet. "Spent three months with him in Iraq. He talked just like that Smith fellow."

"All the man said to us was hello and that he didn't know Honduran immigration law," Ana pointed out.

"He said 'Good to know you' and 'I don't know anything about that.' " Sam's blue eyes shone in the early-afternoon sunlight that filtered through the leaves of the oak tree under which they sat. "He's from Boston, I'm telling you."

She chose a chicken leg. "Okay, Boston. Whatever. You're from Wyoming, and I'm from Texas. People move."

"Yeah, but how come Jim never mentioned having a branch in Arkansas? He's told me a lot about his agency, and he never said anything about that. And he *was* trying to evade your questions, by the way."

"You think so?"

"I know so." Sam reached out and took Ana's hand. "I'll ask the blessing."

As he bowed his head and spoke words of gratitude to God, Ana pondered the amazing power of human touch. Since leaving home, she hadn't made it a custom to say grace in public, and she certainly never held anyone's hand while praying. Now she realized how much she missed both. Sam's heartfelt offering touched her deeply. When he finished the prayer, she almost regretted its end.

"I'm curious about something," she said as he began to eat. "What do you think God is like?"

"I know what He's like. The life and teachings of Jesus Christ couldn't be more clear."

"Love?"

"Power."

Ana picked up a piece of chicken. "I don't agree. I see God as my savior. My shepherd."

"You're not a little sheep, Ana. God is a vigilant protector. His character is that of a warrior."

"He's my authority, sure. But I don't see Him the way you do—as some sort of drill sergeant."

Sam gazed up into the treetops for a moment. "Maybe He's both, Ana. When we need love, He's there for us. When we need power, He provides that, too. I don't look to humans for either."

"No? Not even in church?"

"Some of the most ungodly people in the world hold positions of authority in our churches, Ana. God put

His Spirit inside us to provide discernment. You can't trust everyone."

Ana grabbed her soda and took a drink, hoping to wash down the lump that had risen suddenly in her throat. "I know better," she whispered, "but I guess I've spent most of my life looking for someone to trust."

Sam eyed her. "I said you can't trust *everyone*, Ana. But there are some reliable, honorable Believers on this earth. You can trust those people. I'm one of them."

"According to you." She tried to force a smile. "Maybe you're right, Sam. I'm not sure. I haven't ever known anyone like you."

"That's how I felt when I met Terell. He lived his faith. He was all about surrendering his own desires and being obedient to God's guidance. I knew God . . . Terell introduced me to Jesus Christ."

"But you said he had messed up his life while he was playing pro basketball."

"Christian faith is a straight and narrow path, and Terell decided to take a major detour. Women, two big houses, a fleet of luxury cars, nightclubbing. Drugs. Booze. He was sinking fast. As he tells it, God finally got his attention by throwing his sorry hide into a jail cell."

Ana straightened, recalling her suspicions about Terell's behavior at Haven. "What did he do?"

"Drugs. Steroids. Gambling on his games. You name it. He got kicked out of the league, lost his houses and cars, emptied his bank accounts to pay attorneys. He was living with his mama, working at a convenience store and playing pickup games on a playground court when I got back from Iraq and went looking for him."

Sam stuck his fork in the mashed potatoes. "By that time, Terell had focused himself in the right direction. He and I talked a lot during those months. We decided we wanted to do what we could to change not only our lives, but also the lives of others."

"So running Haven is your 'good deed' ladder into heaven?"

"There's no ladder like that, woman, and you know it. Surrender is what gets a person into heaven."

"We're back to your drill sergeant God."

"That's right, and there are only two armies, Ana. You have to choose. As a Christian, you've given God control of your life whether you like it or not. If you keep trying to manage it yourself, you'll end up like Terell did. Or worse. Homeless. Hopeless. Helpless."

Ana ate in silence, unable to speak. Better than most people, she understood helplessness. She had battled it all her adult life, fighting to hold on to a sense of control. The idea of total surrender frightened her. Yet, Sam spoke with such confidence. His life gave every evidence that what he said was true. In her heart, she knew that total surrender to Jesus Christ's authority would bring a deep peace and a security she had never known. Yet, she wasn't ready to hand Sam the victory.

"Do you believe surrender to God is the answer to the problems the children at Haven face?" she asked.

"Sure I do."

"I can't agree with that, Sam. *Physical healing* requires a doctor. Tenisha needs to work with a physical therapist for her cerebral palsy, and Gerald ought to have braces. There's no excuse for the emotional trauma that little boy is enduring—and he's taking out his hurt on others. *Psychological healing* can't happen without counseling. Those children need to revisit the past and work on the issues that could be stumbling blocks. As for *spiritual healing*, I agree that's God domain. But please don't tell me you're relying on Him to take care of all three areas for them. That's naive."

Sam set down his plate and stretched out on the blanket he had taken from the trunk of his car. Hands behind his head, he spoke in a low voice. "Ana, I trust that God can bring physical, psychological and spiritual healing. I also think He wants us to use doctors and therapists. But the main thing I believe is that these kids need to be given the tools to move forward."

"Basketball and crochet?"

"Those are lures to get them into the program."

"Aha. I knew you had an ulterior motive."

His mouth formed a lopsided grin. "Sure I do—and it's devious. My ulterior motive is to equip the kids with what they'll need to step out into the world and be successful. Yeah, we play basketball. But along with the game, we're teaching teamwork and responsibility. We're breaking down gang lines and insisting on respect for authority."

"What about crochet?"

"Granny's class puts boys in a traditionally female role, once again to break down accepted patterns. Respect for elders goes along with it."

"So that's it, then?" she asked. "You're relying on your classes and your basketball games to create a future generation of successful young Americans."

"We've only started," he said. "I have a lot more in mind. I want to provide a stronger GED program, resources for expectant mothers, job training opportunities. We need more teachers and greater financial backing. When the whole place is functioning, yes, we will be helping create a successful future generation of young Americans."

"That's why you need to fix your lead paint problem."

"Definitely."

Ana picked up the used plates and stuffed them into the plastic fast-food bag. "It sounds good. But I have trouble believing this can help a child like Flora. Something terrible has happened in her past, Sam. She needs to deal with that."

"I don't believe in digging around in the past," he said. "I'm for starting where you are and moving ahead."

"You can't move forward until you've healed your past. You can't ignore it, Sam. It's part of who you are."

"You think everyone needs to spill their guts to some psychologist in order to get healthy? I don't give a rip about my past. It's over and done. I never look back."

"Liar." She crossed her arms and set her jaw. "You look at it every day. You can't stop thinking about it."

He sat up suddenly, leaning forward and jabbing a finger at her. "My eyes are wide-open, Ana. I do not want to look back. I will not do it!"

His words chilled her. "Why not, Sam? What are you afraid you'll see?"

"Nothing." He lowered his head. "There's nothing to see, because I'm not looking."

"Like the old peekaboo game? If I close my eyes, then you can't see me?" She reached out and laid her hand on his arm. "Sam, I don't like to look back, either. It hurts. But I've learned if I try to ignore what happened, I get stuck. There's no way I can move forward."

"You mean your sister? You think it's important to keep looking back at that?"

Falling silent, Ana studied a group of children playing tag on a patch of green grass in the distance. They were running back and forth, shrieking, laughing, falling down and then running breathlessly to their parents. A happy scene, and one that should have lifted her spirits.

Yet it brought back too many memories. Ana didn't like to think about what had happened, and she never discussed it with anyone but the counselor she had seen for a couple of months after her hasty move to St. Louis. People didn't have a right to know about her private life, and she had no intention of sharing it.

She folded her arms across her knees and rested her cheek on them. Eyes closed, she felt Sam cover her hand with his own. In that instant, Ana knew a sense of comfort that she had never felt before. His fingers over hers were strong and solid, a barrier against anything that might cause her pain.

"My sister committed suicide," she whispered. "She was in college . . . but she was drowning in drugs, alcohol, parties, one man after another. I worked at the *Brownsville Herald* and rented the guest cottage behind my parents' house. So mature, you know."

Struggling against tears, Ana reflected on those months in the little Tudor-style home with its broad wood beams, white walls and lace curtains. "I begged my parents to let my sister move in with me. I'd keep an eye on her, see that she stayed straight and went to counseling appointments. I knew I could keep her clean. So, she moved in. I cooked and cleaned and kept a close watch on her."

"The perfect sister," Sam said gently.

"Oh, definitely." Ana discovered she was squeezing his hand. "My work at the newspaper got more demanding. I was assigned bigger stories, and I earned a raise. The editor promoted me from features to the city beat. I began an investigation into smugglers who were using the maquiladoras—the twin factories based on either side of the U.S./Mexico border—to move drugs. I threw myself into the assignment. And I started dating another reporter—we were working together on the story."

"You started living your own life."

Ana nodded. "My work became my focus. Just like here—it's all I do. It's all I have. It's all I want. I'm not able to sustain any real relationships."

"What happened to your sister?" Sam asked.

"One evening I came home from the newspaper. I walked through the door of my cottage . . . and her body was hanging from a beam . . . and it was too late . . . too late to save her . . ."

As she brushed away a tear, Sam drew her into his arms and held her close. The memory of her horror and shock at seeing her sister's dead body swallowed Ana up, as it always had. How hard she had tried to revive that lifeless form. How deafening her mother's shrieks. How painful the hours and days and weeks that followed.

Awash in agony, Ana sank into Sam, burying her face against his shoulder and choking on the sobs. His hand caressed her back, soothing and warm.

"Stop blaming yourself, Ana," he murmured. "You couldn't have saved your sister. When people want to die badly enough, they find a way. Something drove her to end her life, a blackness she couldn't see through, a hopelessness . . ."

He fell silent, his arms wrapped around Ana so tightly she could hardly breathe, and she sensed that he, too, had known such blackness. He heaved a shuddering sigh.

"Bad things happen," he said. "Things that set us up for even more pain. I blamed myself for what happened with my mother. When I was a kid, she got this crazy idea that she wanted to go to Hollywood. She met up with some man who turned her head. He convinced her she was too beautiful, too special to live in a trailer in Wyoming with a drunk, out-of-work cowboy and three little snot-nosed kids. So, they decided to take off. I remember that day . . . the wind was blowing through Cheyenne like it does, and my mom's long blond hair was whipping around her face. She knelt down in the dirt to kiss me and my little brothers, and she was crying. But she got into that man's car, and they drove away, and I didn't say a word. Didn't beg her to stay. Didn't pitch a fit. I just stood there watching as the car left the trailer park and disappeared around a bend in the road."

"How can you blame yourself for what your mother did?" Ana asked. "Leaving was her choice, not yours."

"Somehow I thought that if I had been a better son—smarter, more obedient, a better athlete—she'd have loved me more. And she would have stayed. I figured if I'd thrown a tantrum and clung to her leg, she would have known I didn't want her to leave. I kept thinking I could have done something. If only I could have figured out that one perfect thing—whatever it was—then she never would have gone off with that man and gotten killed in a car wreck in Nevada."

"Oh, Sam. She never made it to California?"

"Nope. She just left us and went off and died."

"So it was like my sister—you had no chance to fix it. No way to close the wound. You couldn't bring her back."

He stroked his hand down Ana's hair. She shivered and snuggled closer into the cocoon of his embrace. For the first time in her life, Ana relished the nearness of a man, the faint scent of spicy soap on his skin, the unyielding mass of biceps beneath his shirtsleeve, the heat of his breath against her ear.

"That's why I don't look back, Ana," he said in a low voice. "I can't change what happened. And the pain is . . . it's bad."

"Maybe now that I know, I can bear it with you a little bit."

"Bear one another's burdens," he murmured. "It's in the Bible. I suppose you could be right about facing the past. Reliving the nightmare again and again doesn't help, but talking about it to someone. A person you can trust . . ."

His blue eyes were depthless as he bent and kissed her lips. It was a soft, almost imperceptible touch, and Ana held her breath at its sweetness. Her heart throbbed, her fingers tightening on his arms as she waited for a second kiss. But he drew away and released her.

"I'd better get over to Haven," he said, getting to his feet. "Terell will wonder what's up."

"Of course." She swallowed down her regret and folded the blanket. Sam took the trash, tossed it into a receptacle and started for the car.

Ana followed, clutching her purse tightly. She couldn't understand why he had broken away from her. Or why she was so unhappy about it. What was it about this man?

As the car started back out into the street, she trained her attention on the passing scenery. It was impossible to feel this way. She never had before. She'd told herself she never would. Physical affection repulsed her. People got too close, too pushy, too clingy. She had accepted and tried to enjoy the light, playful romance of the first few dates with a man. But she never let anyone close enough to touch her heart. Yet, a few moments alone with Sam Hawke, and she was aching for his touch and mourning the loss of time she could spend with him.

"So, Ana," he said as he steered the car into the small parking area near the recreation center. "Do you think you'll be coming back to teach your—"

"Yes," she blurted. "Well, I thought I might. I like the kids, and they seemed to respond well."

"Good." The blue light in his eyes flashed in her direction.

She sank down into the seat, hugging her purse tighter. She shouldn't have agreed. Didn't have time. The lead paint series was due, and she had barely begun to write. She would turn it in to Carl on Friday, and it would be all wrong, and she would lose her job and have to move back to Brownsville. Absolutely, she should not teach that class.

"When do you want me?" she asked. "To come over and work with the writers, I mean."

He smiled, and the parentheses at the sides of his mouth deepened. "When do I want you?" he asked, glancing at her with another flash of sapphire. Then he shrugged. "Always."

"Well, what do you know?" Sam said as he and Ana stepped through the metal detector. "Jim Slater and Jack Smith are here."

She spotted the two men at a distance. "Maybe they're asking Flora about Honduras."

He peered into the far corner. "Nope, she's not there."

"She's not?" The huddled figure in the tight green skirt and pink plastic sandals was absent from her usual spot. Ana's stomach constricted. "Doesn't Flora come on Sundays?"

"I don't think she's missed a day. Sunday afternoon would be a busy time for her young friend."

Horrified at the thought, Ana saw Sam lift a hand in greeting as Terell strode out of the office and headed in their direction. As usual, the man was laden with children who clung to him like barnacles to the sides of a fishing boat.

"What's up, T-Rex?" Sam asked. "I see Slater's here."

"He and that other guy showed up a while back. Maybe an hour ago . . . Just a sec, Sam." The towering man set down one little boy who had been riding on his shoulders and another who hung on his back. Then he pried little golden-haired Brandy loose from her stranglehold on his leg. He gave each of the children a pat on the back and a dime and sent them off to get popcorn.

"Anyhow," Terell continued. "I figured Slater and his pal were here to deliver that check, so I took them on a tour and explained about our lead paint problem."

"Someone actually got to see this infamous lead paint?" Ana piped up. "How nice for them."

Terell ignored her. "Slater never got around to giving me the money. About halfway through the tour, when we're up on the third floor, he tells me to go ahead and get back to what I was doing. He says they'll finish looking around the building by themselves. So, I leave, thinking that's cool. Okay, so I go back downstairs to work on next week's schedule—which is all messed up, by the way, because Granny's got a head cold, and no way can she come tomorrow or Tuesday—and I get to remembering that place where the rain's been coming through the roof upstairs. You know what I'm talking about?"

"Where the floor is rotted out."

"You're with me, man. So, I double-time it back up there to warn those dudes against falling through the floor, and guess what they're doing? They've been down to the second floor where one of the volunteer groups is rehabbing Lulu's new dance studio, and they found themselves a hammer.

And now they're pounding away, trying to break the padlock off that fire escape door."

"Break the lock? I paid good money for that padlock."

"I know, and I said to them, 'Hey, what're you guys doing?' And Slater looks shocked that I caught him, like a crack dealer just been spotted by the police, you know. So then he says, well, it's a fire escape, so the door ought to be unlocked."

"Did you tell him we keep the key in the office?"

"I told him everything, man. I said the third floor isn't in public use yet, and we don't need that fire escape. I explained how the fire inspector came over and looked at the building and said we ought to keep a padlock on that door until we can get one of those self-locking handles installed. And you know what Slater did? He just turned around and gave that lock one more whack, and busted it clean off the door!"

"No way!"

"I was so mad, I could have punched him. I started yelling at him, man, just letting him have it. I know I shouldn't have, but I couldn't help it. You know all we've done to get this place going, and we don't have two dollars to spare, and then he up and smashes our lock! And those vandals are probably gonna get back in, and spray-paint gang signs on everything we did."

"What did Slater say?" Sam demanded. "How did he justify that?"

"He tells me, well, a little girl came running up the stairs past them, right up to the third floor, and they were worried about her. They didn't know where she went. They figured maybe she jumped out a window or something, so they decided they'd climb down the fire escape and look for her. But when they found it locked—"

"Which little girl?" Ana cut in. "Who was it?"

"How should I know? I never saw anything but the usual activities we've got going on, and all the regular kids. And I'm just trying to keep the place running smooth, and . . . where've you been, anyhow, Sam? We opened up more than an hour ago, and Raydell didn't show up, and Granny's grandson called in about her sore throat, and—"

"Where's Raydell?" Sam glanced back at the front door. "I saw Ahmed out there. I figured Raydell had taken the day off."

"No, man, Raydell signed himself up for Sundays from now till kingdom come. I had to put Ahmed outside on guard duty, even though he was bound and determined to play ball. He's spittin' nails about the whole thing, but he agreed to it anyhow."

"Here comes Slater," Sam said in a low voice. "He and his pal have got some explaining to do."

Ana touched his arm. "I'm going up to look for Flora. Maybe she's the girl they saw."

"Stay put for a minute," Sam said under his breath.

Lacking his usual warmth, he greeted the two men. As Jim shook Ana's hand, she noted how clammy his palm felt. Sam had been right. He was ill.

"I'm sure Terell told you about the little problem we had," Jim said, taking a handkerchief from his back pocket and blotting his brow. "My, it's muggy in here, isn't it?"

"The air conditioner doesn't work right," Terell groused. "A lot of things are broke around here."

Sam shot his friend a look of caution. "What's this I hear about a child on the third floor and you breaking our fire escape lock?"

"We saw a little girl. She was a small child, seemingly quite frightened. We followed her, but we lost track of her on the third floor. We checked in all the rooms. Then we decided we ought to try to see if she had gone down the fire escape."

"Why?" Ana asked. "If the girl wanted to leave Haven, she was free to go."

Jim stared at her for a moment. "Well, we were concerned, of course, Ana. We still are, in fact. Jack and I would very much like to find this child to make certain she's safe."

"That's right," Jack Smith put in.

"Was this the girl you saw in the corner the other day, Jim?" Ana asked. "I mentioned her to you at church this morning. The child from La Ceiba, Honduras."

He closed his eyes, brow furrowed. "I believe so. Yes, now that I think about it, I'm sure it was that girl. What did you say her name was?"

"Flora."

"Flora—that's it! Yes, she was running up the stairs, and we called out to her. But she kept going all the way to the third floor."

Sam let out a breath of frustration. "She probably went out through a window. We've tried to board them up, but I'm sure there are some she could have gotten through, especially on that third floor. Did you see anyone chasing the girl?"

"No," Jim said. "We'd have stopped him at once if we had. But no, there was no one following her. I just hope she's all right."

"I want to go up and look for her, Sam," Ana said.

"We searched everywhere," Jack Smith spoke up. "She's not up there. She's probably long gone."

"Which is exactly where we need to be." Jim nodded at Sam. "I'll be back later this week with your check. I wanted to bring Jack by first. He has several connections who may be interested in helping fund the paint removal project."

"That would be great." Sam turned to the other man. "I'm glad you dropped by."

"It's a great place you got here," Jack said. "Real nice. I'll talk to my friends and see what they can do."

Ana studied the two men again as they headed for the door. Terell gave a snort of disgust.

"Bustin' our lock is about all they've done for us so far," he said. "If we get one penny out of Jim Slater, I'll be amazed."

"He paid for the new tiles we're putting in the bathroom, T-Rex," Sam reminded him. "And he comes here to work with the kids as often as he can. He's a good man. He'll give us that five grand, I guarantee."

"And I'm Santy Claus," Terell said, walking away. "I'm outta here."

"Be with you in a sec," Sam called after him. "Listen, Ana—"

"I'm going upstairs to search for Flora," she repeated. "Please don't say no to this, Sam. I need to find her."

"Ana, she may not have been here today. You don't know. Don't go up there. It's not safe, and I'm not talking about lead paint. That door is probably wide-open." He caught her shoulders. "Look, Ana, you went through a lot last night. Why don't you go back to your apartment and rest your arm? I'll walk you to your car."

"You know Flora's in trouble, Sam. I want to look for her. Let me start upstairs."

"All our children are in trouble." He swept the room with his arm. "Brandy's dad slaps her around, Gerald's mother is a crackhead, Ahmed lives with his brother in the basement of a condemned liquor store, Tenisha has cerebral palsy, Donnetta is thirteen and pregnant by a pimp . . . . Shall I go on?" He lowered his voice. "They're all hurting, Ana. Every one of them. That's why we're here—to give them a future and a hope."

"You're here for all of them," she said. "I can only

take one. I can take Flora. I care about her, and I'm going to find her."

"Flora is not your sister, Ana. Nothing you do will bring her back."

At the words, Ana bit her lip and stared at him. Sam ran his hand down her bandaged arm, lifted her fingers and kissed them. "This is the best any of us can do," he said. "*Haven.* It's what we have. It's what God gave us. We have too many kids and not enough volunteers. We can't take care of each individual needy child. We have to help them all."

"Not me. I can help one. I can, Sam." She pulled her hand away. "And don't ever mention my sister again."

His expression softened. "Go look for Flora. Help one, Ana."

Squaring her shoulders, she headed for the staircase that led to the third floor.

Chapter Thirteen

Sam set the schedule book down on the desk in the front office. "Victory," he said. "Cleopatra's changing. We might make her into a tenderhearted volunteer yet."

"What did she do?" Terell asked.

"Before she left Haven today, she went hunting for Flora."

"The woman's hunting for a kid." He chuckled deep in his chest. "And you're hunting for the woman."

"Nah. I just want Ana to teach that writing class. I

wish she hadn't gone off without giving me the final word on it. If Granny's cold keeps her away for a few days, an extra class would help us out."

"Tenisha can manage the crochet bunch," Terell said. "She's talented enough, and being in charge would do a lot for her confidence."

"Good. I'll set that up."

Sam lifted his focus from the schedule book to his friend. Terell was leaning with one hip against the desk, his arms crossed, a smirk tilting a corner of his mouth.

"Okay," Sam conceded. "You think I like Ana Burns, and you're right. But she's not for me. I'm glad she cares about Flora, but I don't want to get tangled with a woman whose whole life is her work."

"And this place isn't *your* whole life? Look, the lady's got a job. A deadline. That doesn't make her a bad person."

Sam had to acknowledge that much was true. "I'm willing to open the door to the right relationship—but this isn't it. You know how I feel about getting involved. We're the same, Terell."

"The same? Did I go off on a picnic today? Did I laze around in the park and enjoy the scenery? No, not good ol' T-Rex. I was here opening the building and starting up the groups. While I'm patrolling classrooms, breaking up fights and keeping basketball games on a fair rotation, you're out having coffee with some lady you claim you don't even like. You order everybody in the building to steer clear of her, and then you turn around and invite her to teach a class. What's up with that, dog?"

"It's complicated."

"Don't even start with me, because I don't wanna hear it. It's love, and no one can explain that."

"Love? Are you kidding me? I've known the woman a week, and she's driven me crazy the whole time."

"Like I said."

"It's not love, Terell. Believe me. Ana Burns is a pain. She insisted on searching for Flora even though she knew Slater and his pal had already combed the place. Then she vanished. Didn't even stop in to say goodbye. Nothing."

"So, the picnic . . . did you kiss her?" Terell's smirk split into a wide-open grin. "Come on, man, tell the truth. You kissed her, didn't you? Ha! I can see it on your face! You kissed the girl, and you liked it. Woo-hoo!"

"Shut up, you."

"Hey, none of that talk allowed here at Haven. You know better, Uncle Sam."

"Listen, did you check the parking lot?"

Sam was in no mood to kid around. Despite what he had told Terell, the thought of not seeing Ana again troubled him. Nor did he like the idea that she had walked to her car alone. By the time she had left, it was dark outside, and the hood at night was no place for a lone woman. The suspicion that Raydell had been behind the previous night's attack ate at Sam.

"I'll see if anyone is hanging around outside," he

told Terell, "and you take a look in the bathroom and the classrooms. When I come back, we'll head upstairs, just in case somebody missed the little girl."

"Meet you right here in fifteen."

As Sam started for the door, he had to acknowledge the toll their work took on the two men. After putting in so many hours at Haven seven days a week, both men were exhausted. They had set up cots in a large, empty room on the second floor. Despite the discomfort of their feet hanging off the ends of the narrow beds, they usually fell asleep immediately. Sometimes, though, Terell talked about his past life in the NBA and his continuing battle against the desires that pulled him toward addiction.

Sam had suggested they work through a Bible study together, and that took them into the book of Acts. Reading about the early Christians endeavoring to live a life wholly dedicated to Christ inflamed their determination to make Haven a success. Praying, reading, eating and sleeping in such close proximity had taken their friendship to a deeper level—a similar intimacy and support he had known with his fellow soldiers in the Marine Corps—and Sam was grateful.

"You gonna get the lights?" Terell called as he headed for the row of classrooms.

"I'll do it when I come back inside. I hope I don't run into that bunch we had out there a few nights ago," he said, referring to a group of belligerent teenagers who had chosen the Haven parking lot as a place to sell drugs.

"I'll listen for your death screams," Terell said as he headed toward the classrooms.

"Funny."

Sam pushed open the front door. It bothered him that Raydell hadn't appeared the whole evening. No one seemed to know where the boy was, though Sam heard a rumor that his father had turned up drunk and beaten him to a pulp. That didn't seem likely, Sam thought as he stepped out onto the sidewalk. Raydell said he hadn't seen his dad for nearly five years. The man wouldn't suddenly appear out of nowhere and start knocking his son around.

Unless he had just gotten out of prison. The thought sent a sick feeling through Sam's stomach. He recalled all too well the many nights his own father wound up in jail for driving with a revoked license while under the influence of alcohol. The man would head straight from the pokey to the bar, then he'd stagger home, tear up the trailer and cuff his three boys until he passed out on the couch. If Raydell's father had been in prison, such a scene was possible.

Sam made up his mind to find the young man the following morning. He feared Raydell might have been hurt by his father—or that the boy might have fallen in with gang members on the streets. Worse, the possibility that Raydell had been part of the plan to attack Ana troubled him.

Except for Sam's car and Terell's truck, the parking lot was empty tonight. Sam studied the moon and wondered if Ana was safely tucked away in her clean little apartment. He hoped so. A muffled sound drew his attention to the large metal garbage container leaning against a brick wall of the building. Cats, no doubt. He hoped it wasn't rats. Either way, the pests wouldn't find much. The trash truck had come around on Saturday.

Sam was headed back toward the door when he recognized the sound in the Dumpster as a sob. A human sob. A chill racing through him, Sam thought instantly of Raydell. Injured? Thrown into the trash? Heart hammering, he hurried back across the parking lot.

What if it was Ana?

Dear God, please don't let it be Ana, he prayed. Don't let her be hurt.

Or maybe someone had put a baby in there. It happened. The idea scared him to death. He had no notion of what to do with an abandoned newborn. Call the police? Take the infant to a hospital?

His breath hanging in his chest, Sam peered down into the large receptacle. Someone gasped.

"Okay, who's in there?" he demanded. "Talk now, or I call the police."

"Sam, it's me!"

"Ana?" Her face moved out of the shadows into the moonlight. "What are you doing? Are you all right?"

"I'm fine. Flora and I are talking."

"Inside a garbage bin?"

"Shh." Her dark eyes met his. "I found her here when I was leaving. She's hiding. Come on in. I'll tell you what I know."

Sam stared into the reeking metal container, its walls stained with every kind of nastiness known to man. The last thing in the world he wanted to do was climb down into it. But Ana was beckoning, and he saw that she and the child were seated side by side, the woman in her beige linen Sunday dress and the child in her green skirt, white T-shirt and pink plastic sandals. Both were gazing up at him, their brown eyes large and glowing in the moonlight.

Hoisting himself up, he swung one leg and then the other over the steel side. As he dropped down into the receptacle, Flora whimpered and shrank into Ana. Sam hunkered down, tried to ignore the stench and smiled at the two females across from him.

"Hi, Flora," he tried, adding the only Spanish he knew. *"Buenos noches."*

Her dark eyes blinked up at him.

"She's afraid of you," Ana said. "She says you know the man who hurt her."

"I do? Who is he?"

"I'm not sure. She keeps talking about Primero and Segundo, the First Man and the Second Man. That's all I can get her to say."

"No one I know would hurt Flora. Not ever. Please tell her that."

Ana translated his message in a soft voice. As Flora responded, she shook her head adamantly and pointed in the direction of Haven.

"She insists the man is inside there," Ana said. She touched his arm. "Sam, what if it's Terell? You know my concerns. I'm afraid he may have hurt her."

"No way," he flung back.

At the harsh response, Flora cried out and buried her face against Ana's shoulder.

Ana gathered the child in her arms. "Sam, you're scaring her."

"Terell would never mistreat a child. He's a good man. I've known him too many years to believe he would lay a hand on anyone."

"I don't think this is physical abuse. I think Flora's been molested."

"Terell would *not* do that. He likes women—adult women. That was a big part of his problem in the past. His craving for women, drugs and booze took him far from God. In the past year or so, he's had to do a lot of repenting. Even though he knows how harmful that life was, it hasn't been easy for him to surrender. He's just now getting things under control."

"That's what I mean. What if he's been using the children as a way to—"

"Don't even think it. He would never do that. Terell is a Christian man, Ana."

"Christian men abuse children." She ground out the words. "It's possible. It happens."

"I admit a Christian can walk away from everything he knows is right. But for a God-fearing, Bible-believing man to actually touch a child? Like that?"

"Yes, Sam. One in every four adult women has been sexually molested in one way or another. Don't think it doesn't happen in the church."

"How do you know that statistic?"

She looked away. Then she laid her cheek on Flora's head and closed her eyes. "I know, Sam. Trust me."

At her words, fear erupted in his chest. Before he could speak, she was at him again.

"I'm talking about Terell, Sam. Flora says there's a man at Haven who hurt her. Look . . . look at her arm. I found this child out here cutting herself with a shard of glass. This time she went deep. I know Flora doesn't want to die, Sam. She's looking for some way to relieve the stress, the anguish. She needs help—an advocate."

"I saw Flora's friend looking for her this evening. The one who drops her off every afternoon. She called herself Gypsy. Tell Flora that Gypsy is worried about her."

Ana spoke to the child again. Flora nodded.

"Hipsy," she whispered.

"She's giving it the Spanish pronunciation," Ana explained. "Flora's been telling me about her life. She's a runaway."

"Are you sure? They're usually not this young."

"Or from Honduras," Ana added. "Flora told me she did a bad thing at the house where she lived, and after that she ran for a long time down many streets. It was night. A woman driving a truck picked her up on the side of the road and brought her here. She doesn't know where she is, Sam. No idea."

"Honduras. She couldn't have run away from Honduras and hitchhiked to St. Louis."

"I don't understand it either. She says she lived in a house in La Ceiba, and she has a . . . a little sister."

"Ana." Sam reached out and touched her arm. The two in the garbage bin, he realized suddenly, had matching wounds on their arms. Flora's was self-inflicted. But Ana . . . she had insisted she'd been attacked.

"Flora isn't sure what happened to her original house and family," Ana was telling him. "She and her sister rode on an airplane together. I can't get past that, because every time she mentions the little sister, she starts crying."

Sam's heart melted—not only for Flora, but also for Ana, whose own pain and grief were obvious. "What happened after the woman in the truck dropped her off in St. Louis?"

"She slept in a trash container like this for two nights. She was very frightened. On the third day, when she was looking for food, she met Hipsy. *Gypsy.* Gypsy has a bad life, Flora told me, but she is a friend. They sleep in a room together, and they share food. Gypsy brings Flora to Haven and then goes to work during the afternoon and evening. Her employer is a cruel man who scares Flora. Gypsy says that Flora is going to have to work for this man in order to pay for the room and food."

"The man is Gypsy's pimp. They're grooming Flora." Ana nodded. "They've told her she's too small right now. She's only ten, Sam. Gypsy is thirteen."

He forced down his revulsion at the idea that men

would use children in such a way. "Ana, why does she say someone at Haven has hurt her?"

"Let me ask one more time." Ana bent and spoke in the child's ear. Flora whispered a response.

"She says Primero is there. The First Man."

A terrible thought hit Sam. "Could it be Raydell? She sees him at the door. It's hard for me to accept, but he may have been involved in the attack on you—and he didn't show up for work today. That's not like Raydell, Ana. Maybe he's been hurting Flora . . . though I can't believe he would do that. Raydell has a rough life, but he's got a good heart."

"Men who prey on children focus on places like Haven," Ana told him. "That's why I've been concerned about Terell. A predator who has constant contact with kids can spend a long time preparing his victim. He can use gifts, bribes, threats. He can begin the grooming slowly and move forward with such subtle steps that the child doesn't realize what's happening. It's like a cat stalking a mouse—toying with it for a long time before he eats it."

Sam tried to imagine this kind of behavior from Terell, and it was unthinkable. With Raydell, though, anything was possible. The boy came from a troubled home, and he walked the edge. If he had been molested as a child, maybe he was now choosing to act out his aggression by preying on others.

"Can Flora give us a description of Primero?" Sam asked.

"I've tried, but when she starts talking about him, a vacant look crosses her face and then she—"

"Sam?" Terell's tall form appeared over the edge of the trash bin. "Sam, you in there?"

"Ai! Ai!" Shrieking, Flora scrambled onto Ana's lap, stepped on Sam's shoulder and vanished over the metal side.

"Flora?" Ana leaped to her feet. "Flora, wait!"

"What are you two doing in the garbage can?" Terell demanded.

Sam hoisted himself up. "That little girl—which way did she run?"

"Girl? I thought that was a dog."

"It was Flora." Ana's voice wavered on the brink of hysteria. "Sam, we've got to find her."

"She went that way," Terell said.

"Hang on to my shoulders," Sam told Ana. Setting his hands around her waist, he lifted the slender woman out of the trash receptacle and set her on her feet in the parking lot.

Terell had already started down the street, and Sam took off at a dead run, catching up easily. He could hear his friend's heavy feet pounding the pavement beside him, but in a moment, Ana overtook them both. Holding her sandals in one hand, she tore barefoot along the sidewalk, her hair flying behind her.

"Flora! Flora!" she shouted. She called to the child in a stream of Spanish words Sam didn't understand, and he could hear the tears in her voice.

In the next half hour they searched side streets and

alleys, but Sam knew it was futile. The girl had vanished. Gone into the night, like so many others who lived and died in this neighborhood. What had frightened Flora into climbing straight up over two adults and hurling herself out of the trash bin? he wondered.

Terell.

Surely it couldn't be. Not his friend. Not his basketball teammate. Not the man who knelt beside him in prayer every morning and every night. No.

Sam stopped to catch his breath. He could see Terell and Ana far down the street, searching under cardboard boxes and lifting trash can lids. Both were calling for Flora, but they wouldn't find her. Soon, they would give up, and then Sam would have to face his friend.

The one who looks like me is my sister. I see her clearly now. Even though my head aches and my eyes blur, I understand that Aurelia stands before me. He has brought her to this place. He will hurt her in the same way he hurts me. She will know the same fear, the looming, choking, suffocating fear.

Aurelia smiles at me, and she shows me her new toy. A doll with long golden curls. The very doll she has been wanting for a long time. He gave it to her.

"Look!" she says. "See what I have! It's mine."

I nod. She wants me to be jealous. She wants me to cry and beg to play with the doll. Then she will have power over her big sister.

I came home with a new toy once, too. I had a bear

with thick brown fur and a bow around its neck. I put the bear at the back of my closet, and I sat down beside it. Then I pulled clothes over my legs, my stomach, even my head. I shut the closet door, and I sat beside the bear. For a long time we sat, the bear and I. There was nothing to do, nothing to say. Only the memory of what had happened to me on that day.

The bear knew. It had seen what the man did to me. But it would not speak, and neither must I. The man said he would hurt my mama and papa if I ever told them about the lightbulb room and the thing that happened there. The man would kill my parents. He showed me the gun, long and black, with bullets inside it. And I believed him.

So the bear and I sat inside the closet in silence. We kept our secret.

That evening, I stayed in my closet until my mama called me to supper. I didn't want to go to supper or anywhere ever again. I wanted to stay in the darkness under the pile of clothes forever. How could I go out? My parents would see my face, and they would know what had happened to me. Then the man would kill them.

But my mama was calling, and I knew that soon she would come to search for me. She would ask why I was hiding in the closet, and I would tell her. And the man would shoot my parents with his long, black gun.

So I opened the closet and pushed the clothes away. I crawled across the floor like a puppy. I pulled on the knob of my bedroom door to help myself stand up. I went to supper.

And they did not know. They saw nothing on my face. Nothing.

The toy bear who lives at the back of my closet kept the secret.

So did I.

But now I understand that I made a mistake. I should have told Aurelia. I ought to have warned my sister. Now the man has brought her. He has given her the golden-haired doll. And he will hurt her in the same way he hurt me.

She smiles at me again. “Look,” she says. “Look at me!”

The man pats her on the head. Then he gives her braid a tug. He says, “Come with me, Aurelia. Your sister will wait for you here.”

I cannot move. I can do nothing but watch Aurelia skip across the floor and go into the room with him. It is the lightbulb room. The lightbulb is there, and it can save her. But I have forgotten to tell her this! I jump to my feet and run to the door—

And then I hear her scream.

Aurelia’s cries tear through my ears and fall into my heart. I stand numb, listening to my sister’s pain. I hear the fear as it rips into her body. I have not saved her. I have not protected her. I allowed her to go into the room with the man.

Slowly, I turn around and lift my head. Here is another lightbulb behind a white glass globe. I stare at it.

Come to me, dear God, I pray. Come to me and take me away. Take me to the sunshine and the beach and the happiness.

But nothing happens. I still stand beside the door. I still hear my sister in the other room, sobbing now, groaning, whimpering. I still wait, like a statue, staring at the white paint on the door.

The grain of the wood runs up and down. The brass handle gleams. The room behind the door is silent.

I stand and wait. I wait longer. I wait until fear has grown into a mountain inside my chest. And the door opens.

Aurelia steps out. She stares at me, and I see that my sister and I are exactly the same now. The golden-haired doll hangs limply from her hand.

I move toward her. "Aurelia."

"Stop." She looks at me with sad eyes. She is not angry that I failed her. She does not shout at me for letting this thing happen. Instead, she walks past me across the carpet.

"Come," she says. "It is time for us to go home."

I decide that I will show her where the toy bear lives. I will take her into the closet and hide with my sister under the clothes. We can sit there until suppertime, not talking, not crying, not moving. Then we will walk together to the table, and we will eat with our mama and our papa.

We will not speak of this thing in the room with the lightbulb. It must be our secret. Aurelia's and mine, the bear's and the doll's.

Chapter Fourteen

Ana stared down at her bare feet and wept. Flora was gone, and nothing could be done to save her. Nothing.

She felt Sam's arm slip around her shoulders, drawing her close. Unable and unwilling to resist him, she sank into the comfort of his embrace. Clutching his sleeve, she gathered the soft fabric in her fist as the tears ran down her cheeks.

"It's okay, Ana," he whispered. "It'll be okay. We'll find her."

"What's going on?" Terell asked, arriving back from his search down an alley. He was breathing hard, sweating, his brow furrowed. "Who are we looking for anyhow?"

Ana studied Sam's face as he greeted his friend. She knew he was trying to see evil in a man he had loved so many years. No doubt the long arms, the big goofy grin, the chest-deep guffaws all meant warmth, comfort and companionship to him. And perhaps Terell was innocent.

Children clung to the big man, laughing with him, poking him, begging him to rub their backs or give them a piggyback ride. Though Sam said his friend had chosen to stray from the straight and narrow path for a time, Terell appeared to be living like a Christian again. Ana could not deny that every word from his mouth, every expression on his face, every touch of his hand conveyed empathy and love for those around him. Could Terell Roberts be a fraud?

"What do you know about Flora?" Sam asked Terell. Ana read the note of accusation in his voice.

"The girl who was bleeding in the bathroom the other day," she clarified. "The one Jim Slater was—"

She caught her breath as her own words sank in. Jim Slater had been chasing Flora. *Chasing her.* Determined to catch her, he had followed the child up the steps to the third floor. He broke the fire escape padlock with a hammer to get to her. Why?

Fast on the heels of that revelation came another. Flora had said Sam knew the man who had molested her. Jim Slater visited Haven often. He talked to Sam. And Flora watched them from her corner.

Then a third piece of an emerging puzzle fell into place. Jim Slater transported children from Honduras. On airplanes.

"I don't know much about Flora," Terell was saying to Sam. "I'm not even sure I saw her in the corner today."

"But she ran past you while you were talking to Jim," Sam countered.

"Listen, dog, I never saw Flora or any other girl running anywhere. I was on the second floor with Jim and his friend when they asked me to leave. Next thing I knew, they were busting our padlock on the third floor."

Terell let out a breath and focused on Ana. "I don't know what you're after at Haven, ma'am, but I can tell you this. I played pro basketball for the Orlando Magic, and nobody runs past Terell Roberts without me seeing 'em."

Sam nodded in confirmation. "Jim must have spotted Flora after he and Jack Smith went up to the third floor."

"But that's not what he told us," Ana stressed. "I distinctly remember him saying they saw her run up to the *third floor.* After Terell left the two men alone, they must have searched the third floor. When they couldn't find Flora, they went back downstairs to get a hammer and break the padlock so they could follow her."

"Ana, what are you getting at?"

"Jim lied to us, Sam."

He shook his head, his focus on Terell again. "I don't think so. Jim was probably confused. Besides, the girl Jim saw might not have been Flora. You don't know for sure."

"Of course it was Flora. Jim Slater was chasing her. She was so frightened of him that she climbed through a broken window, hid in the garbage bin and slashed her arm with a piece of glass."

"You're saying Jim was chasing Flora? That doesn't sound like something he would do."

"At this point I wouldn't put anything past the guy," Terell groused. "I couldn't believe he and his pal were tearing down our fire escape door. The last time I saw Jim Slater, he was over in that far corner with—" He paused and a light flickered over his face. "Wait a second. I *did* see Flora today. Jim Slater was in the corner talking to her."

"Terell," Ana asked, her heart thumping heavily. "What do you know about Flora?"

"Not much. She slips into the building and goes right to her corner. Most of the day, Flora stays huddled in a ball with her forehead against the wall. I've gone over there a few times and tried to talk her into playing basketball. She curled up like a dead spider and wouldn't even look at me. Never said a word, just sat there trembling all over."

"We think Flora's been molested," Sam said.

Terell's face went hard. "Molested? At Haven? Inside our building?"

"It's possible."

"No way. You and I rotate all the time, Sam. We look in on the bathrooms and the classes. I'm always checking things out—though I have to admit I've mostly been looking for drug deals going down, fights breaking out or kids passing booze around. Maybe a volunteer could have taken a kid up to the third floor and . . . Well, that's perverted, Sam. I don't even want to think about it."

"Somebody hurt Flora." Sam's words held a note of veiled accusation. "She told Ana she sees the person at Haven."

Terell crossed his arms over his chest. "We'd better find that sicko, and quick. Did Flora tell you who it was? I guarantee, I'll wrench his neck right off his body."

"Sam suggested Raydell," Ana said.

"Nah. Not him. He's been in trouble before, but we count on him. Raydell wouldn't hurt a little girl."

Sam swallowed. "She was afraid of you tonight, Terell."

"She about scared the living daylights out of me, too.

First I hear voices coming from the trash, and next thing I know something comes flying out at me." He paused. "Wait a minute. What are you saying, Sam? You think she was scared of *me*. You think *I* might have molested Flora?"

"Did you?"

The men eyed each other. Terell's fists were clenched, and Sam had leaned forward as if ready to take on the taller man at the first flinch.

"You work at Haven," Sam said. "You've had problems in the past—drugs, women. Kids hang on you—especially the little ones. And tonight Flora screamed and ran off when she saw you. We've been friends most of our lives, Terell, but right now I don't know what to think."

"I know what to think. You're nuts." Terell stepped toward Sam menacingly. "*You* work at Haven, man. You've had problems. Kids hang around you. So explain why you're blaming me for this girl's problems."

Ana cleared her throat. "Sam, I'm beginning to think Jim Slater might have something to do with it."

"Jim Slater runs an adoption agency," Sam growled,

his eyes still on Terell. "He cares about kids."

"I may have been wrong about Terell," Ana said. "Jim fits the profile much better."

Terell turned on her. "*You're* the one who put all this in Sam's head?"

Ana blanched. "The abuser could be anyone, Terell. I don't like to make accusations, but Flora is terribly frightened. She's hurting herself because of it—and she says someone at Haven is responsible. I'm beginning to think we ought to consider Jim Slater as a possibility. He's always around kids—his adoption agency, the church nursery, Haven. Flora said she sees Primero at Haven, and you told me Jim's there a lot. The most significant thing, Sam, is that Jim brings children to Missouri on airplanes. From Honduras."

"Come on, Ana. You know Jim. You go to church with the guy. You've worked together in the nursery. If he'd been inappropriate with a child, you would have noticed. He visits Haven, sure—but his goal is to improve the place, not molest the kids. Jim is a good man. You've said so yourself."

Ana raked her fingers back through her hair. The night was hot, and the men's tempers had flared to the point of combustion. Worse, she had begun to believe that Terell was innocent, and that Jim Slater—one of the most upstanding men in St. Louis—might be a pedophile.

"Let's all go get a root beer," she suggested. "We need to sit down somewhere cool and quiet to talk this through."

"I'm not going anywhere," Terell said, his dark eyes locked on his friend. "I'm not moving till you apologize to me, Sam Hawke."

"I'll apologize when I'm sure you're not touching our kids," Sam retorted. "When Flora saw you, she took off like she'd been bit."

"Sam," Ana said, "she reacted the same way to you. Remember when you looked into the trash bin? Flora gasped, and it was all I could do to hold her down. She's afraid of men. All men."

Looking down, Sam shook his head. "This is unbelievable. We run hundreds of teens through Haven every day. The abuser could be anyone. Listen, Terell, I apologize for jumping on you. When I heard Flora scream and watched her climb out of that garbage bin like the devil was after her, I was freaked out. You can see how things seemed to add up."

"All I can see is a false friend. And for the record, I would never accuse you of anything like that. Never—not ever. I love you."

"T-Rex," Sam said, his shoulders sinking. "I love you, too. You know that."

"Nah, don't even go there, dog. It's like those verses we read in the Bible the other day, and I said that's how I felt about you. If you love someone, you'll always be loyal to him, you'll always believe in him, always expect the best of him, and always stand your ground in defending him."

"First Corinthians, thirteen. Terell, I'm sorry, man."

"Sorry nothing. You showed your true colors." He turned away. "I'm going to bed."

Ana's heart ached as she watched the tall man stride to the front door and disappear through the metal detector. The sting of betrayal was written in every footstep. As she faced Sam again, she read the misery on his face.

"I blew it," he said. "I'd better go try to talk to him."

"It's my fault, Sam." Ana hugged herself. "I shouldn't have been so insistent about Terell. The thing is, you're responsible for the children who come into Haven. You have to keep your eyes open. Abusers work hard to look normal. They hold good jobs, go to church, sit on boards, play active roles in their communities."

"How do you know all this?"

"They date, marry, have children," she went on without answering his question. "All the while, they live a secret life. There's a desire . . . a lust . . . for children. Pedophiles don't see kids as humans. A child is an object. These men find ways to be around children . . . and they keep collections of . . . of . . ."

She covered her mouth with her hand. "Oh, Sam! Jim has a doll collection. And those cherubs. They're statues of children."

"He told us his wife collected them."

"What wife? Have you ever seen a wife?"

"She died, remember?"

"How do we know that? Maybe he never had a wife."

She clasped her hands together, trembling without

even knowing why. "It's got to be Jim Slater."

"Now you're jumping from Terell to Jim? Think what you're saying, Ana. Remember at Jim's house we saw those little girls waiting for their adoption paperwork to clear? He was watching them for their foster parents—providing respite for the caregivers. How much kinder can a man be? The girls had toys to play with and nice clothes. They didn't look anything like Flora. They weren't scared. They were happy."

"But Sam, everything Jim does is about children. He's Primero, don't you see? He's the first man Flora knew in this country. He brought her here on an airplane . . . with her sister."

He caught her hands in his. "Ana, you've accused Terell and now Jim Slater. Are you going to run through the list of every volunteer at Haven? Is every male who walks through that metal detector a suspect? We're not even sure what Flora told us is true."

"But you've made things too easy for a predator. Despite your metal detector, your dog and your constant patrolling, Haven isn't safe."

"Is any place completely secure? We're doing our best." Sam shook his head. "Terell is all over the building. He has time and opportunity. So do I. Why do you doubt him and trust me?"

"I've watched you. Studied you. Listened to you. I've done the same with Terell."

"You've been onto this for a while—this situation with Flora. Why didn't you speak up?"

"Because I'm not sure, Sam. Flora says she's been

molested by someone at Haven, but she's uncertain of details. What she says sounds far-fetched—unless you fit Jim Slater into the picture."

"Terell's the man with a past. Slater's an outstanding citizen of this city. So why have you changed your mind about Terell and decided Jim is the culprit? What's the difference?"

"Empathy. When I first met Terell and saw that little blond girl with a slap mark on her face, I suspected him of abuse. I didn't like the way Brandy was sitting on his lap, either. But since then, I've seen her tagging after Terell like a little puppy. Brandy's not afraid of him. She adores him."

"I can clear Terell of that charge right now, Ana. I saw Brandy come into the building with a bruise on her cheek that day. She was sobbing her eyes out, and she walked from the front door right to me. I was busy sorting out a fight, so I gave her . . . well, I gave her to Terell. That's what I do with all the sobbing kids."

Ana nodded. "Because you know he cares about them. They know it, too. That's why they hang all over him. A molester may have children around him, but he has lured them with toys or candy. Teens can be seduced by drugs, alcohol, pornography—or just a place to get away from their own horrendous home lives. Money can be the draw, like with Gypsy. But there's always fear. Fear lurks under the surface of all abusive relationships, and you can see it in the kids' faces if you look closely."

"Gypsy," Sam said, his eyes focused in the distance. "She lives in fear for her life."

"Her pimp is exploiting her. He uses her and keeps her on the edge of terror."

"Terell's not taking advantage of anyone," Sam said. "Even when he was living down and dirty, he paid good money for his vices. That's why there's nothing left but his Rolex watch and an empty bank account. He sold his house in Miami to pay off his debts, and he gave me what was left as a down payment on the Haven building. If anything, other people exploit Terell. He's so good-natured they use him to get what they want."

"Sam, I think I steered you wrong about Terell. When he found out about Flora's abuse, that was genuine horror, disgust and rage on his face."

"But Jim is empathetic, too. You heard him talk about the orphaned children he brings into the country. He's motivated by their plight, not by some scheme to molest them. If Jim wants to abuse a child, why not pick up a girl like Gypsy? He doesn't have to go all the way to Honduras for that. Remember what he said about the red tape he wades through? Those immigration laws."

Her brows lifted. "This morning in church, Jim didn't know a whole lot about Honduran immigration law. Ran from the question like he was about to be stung."

"He had to take his buddy to lunch." Sam rested his hands on his hips. "Listen, Ana, if Flora said this

Primero is at Haven, I won't argue. But we can't accuse people left and right. I've hurt my best friend, and now you're ready to pounce on a man who supports Haven with both his time and his money. If there really is a molester, Flora's going to have to point him out."

"If she ever comes back."

"I think she'll be back," he said, "because of you. You're the only one who's gotten through to her."

"I don't know. She's terrified of Primero, Sam. After I got down into the trash bin with her, she literally clung to me. And the tears . . . she broke my heart." Ana looked away. "I'd better get home. I have an article on lead paint to write."

"I'll walk you to you car."

He took her arm as they started down the sidewalk. "Do you think Terell will forgive you?" she asked. "He was very upset."

"I've never seen the guy hold a grudge longer than five minutes. I'll apologize again, Ana, but I'm going to keep an eye on him, too."

"You and Terell both need to be watching for trouble."

"And then there's Raydell. I've got to find that boy. From the time he first showed up at Haven, he hasn't missed a day. Even when he wasn't working the front door, he came to play basketball or just hang around and talk."

"Let me know how it goes, okay? And if you see Flora . . ."

"I'll call you immediately. Will you be coming in to teach your writing class?"

They paused beside her car. "Next Saturday," she said. "I'm glad I had a chance to talk to the kids. The article will be better for it. I'm in great shape now."

He grinned, scanned her up and down, and wiggled his eyebrows. "Can't deny that one."

With a groan, she rolled her eyes. "Have a good week."

"You, too." Hands in his pockets, he eyed her as she unlocked the door and slipped into the driver's seat.

As she pulled out into the street, she glanced in her rearview mirror. Sam was still standing there watching her, and a pall of loneliness filled her chest. How could anyone miss a broken-down building with a basketball court and a bunch of ragtag kids inside? How could she feel empty inside at leaving a neighborhood filled with muggers and teenage prostitutes? And how could the sight of a man in her rearview mirror make her want to jump out of the car and run right back into his arms?

Shaking herself, Ana focused on the road ahead. She needed to change the bandage on her arm. Get out of this filthy dress. Take a shower. Review the notes she had taken. And browse the Internet for a former resident of Aspen, Colorado . . . one Jim Slater who had been a successful building contractor.

Or had he been a real estate agent?

• • •

He put down the phone and stared at Bering. "The Feds got Stu. Picked him up a few minutes ago. His wife said they took his computer and all his files. Everything out of the home office."

Cursing, he shook his head. The idiot! How many times had Stu been warned? But he was too stupid to understand the danger. Too obsessed with his hobby to destroy the years of evidence he had collected. No doubt some of it could be linked to its source.

"I bet the wife is freaking out," Bering said.

"Who cares?" he snapped. "He was a fool."

"I didn't like him, either. Creep."

"Forget Stu. You've got a job to do, and there's not much time. The Feds will be heading this way. I want you to do the first two tonight. Then follow the woman, and do her."

Bering shifted in the chair. "You sure about the two? I mean, they're kids."

"A couple of bad headaches." He grimaced. "Just get 'em out of here. Go out of town, and get rid of them. Make sure you dispose of the bodies adequately, too. We can't have those coming back to haunt us."

"Sure."

"In the meantime, I'll be working on the woman. Her phone is unlisted, but I can find out where she lives. I'll have it for you by the time you get back."

"You want me to do her in the daytime? I usually take care of my business at night."

"Do you see that suitcase, Bering?" He gestured at

the large black leather wheeled bag beside the front door. "In it, I've packed every article of clothing I will need to begin my new life. I have a safe containing my passport and all my documents. Tomorrow, I'll visit my bank and withdraw the money I intend to take with me when I step out of that door tomorrow night, get into my car and drive to the airport. If you don't have everything taken care of by that time, I won't pay you a red cent. I'll transfer your name and all identifying information to the St. Louis chief of police, who is a personal friend of mine. Do you understand me, Bering?"

"You're a friend of the police chief?"

"Him and everyone who matters in this city. I sit on seven boards—a bank, a civic foundation, a newspaper and several others. I attend one of the oldest churches in the Midwest. I'm a member of two country clubs. And I volunteer my time and money to almost any organization that needs help. I am a good man, Bering. People respect me, and they seek my favor. My clientele are men like me—men who rule their worlds and pay very well for my services."

He sat back in his chair, relishing the recitation of his accomplishments. Then he looked across at the lowlife he was paying to secure his future.

"You are nothing, Bering," he said. "Nothing and no one. You have no significance in this world other than to do what you're told. If you succeed, you'll be paid well. If you fail, I will ruin you. Do you understand this?"

The man nodded. "I understand you got no conscience."

"And you do, Mr. Murder-for-Hire?"

"I got my morals."

"As do I. Our morals are different from the norm, aren't they? But we have morals all the same. Our morals tell us that what is right is to take care of ourselves, to make certain our needs are met, to see that we live well and are paid the best possible price for our services. Our morals tell us that what is wrong is to fail. To be weak. To give others the upper hand. Am I correct, Bering?"

"Yeah, sure."

"So, do you intend to sit there and talk to me all night? Or are you going to do what I've asked?"

The man nodded. "I'll take care of everything." Standing, he grabbed a black leather jacket from his chair and shrugged it over one shoulder. "The two are in the back there? Down that hall?"

"Asleep in their bedroom, yes. Here's the key. And be quick about it."

"No problem."

Bering took the key and crossed the room. As he vanished down the hall, silence overwhelmed the room. The call of the martini closet rang loudly. The beckoning pills lured with an undeniable urgency. But he must deny them. He must focus. Stu was gone, and the enemy would soon be at his own door. No one could save him now. No one but himself.

Chapter Fifteen

By late Monday afternoon, Ana had nibbled her fingernails down to the quick. After deleting the story she had started the previous week, she managed to force out one complete article on lead paint—but she wasn't happy. Trying to fit in enough factual detail to satisfy Carl Webster, she had struggled and failed to cut the piece down to a reasonable length. She could find no place to shorten it, yet what sane reader would want to plow through the endless inches? Quotes from health department supervisors came off as dull and trite. Statistics read like a roll call of indecipherable numbers. Even facts about detrimental effects of the paint were less interesting than the nutrition label on a box of cereal.

What was she doing wrong? Ana slammed her fists on her desk and then dropped her forehead onto her hands. She knew the problem, of course. Flora had been calling to her all day. Tenisha and Gerald pleaded to come alive on the page. Raydell demanded to have his say, too. Sam and Terell insisted on broadcasting their mission. All of them cried out to be heard, and she had promised herself to write about them—no matter what.

But this morning as she had faced the computer, fear came to life in her stomach. Unless she satisfied her editor, she would lose her job. The scenario played out in her mind. Carl calling her into his office, tossing the hard copy of her series into the trash can, and then curtly dismissing her from her position at the *Post-Dispatch.* Boxes and bags stacked at the entrance to her empty apartment. Miles of Interstate highway taking her away from the independence and hope she had so desperately sought. Her mother and father welcoming her back with open arms, smiles . . . and tears. A search for a job, perhaps back at the old *Brownsville Herald.* Memories taunting her, unforgotten failures tapping her on the shoulder, and the agony of the pain she could never escape haunting her . . . always lurking just beneath the surface . . .

"Lead paint," she hissed through clenched teeth as she pounded the words into her computer. "Lead paint, lead paint, lead paint!"

She had to obey Carl.

But Flora wouldn't let her. The child's voice whispered inside Ana's head. A fragile little girl hiding in a trash bin. How could anyone need Ana more?

"The man put his hands on me," Flora had whispered, her cheek pressed against Ana's shoulder as they sat in the darkness of the empty container. "It was Primero. He hurt me so much that I screamed. My shame is great, but I deserve it. Primero offered me the chocolate, and I took it. And so it was my fault that he hurt me."

Recalling the trembling girl in her arms, Ana gripped the vinyl armrests of her office chair. She squeezed her eyes shut and tried to block the image of that small, frightened body huddled so close to hers inside the reeking steel womb.

"Oh, Flora, it's not your fault," Ana had told her. "Please believe me. That man is bad—not you."

But sobs rose from deep in Flora's chest. "Before I went to live with Segundo, he took away my sister."

"Who took your sister?" Ana asked.

"Primero took her. I did nothing to stop him. I lost my sister, and I don't know where she is . . . and it is my fault . . . ."

That night in bed, Ana had stretched out like a corpse, unable to move, hearing the words over and over. I lost my sister. I lost her. It's my fault.

How could Ana turn a deaf ear to Flora's cries when her own pain hammered at her day after day? Was there any hope for relief?

God had saved her from the brink once, not many days after her sister's death. Ana, too, had heard the sweet siren serenade of suicide. How nearly she had succumbed. Yet, God's hand had reached out to her, and she had taken it. He had lifted her up from the murky, sucking sea of her despair.

But what was the true nature of her rescuer, her Savior? Was Sam right in his view of God as the strong force who could triumph over all? Or was He the softly cradling arms of love she once had felt?

Sam's message of surrender echoed in Ana's heart. Surrender everything to God, he had told her. Ask Him to take control of your life. Surrender was the opposite of welcome warmth, wasn't it? Did God have both traits within Himself—the loving Father and the vigilant Protector?

At her desk, staring blankly at the text that covered her computer screen, Ana at last understood the truth. Closing her eyes, she opened her heart in prayer. Jesus had lifted her from the depths and embraced her. He was Love. But He was also power and authority. Ana and Flora both needed God's love . . . and His strength. Surrender, she realized, meant laying down her own efforts to protect herself. It meant allowing the God of love to do battle on her behalf. And so, in the busy crowded newsroom, she submitted to Him, surrendering herself to His compassion as well as His commanding rule over her life.

When Ana lifted her head, she saw that nothing had changed. The cursor still blinked at the end of her lead paint article. Her deadline still hovered. And Flora was missing.

But something had changed. Ana could feel God's presence. Not only His compassion but His strength. It was as though He had opened another part of Himself to her, like a curtain drawing back from a shrouded window to reveal the sunshine. Joy flooded her . . . yet at the same time, her heart ached. Amid the bustle, she still heard Flora's voice.

Primero took my sister . . . Primero . . .

Primero. The first man. Flora said she had seen him there—at Haven. Who was he, then? Terell Roberts? Raydell Watson? Sam Hawke?

No. Not one of them fit.

Ana clicked out of her word processing program and

called up an Internet search engine. Possessed with a determination that almost frightened her, she typed in a few key words. James Slater Aspen Colorado. A list of entries appeared—a genealogy record, a travel agency, a bed-and-breakfast guide.

Her heart racing, Ana added more words to define her search. Building contractor. Real estate agent. Again, a random group of references materialized. She opened several and read them carefully. Not one could possibly refer to the man who now lived in St. Louis and operated Young Blessings Adoption Services.

Precious minutes ticked by, and Ana knew she should be editing the lead paint article and starting others that must accompany it. But she couldn't make herself stop. After printing out what she had uncovered, she located phone numbers for the Aspen chamber of commerce, real estate and builders associations and the city's finance department.

An hour and many phone calls later, she had learned that no one by the name of Jim Slater had ever belonged to any organization in the town of Aspen, Colorado. He had never applied for or received a business license there. No address or telephone number had ever been recorded in his name. Nothing open to public investigation revealed that anyone by the name had ever lived in Aspen. Widening her search, Ana checked the same information in the nearby towns of Woody Creek, Snowmass, El Jebel and Carbondale.

Nothing.

Now she turned her attention in another direction. Locating Web addresses for the sheriff 's department of every sizable city in Colorado, she searched sex offender registries. Names and addresses marched across her screen. One criminal after another. But Jim Slater?

Nothing.

She entered the names of newspapers and went through their archives looking for the man's name. Had Slater committed crimes in the state? Had he been tried? Served on a jury? Received civic awards? Been nominated for committees, sat on boards, made comments about anything anywhere? Had he even advertised the company that had earned him such wealth?

Nothing.

Jim Slater had not lived in Colorado. Ever.

Letting out a breath, she picked up her phone one last time. As she dialed, she realized she was hungry. Her head ached, and her heart had been beating so fast for such a long time that she felt as though she'd run a marathon. One whole day had vanished, and all she had to show for it was a lengthy, unreadable article and a fruitless search of the state of Colorado.

"Haven, how may I help you?" The voice belonged to young Caleb, the volunteer who had come from New Mexico.

Ana's shoulders unknotted as she envisioned the technical wizard with his head of dark curls. She could see the boy staring at a stack of computer hardware while fuming and fussing at the pile of junk he'd been handed.

"Hey, Caleb," she said softly. "This is Ana Burns at the *Post-Dispatch.* Is Sam there?"

"Is Sam here?" the youth scoffed. "Of course he's here. He's never anywhere but here. Just a sec."

She could hear the teenager yelling. "Yo, Uncle Sam, it's your hot chick! She wants you, man! She needs you!"

Mortified, Ana felt her cheeks blaze. Good grief, is that how they viewed her? The hot chick who was chasing Uncle Sam? Great. This was terrific.

"Ana?" Sam's voice jarred her. "Is everything okay?"

"I'm not a hot chick," she informed him.

He was silent a moment, and she could almost see those parentheses in his cheeks deepening. "I beg to differ," he said finally. "Is that why you called?"

"No, but . . ." She nibbled her thumbnail for a moment. "Jim Slater never lived in Aspen."

"He didn't? Are you sure?" His voice deepened. "How do you know this?"

"I gathered data, made phone calls. I found no record that anyone by that name ever lived in Aspen. I looked in bigger cities, too. No evidence of his existence. Jim Slater is not who he claims to be."

"That's a serious accusation about a man of his stature, Ana. Can you disprove the things he said? He gave us details, remember? His family lived in Aspen's Santa Lucia subdivision. The cherub collection belonged to his wife. They had three daughters, and we saw their photographs. He ran a multimillion dollar company."

"So, was he in real estate, or was he a building contractor? Sam, he told you one thing and me another. He made a mistake, because he was lying."

"He told us he did both."

"He lied to us."

"Why would he do that?"

"Sam, I think the person we know as Jim Slater is the same man Flora calls Primero. He brought her on a plane from Honduras to St. Louis, and he transferred her to another man, Segundo. Both of them molested her. She ran away, and ended up on the streets. Gypsy found her and took her in. While Gypsy works, Flora stays at Haven, and sometimes she sees Primero there. Jim Slater."

Sam was silent.

"Do you remember the time I found Flora in the bathroom?" Ana asked. "Jim had been at Haven that afternoon. Flora saw him, Sam. I'm sure of it—that's why she was so upset. And yesterday, she saw him again."

"Are you saying Jim Slater chased Flora up three flights of stairs and tried to break our fire escape door because Flora knows who he is? Because she can ruin him?"

"He's terrified of her."

"And she's terrified of him," Sam said, his voice almost a whisper. "Ana, this is serious."

"Jim isn't running a legitimate adoption agency,"

she told him. “Something else is going on. I’m not sure what Jim is up to, but Jack Smith is part of it. You told me that God is our protector, a warrior in our defense. Sam, I believe He put us together to save Flora. We have to stop Jim.” She pursed her lips together, fighting unexpected tears. “Please, Sam. Help me.”

She could hear the torment in his voice as he spoke. “Ana, you realize what you’re asking me to do. Jim Slater and his donation to our lead paint rehab fund are my only hope for keeping Haven open. My kids are fighting to have decent lives, and I’m doing all I can to open doors for them. We can’t make an accusation against Jim without absolute proof. We could ruin an innocent man and destroy a better future for hundreds of kids.”

“How can we get absolute proof, Sam?”

“I don’t know. But we can’t point the finger at Jim and then walk away unscathed if we’re wrong about him. Remember I told you how easily Terell forgives? Last night, he refused to talk to me. He won’t look at me today. At lunch, I found him up in our room reading his Bible and crying.”

“Oh, no.”

“You know what he told me? Terell said if anyone ever believed he had done such a thing, his life would be over. The hint of a rumor, any kind of accusation can destroy a man. Terell has worked hard to rebuild his reputation. He’s convinced if he ever messes up again, he’ll never be able to get a job. Or a wife. His family would disown him. He’d lose everything.”

Ana heard the pain in Sam's tone. He had wounded his best friend, and he didn't know how to heal the rift.

"I'm sorry Terell is hurting," she said gently. "But you heard Flora's screams. We were right to question him."

Again Sam fell silent. When he spoke, his words came slowly. "Jim Slater holds the future of Haven in his hands. I've given all I have to that place. Tenisha, Gerald, all of them—those are my kids, and I'll do anything to make their lives better. I can't risk Haven's future just because Jim Slater lied about living in Aspen. Ana, give me proof he's the man who hurt Flora. If you can tie it together, I promise I'll go after him with everything I've got."

Ana clamped her mouth shut as Sam's demand reverberated in her brain. She had heard such words before. Knew well the disbelief and denial that could accompany an accusation. Understood the impossibility of utter, absolute proof.

"It's getting late," she said finally. "I need to get back to my article."

"I'm sorry, Ana."

"Save it. I've got hours of work ahead of me here tonight. I'd better go."

Before he could respond, she set down the receiver and let out her breath. As much as she hated to admit it, Sam was right. Accuse someone wrongly and you'd ruin his life. Accuse Jim Slater and she'd shut down Haven.

But her heart cried out in defiance—allow a

pedophile to go free, and ruin the life of a child. Many children. Perhaps hundreds.

Ana picked up her purse and stood, hoping to find something to eat in the snack machine on the first floor. She headed for the stairwell, pushed open the door and started down. As she reached the first landing, she saw Jack Smith leaning against the wall.

He smiled. “Hello, Anamaria Burns. Just who I was coming to see.”

Her heart stumbled. “You. You’re working for Jim Slater, aren’t you? You’re part of his pedophile ring. You’re the one Flora calls Segundo. The man she escaped from.”

“Right on the first charge. Wrong on the second. I don’t know who had the girl, but I would never touch a kid. Guys who do that are sleazebags. I’m a hired man, and I don’t ask questions. If I’d known who I was working for when I signed on, I would have turned down the job.”

“How . . . how did you get into the building?” She backed up a step, clutching the handrail for support.

“You’re almost as good as me,” he continued. “Almost. See, I figured out how to get into this place, no problem. And you figured out about Jack. Only difference is, I’m right on time. But you? You’re just a little bit too late.”

“What do you mean I figured out about Jack? That’s you, right?”

“Nah. Name I’m going by in St. Louis is Don Bering. Even got a driver’s license to prove it.”

Ana stared at the smirking man, trying to drink down enough air to think clearly. Though he had said nothing menacing, she recognized the look on his face. He was planning to hurt her. Kill her, perhaps.

Without turning her head, she made a mental search for an escape. The night cleaning crew would be somewhere nearby, emptying trash cans and vacuuming floors. Her pepper spray can lay at the bottom of her purse. And she could run.

But Bering—or whatever his real name might be—was big, stocky, layered with thick muscle. He was close, too. feet away, at the most. Then she saw the gun in his hand. A small, silver pistol with a silencer on the barrel.

Desperate to buy time, Ana asked, "What can you tell me about Jim Slater? If you're not Jack, who is he? You said I figured out . . ." Realization washed over her. "It's Jim, isn't it? Jim Slater. Jack is his real name."

Bering chuckled. "Slater was born Joseph Slaughter, and he grew up in Philly. The city of brotherly love, they call it, but Jack's more into children. You pegged him, lady. He runs a big operation, lots of clients, wads of money. Strictly cash, of course."

"He trades in children. Brings them in from Honduras. I suppose he sells them. Or is it a rental agreement?"

"I don't know the details. All I know is that we're alone. It's just you and me."

Ana edged her purse around, hoping to be able to

grab the pepper spray. "What do you want with me, Don Bering or whoever you are? Did Jim—Jack—send you here?"

"First, I want you to put down the bag." He gestured at her purse with the gun. "Set it over there. Farther. That's a good girl. Now, you're coming with me."

"Where are you taking me?"

"You do what I say, and don't ask questions. We'll go down to the first floor, and we'll step outside and get into my car. Nice and easy. Happy face, you know? Don't even think about screaming or trying to run, because this little baby is equipped with a very sophisticated silencer. You'll be dead before you hit the floor, and no one will hear a thing. Now, let's start walking, shall we?"

With a last look at her purse—where her pepper spray, car keys and cell phone were stashed out of reach—Ana stepped away. As she did, her phone rang. She glanced at Bering.

"Sam Hawke knows I'm here. I told him I'd be working late."

He frowned. Kicked at the purse. Dug around inside until he found the phone and tossed it to her. "Take it. Watch what you say. One hint and I drop you right here."

Praying hard, she spoke into the phone. "Hello. It's Ana Burns."

Sam's voice was tight. "I called Jim's house. He's not there. I talked to a housekeeper. She said he'd been planning a trip, a vacation, but she wasn't sure he'd left yet. Those two girls we saw? They weren't with a foster family. They'd been living at Jim's place. Now they're gone."

Ana swallowed. Bering was motioning her to cut off the conversation. "Okay. I'd better get back to work."

Bering grabbed the phone and snapped it shut. "Get moving." He grabbed her by the upper arm and jerked her down to the landing again.

"Hey, you're hurting my arm," she protested. "I got cut with a knife right there the other day, buster. Move your fingers."

To her surprise, Bering dropped his hand but jammed the pistol into her side. "Walk," he said.

"So, what happened to the two little girls?" she asked as they started down together. "Slater was keeping them at his house."

"I don't know anything about that."

"Did you kill them?"

"Just keep moving!" he barked, giving her a shove. Using the momentum, Ana leaped over the handrail and dropped to the lower flight. Her feet flew down the steps, light, hardly touching, taking them faster than she ever had. The pounding of Bering's feet above her echoed through the stairwell.

A chunk of concrete exploded just in front of her face. He was firing at her, using the silencer to muffle the shots. Ana coughed and stumbled forward. A spray of powder erupted two feet ahead. She grabbed the metal railing, used it to propel herself faster.

His breath was labored now behind her, and she

thought she had a chance. A few more steps to the door. She reached for the release bar. A bullet slammed into her hand. Flesh sizzled. Bones snapped. Blood sprayed across the exit door.

She threw a hip against the bar and burst out into the parking lot. “Help me, help me, dear God!” she choked out. Her legs moved of their own accord, conditioned by years of training. Instinctively, she reached for her purse.

No purse. No keys.

A bullet hit a streetlamp post and ricocheted past her thigh. Bering’s voice rang out. “Hey! Stop right where you are.”

Her hand knew no pain, only the dull shock of injury as she rounded a corner. Not a single store was open. No cafés. Nothing. And then she spotted the city bus pulling away from the sidewalk.

“Wait!” Ana shouted. She waved her wounded hand, sending flecks of blood arcing through the air over her head. “Please wait!”

The bus brakes squealed, and Ana sprinted into the street. She slammed a shoulder into the bifold door and wrenched it open. Her foot hit the metal step, and she launched herself up and through. Swinging around, she threw herself against the door as Bering’s fist began hammering on the glass.

“Drive!” Ana screamed to the startled woman behind the steering wheel. “He’s trying to kill me! Please go.”

The driver stomped on the accelerator. Ana tumbled

to the rubber-matted floor, clutching her hand to her stomach.

"You bleeding?" the driver demanded, glaring over her shoulder at the new passenger. "Bleeding on my bus?"

"Go," Ana croaked. "Just keep driving."

"I'll have to clean that up. Get into a seat. We don't allow riding on the floor." She clicked her tongue against her teeth.

Ana staggered up and fell onto a seat. Except for an old man snoring in the back row, the bus was empty. She clamped her good hand over the other, trying not to cry from the intense pain that now shot through it, elbow to fingertips.

"Where you goin', lady?" the driver called. "You got money to pay the fare?"

"Can you take me over to Haven on Martin Luther King?"

"That's not on my route."

"Please. There's a man who can pay you."

"You telling me you ain't got the fare?"

"I can get the fare."

The bus pulled over to the sidewalk. "Get out, lady. You're my second gunshot this month, and I ain't taking you nowhere. People bleeding all over my bus . . . forget that."

Ana lurched forward, grasping the steel bars that rose from one seat back after another. Her hand was on fire. The door swung open. Gritting her teeth against the pain, she turned to the driver.

"A man is trying to kill me. I need to get to Haven. And you won't help me?"

The driver looked at her in distaste. "I'll radio the police. Now get out."

Unable to stop the tears, Ana worked her way down the steps. The bus had traveled only a couple of blocks from the *Post-Dispatch* building. For all she knew, Bering would round the corner at any moment. She stepped down onto the sidewalk and realized immediately that she was standing in the heart of a run-down, drug-infested neighborhood with only a few streetlamps to light her way. Ragged children paused in a game of tag to stare at her. Three young men lounging against a boarded-up brick building gazed at her beneath hooded eyelids.

"Dear God," she murmured in a prayer born of utter despair. "Please help me. Be my defender."

"Excuse me, ma'am, are you trying to get to Martin Luther King, Jr. Street?" a voice asked behind her.

Ana swung around to find the old man from the back of the bus. His skin the color of dusty charcoal, he wore an old blue suit coat, a pair of plaid trousers and some brown tennis shoes with holes in the toes. He scratched his chin for a moment then squinted at her.

"I know that street," he said. "Want me to help you get there?"

Ana managed a nod.

"Well, come on, then. Let's get moving."

Chapter Sixteen

"Terell, I have to go check on Ana." Sam approached his friend cautiously, unwilling to widen the rift between them. "We were talking on the phone, and we got cut off. I've called her back three times, but she won't pick up."

"Probably mad at you." Terell kept his eyes on the basketball game in progress at Haven. "Wouldn't surprise me."

"T-Rex, listen—"

"Don't call me that name." He swung on Sam, his dark eyes blazing. "Things are different between us now."

Sam looked at his friend, despair heavy in his chest. "I'm sorry. I'll say it seventy times seven if I have to. Please forgive me, Terell. I didn't mean to hurt you."

"It's not about hurt, man. I can take that. This is about trust. You don't trust me. What kind of friend is that?"

"Ana had just told me what Flora was saying in the trash bin. Ana thought—"

"Ana this and Ana that. You trust me less than some woman you've known for a week. Is that it? Huh?"

Sam rubbed his eyes. "You know I trust you, Terell. I believed in you when nobody else would even speak your name."

"Then why would you accuse me?"

"It's Flora. She's one of our kids. And she . . . she reminds me of . . ."

Unable to speak the words, he shook his head. How could he justify accusing his best friend of molesting a child? But how could he live with himself if he didn't try to find the man who had assaulted Flora?

"What—she reminds you of that little girl you shot in Iraq?" Terell tossed out. "You'd better get over that, Sam. You killed a kid and nothing you do can change it."

"Shh." Sam stiffened. "Drop it."

"You killed her on accident," Terell went on, throwing the words at the man beside him. "The military knows it. God knows it. I know it, too—and I wasn't even there. I know it, because I trust what you told me. I trust you, Sam, because I'm your friend. I believe you thought that van was full of Iraqi insurgents who were driving toward the roadblock to attack you. I know you shot at the car to protect yourself and your men. And I'm absolutely sure you didn't intend to cause the death of that little brown-eyed girl."

Terell wore a frown in place of the usual grin. "You better just get over it, Sam," he declared. "Get. Over. It."

"I'm trying," Sam hissed through clenched teeth.

"No, you're not. You take one look at that little Mexican girl—"

"Honduran."

"Whatever. And all you see is that girl in Iraq. Well,

you can't bring her back, Sam." He leaned closer. "She's dead! You hear me? Dead!"

"Why are you doing this to me?"

"Because you're so fired up to make amends for a dead girl that you would accuse me of the worst thing a man could ever do! Your guilt has eaten holes right through your brain, man. You know me. You know who I am. You know I would never do that."

"And I know I would never shoot a full magazine of bullets into a van carrying a poor Iraqi family. But I did. I did it, Terell. Sometimes we do things we never thought we would in a million years."

"What you did was a mistake. What you're accusing me of is a vile sin. I'm a forgiven sinner, but not that kind. And you know it."

Sam stared into the dark eyes of the friend he had loved so many years. He sensed the cluster of children growing around the two of them. They had never seen Uncle Sam and T-Rex angry at each other. One of them started to whimper. Another kept tugging on the hem of Sam's white T-shirt. Sam searched his brain, trying to erase the memory Terell had roused from its fitful slumber, trying to replace the image of that bloodied, lifeless child with an explanation that would satisfy his friend.

"I know you didn't hurt Flora, Terell," he repeated. "I shouldn't have accused you. I wasn't thinking—"

"It's that lady!" someone screamed. "She's bleeding again!"

The children scattered, their shoes pounding across

the concrete floor, their voices pitched high with hysteria. Sam pivoted away from Terell. He spotted Ana as she hurried toward him. One arm cradled the other against her body and pressed her hand to her abdomen. Even from a distance, he could see blood spattered across her face and shirt.

"Sam!" She ran toward him, calling out, stumbling through the mass of shrieking children.

He left Terell, his legs eating up the space between himself and the woman. "Ana, what happened? Who did this?"

"Oh, Sam!"

He caught her, pulled her close. "Ana, Ana."

"You kids get on back to what you were doing!" Terell barked. "You're out of your groups, every last one of you. Am I gonna have to put you on the list?"

With a chorus of cries and shrieks, the children scampered back to their activities. Terell clamped a hand on Sam's shoulder. "Let me look at her, dog. She's pale. She might be in shock."

"I'm not in shock," Ana breathed, her eyes focusing on the taller man. "It was him, Terell. It was Jack Smith." She shook her head. "That's not his real name. He shot me, and I barely—"

Her face crumpled. Caught in Sam's arms, she sagged to the floor. He and Terell followed her down, lowering her gently to the cool concrete. She sat spread-eagled, her shoes missing, her head bowed, red stains spattered across her blouse.

"Get the first aid kit, Antwone!" Terell shouted to a

teenager who still hovered near. "Call 9-1-1, and tell them to get over here with the police and an ambulance."

"No, wait." Ana lifted her head. "It's just my hand. I think I can—"

"Did you hear me?" Terell snapped at Antwone. Then he twisted back to Ana. "I don't care if the bullet went through your hand or your head, woman. You need a doctor."

"But he's after me. He'll find me." She caught Terell's arm, her eyes pinned to his face. "I know who did it. I was so wrong about you. The predator is Jim Slater. He's Primero. He sent the hit man after me, because I figured it out. We have to find Flora! Terell, please help me. Sam, I need you."

"Ana, slow down," Sam said as Terell eased her wounded hand away from her body and began to examine it. "You say Jack Smith shot you? Where did it happen?"

"At the newspaper building. He got in. It was the man Jim Slater introduced as his colleague from Arkansas. He told me his real name—at least the alias he is using with Jim—is Don Bering." She winced when Terell prodded her palm. "Jim hired him. Jim's real name is Jack Slaughter."

"Jack Slaughter? So that's why you couldn't find any mention of Slater in Aspen."

"Yes, and Bering . . . I'm afraid of what he did to those two girls. Now he's after me. He's going to kill me, Sam."

"No way. I've got you now. You're safe."

"These bones are broken," Terell announced. "Bone fragments in the wound. Shredded tendon. Her skin's burned, too."

"But no arteries," Ana said. "Nothing important."

"Nothing important? You're a reporter, aren't you? Your livelihood depends on a keyboard. A surgeon needs to set these bones and stitch the tendons back together if you want to keep full use of your hand."

"I can't. Not now. Just wrap it, and I'll go to the doctor later. We have to find Flora. Bering will be after her, too. We need to look for Gypsy and see if she can tell us where Flora might be."

"The only place you're going, Ana Burns, is to the emergency room," Sam cut in.

"Terell, you seem to know more about injuries than Sam. What do you think?"

"I think Sam ought to stop running his mouth all the time. Making accusations, bossing people around. That's not how we act at Haven. I might have to put Sam on the list." Terell chuckled, the first happy sound Sam had heard from his friend in the past twenty-four hours. "Let me work on this, Ana. I'll make the decision."

Sam digested the shards of hurt that remained in his friend's voice. He suspected the injury to Terell would take longer to heal than Ana's.

His attention riveted on his patient now, Terell began to work. Ana clutched her trembling hand, her pale face contorted with pain. As Sam gently rubbed her back, Terell unrolled a bandage, packed the wound with sterile gauze and began to wrap the hand.

"I know this sounds crazy, but I'm with Ana," he told Sam. "She needs to see a doctor, but if the pain can wait, we've got other business. She's been shot, and that means someone wants her dead. Ana, are you sure you saw who did this to you?"

"Don Bering," she said. "The man we met as Jack Smith. The guy who came here with Jim Slater after church on Sunday."

"I didn't like the looks of him," Terell said. "That dude and Slater were up there like a couple of burglars breaking our padlock. Made me mad."

"They were trying to get through the door and onto the fire escape so they could catch Flora. It's because she can tell police what they're doing. They know I've been talking to Flora, so Bering came after me tonight. He fired at me as I ran down the stairwell. He took my purse, so I didn't have my keys. I barely made it onto a bus, but then the driver made me get off."

"You were bleeding," Terell murmured. "Bus drivers won't do ambulance service. So, how'd you get here?"

"There was a . . ." She looked over her shoulder. "He was a . . . Where did he go? He got off the bus when I did. He led me here."

"I didn't see anyone but you," Sam said. "Ana, I know you want to look for Flora, but you've got to stay here until the police and ambulance arrive. Terell and I will—"

"No, Sam. Absolutely not." She pushed herself up, the end of the bandage floating from her hand like a white banner. "Bering knows I figured it all out—Jack Slaughter's operation. The Honduras connection. Slaughter hired him to kill me, and I have no doubt he's after Flora, too."

"Then we'd better find her first," Terell said, getting to his feet.

"She'll be with Gypsy," Ana told him. "But how can we find her? She could be anywhere."

"Gypsy won't be hard to track down," Terell said. "These girls work regular streets. They stake out a corner, and the pimp protects it. If we can find someone who knows his way around—"

"Raydell," Sam said, standing now. "Raydell knows everything and everyone in this hood."

"You're just breaking Haven's rules all the time, aren't you, dog? Butting in, giving orders, acting uppity." Terell chastised him. "You fall in love, and the rules go right out the window."

"I am not—" Sam bit off the denial. Unable to bring himself to look at Ana, he growled at Terell. "Speaking of rules, T-Rex, it's against the law to shoot someone. Finding Flora is a job for the police. They know the streets better than any of us. And if you think Ana's hand is going to heal right—"

"Those two little girls at Slater's house!" Ana spun around and caught the sleeve of Sam's T-shirt in her good hand. "We've got to go find them, too. Come on, Terell."

"Now wait," Sam called as Ana and Terell started for the door. "You don't have any shoes on, woman. The ambulance will be here any minute. This is a civilian setting. There's a certain order to the procedure."

"Civilian setting? This is war!" Terell yelled over his shoulder. "Come on, Sam, you're the reconnaissance dude. Put on that black beret again, and help us out."

Standing in the middle of the gym, Sam stared at the two—the wounded woman, and the wounded friend. They both needed a haven, and he wanted to provide that for them. But they wouldn't have it.

As Sam hesitated, the words of Jesus filled his head. . . . *The greatest love is shown when people lay down their lives for their friends.* Love. Ana's idea of God was the rescuer, comforter, savior. But now he saw that the two facets of his Lord's character worked together. Love demanded action. Action revealed love.

Sam held up a hand, signaling Ana and Terell to wait. He jogged to the office and pulled Caleb's attention from the innards of a computer. The youth agreed to shut down the building early, to give Sam's cell phone number to the police and to notify the ambulance that a woman with a gunshot wound to the hand would arrive at the hospital soon.

Questioning his sanity the whole way, Sam dug yet another pair of flip-flops out of the lost-and-found box. Though he knew it was crazy to venture out with a woman as badly wounded as Ana, his body hummed with the cry from Terell's lips.

This is war.

And it was. Jesus had ordered His troops to care for "the least of these." Wasn't Flora the very least of all? Didn't she—didn't every child—deserve better?

Jesus had instructed His disciples to clothe the naked, and that description perfectly fit the abused children Ana knew so much about. They had been stripped of everything—their dignity, their self-worth, and most of all, their innocence. They stood helpless, completely defenseless against anyone who meant them harm. Their only hope was that some adult would care enough to reach out and find them, rescue them, clothe them in warm robes of love.

"What was the word in the poem Flora wrote?" Sam asked as he handed Ana the flip-flops.

"*Esperanza,*" she said. Her voice softened as she translated the verse. " 'It comes. Like moonlight. Like wind before rain. Like a green bud on a dead tree. *Esperanza.* Hope.' "

"So, are we gonna talk poetry all night?" Terell asked as he clipped the end of the bandage in place on Ana's hand. "Because I'm ready to get out of this place. Hear the sirens? If we don't beat them, we'll be here for hours."

Ana squared her shoulders. "Let's go find our children."

• • •

The stairwell smelled of urine and vomit. Cockroaches skittered beneath piles of wadded napkins, paper cups, uncapped syringes, beer cans. Ana tried to hold her breath, but for some reason, the effort made her hand hurt worse. She huddled close to Sam as he knocked on the battered apartment door.

Did Raydell Watson really live in this place? She knew such squalor existed in the city, but still it shocked her. How could anyone find hope here? How could a child ever survive? How could a young man build himself a future?

"Who's there?" someone called from the other side.

"It's Uncle Sam and T-Rex."

"Go away."

"Raydell, open the door," Sam told him. "We need to talk to you."

"I did it, okay? I'm the one who set the whole thing up. So, now you know. Just go away and leave me alone."

Sam glanced at Ana. She murmured an explanation. "The attack on me last Saturday. It was Raydell."

"Why'd you do that?" Terell asked. "Miss Burns never did nothing to you."

"I thought . . ." The voice behind the door fell silent.

"Hey, Raydell," Ana spoke up. "I'm okay. It's over. We didn't come here about that. We miss you at Haven. And we want to ask you some questions about the little girl in the corner."

"I never did nothing to Flora," Raydell burst out. "I

heard Sam say he didn't want you coming back to Haven. He was trying to get rid of you, and I figured I ought to help."

"Raydell, open up." Sam rattled the doorknob. "Come on, my friend."

To Ana's surprise, the door swung open. The stocky teenager stood before them, his face swollen and bruised, and his gold tooth missing. Head hanging low, he stepped aside.

"My mama works nights," he mumbled. "You can come in."

Ana followed Sam and Terell into the filthy room. Plywood blocked the windows, and the odor of rotting food drifted from the kitchen. Gingerly, she took a seat in one of the mismatched chairs.

"Who did you, man?" Terell asked the boy.

"Them. I said I'd pay the two of 'em to scare her, but when they told me what happened, I refused." He rubbed his hand over his eyes. "I never wanted them to hurt her. Not even to touch her. I told 'em not to lay a finger on her. But they said what they had been doin', and then they told me how some kind of ghost came out of the darkness at 'em, and how Miss Burns got away. I was so mad that they . . . they did what they did . . . ."

"They didn't hurt me much, Raydell," Ana spoke up. "I'm all right."

As determined as she was to be kind, Ana's agitation was growing by the minute. The pain in her hand was about to make her pass out, and now she noticed lines of baby cockroaches racing up and down her chair. Hundreds of them. Maybe thousands.

"When I told 'em I wouldn't pay," Raydell was saying, "they beat me up."

"You sure it wasn't anybody else?" Sam asked. "We heard your father had come home."

Raydell gave a hiss of disgust. "That loser's got nine more years, man. Even when he gets out, he won't be comin' around here. I ain't seen him since I was six years old anyhow."

Despite the boy's obvious anger toward his father, Ana noted that Raydell knew the exact number of years left on the man's sentence. No wonder the youth had bonded with Sam and Terell. They were his father figures.

"Raydell, you should have asked me about Ana," Sam said. "I'd never want anyone to hurt her. Even to scare her. Never."

"Well, you were yellin' at her. I heard you. You told her not to come back to Haven, and she told you back that she could do anything she wanted. So I thought . . ." Raydell hung his head, the long dreadlocks hiding his features. "Forget it."

"We need you at the door," Sam continued. "Nobody can run it better. We count on you."

"Yeah," Terell concurred. "The place isn't safe unless you're at the door. When you coming back, dog?"

Raydell's chin lifted an inch, and his hooded eyes searched the faces of the three adults. "You want me back?"

"Can't do without you," Sam said.

"And we need your help with Flora," Ana added, deciding to stand as the lines of cockroaches came ever closer. "She usually comes to Haven with another girl. Gypsy."

"I know Gypsy," Raydell said immediately. "White chick, hair dyed black, about so tall. She comes around all dolled up for business. Brings Flora and leaves her at Haven till we close down." He paused. "Gypsy's thirteen. She told me."

Ana swallowed hard. "Raydell, do you have any idea where Gypsy works? We need to find Flora. She may be in danger."

"From who?" He jumped to his feet, the old defensive posture back in place. "Nobody touches our kids."

"Jim Slater," Sam said. "He's not the man we thought he was."

Ana heard the resignation in his voice. She knew how hard he had resisted accepting the truth. The exposure of Slater's pedophilia would rock the St. Louis community. His guilt would wreak havoc in churches across the state. It would affect countless charitable foundations. Certainly it must mean the end of Haven.

"Are you talkin' about the guy who wears all them shirts with the . . . the stripes?" Raydell was asking, his lips twisting into a grin at the memory. "Aw, he couldn't hurt nobody. I could knock him out with my little finger."

“He hired a hit man,” Ana said, lifting her hand. Blood had begun to seep through the bandage. “The guy shot me tonight. Raydell, help us find Gypsy and Flora.”

“Let’s get goin’. I’ll take you to Gypsy’s corner. No problem.” The young man was out the door and down the steps of the apartment building before they’d had time to shut the door behind them.

Ana recognized her sister’s eyes in Gypsy’s face the moment she spotted the girl staring at them from a distance. Dark green eyes, full of spitfire and bravado. And behind the defiance, pain.

“Her pimp’s watching,” Raydell said in a low voice. “Stay cool.”

On the walk to the nearby area of downtown, Sam and Ana had explained the situation to Raydell. The teen was angry but not surprised. He had known men who preyed on children that way, he said. Some of his friends had been lured onto the streets—young boys who had prostituted themselves, sniffed paint or smoked marijuana to stay high and escape the shame they felt. Some had been beaten within an inch of their lives, and then they had vanished. He had no idea where they’d gone.

“I don’t see the pimp,” Raydell told the others, “but he’s around. He’ll peg us right away—knowin’ we ain’t customers. We can’t stay long, or the guy will make her pay.”

“Pay?” Ana asked.

"Slap her around. She's supposed to be hustling."

Remembering herself at thirteen, Ana studied the tall youngster. Gypsy wore a purple satin top, black miniskirt, fishnet stockings and four-inch-heeled ankle boots. The outfit could not have been more different from Ana's prep school uniform—white blouse, pleated plaid skirt, knee-socks and brown leather shoes. At thirteen, Ana had sported a ponytail and a full set of braces. Gypsy's hair, dyed black and starting to show its light brown roots, hung like a curtain over the side of her face. She glowered at the approaching foursome.

"Let me do the talkin'," Raydell said. "She knows me."

Ana stepped back and observed the grimy storefronts and cracked sidewalks that were this child's world. What was Gypsy's real name? How had she fallen into this impossible downward spiral? Was she already infected with HIV or some other disease? Did she use drugs to numb her bleak existence?

Ana's heart ached with the burden of the girl's suffering. Had Christ ever known such hopelessness? Did he understand the abandonment and fear that Gypsy knew? Ana recalled His betrayal and execution on the cross. Suffering, hopelessness, abandonment, fear. Yes, Jesus knew.

But what hope was there for this girl and the others who worked their corners in swaggering pairs or trios? Could Christ really bring healing to children so deeply scarred?

"Yo," Raydell greeted Gypsy. "What's up?"

"Nothing." She eyed him with a mixture of suspicion and curiosity. Tipping a chin in the direction of Sam, Terell and Ana, the girl asked in a low voice, "What ya'll want with me, huh?"

She had a surprisingly familiar accent. Texas, Ana realized. Gypsy was from Texas!

"We're lookin' for that kid you bring to Haven all the time," Raydell said. "Flora. Where is she?"

Gypsy folded her arms across her chest and looked away. "I don't know what you talkin' 'bout, dog. Get outta my face."

"You better tell us where she is. You don't, and we'll stick around till your man gets onto us."

"Hey, I don't know where she is!" Gypsy hissed. She glanced at a group of men down the street. Clustered in a tight group, they were conducting some kind of transaction. "What you want with her anyhow? She never did nothin' to you."

"Somebody's after her. Lookin' to kill Flora. The dude shot her tonight." Raydell pointed at Ana, who held up her bandaged hand. "We wanna take her someplace safe."

"She's safe." Gypsy looked away again and gave an exaggerated shrug. "You don't have to get all punk about it."

"If she's here, she ain't safe. And neither are you."

"Raydell's right," Terell spoke up. "Anyone connected with Flora or Ana is in that dude's line of fire. You know what kind of a place we run, Gypsy. You know we'd take care of Flora."

Sam nodded. "You wouldn't be bringing her to Haven if you didn't care about her, Gypsy. Tell us where she is. Her life is in danger."

"Look, get outta here!" the girl snarled suddenly, her black-lined eyes filling with tears. "All of ya'll, get off my street. An' I mean it!"

Ana noted that a large man had separated from the group down the way and was headed in their direction. As Sam, Terell and Raydell stepped back, she leaned closer to Gypsy and whispered the name of her street and her apartment number. "Tell Flora that Ana is worried about her."

"I can't tell her nothin'. She don't talk English."

"Just say my name."

Gypsy gazed at Ana for a moment, their eyes meeting, locking, recognizing. "I'll take care of her."

"I will, too. You come see me sometime, Gypsy."

Without speaking again, Ana grabbed Sam's hand and turned away. He beckoned the others.

"We need to find the guy who shot you," Terell said as they started back toward Haven. "Whatever his name is, if he's following us, he'll hurt Gypsy to get at Flora."

Ana fought the pain in her hand as she walked. "I'm worried about leaving Gypsy alone."

"Nobody followed us." Sam said it with such confidence that Ana looked up in surprise. "Recon. We're clear."

She let out a breath. "Then we should go to Jim Slater's house. Jack Slaughter—that's his real name.

If he hasn't gone on his 'vacation,' Bering will check in with him. I have a terrible feeling about the two girls, Sam."

His arm came around her, holding her close. On her other side, Terell took her free hand and tucked her arm through his to support her weight as she walked. Raydell strode a few steps ahead of the others, his shoulders casting a broad shadow on the lamp-lit sidewalk.

Chapter Seventeen

Flames lit the night sky, licking the stars and casting an orange glow across the clouds above Ladue. As Sam pulled his car to the curb in front of Jim Slater's mansion, the flashing lights of fire trucks and police cars painted the high stone wall in shades of red and blue. Arcs of water shot through the darkness like crystalline rainbows, and where they ended, smoke billowed upward in feathery gray plumes.

"He burned down his house," Ana said.

"Lord have mercy," Terell whispered.

Raydell whistled. "That dude in the striped shirts lived here? Look at all the statues. Like a graveyard."

Sam opened his door and stepped out into the smoke-filled air. A policeman approached, waving him back. The man carried a roll of yellow tape in one hand, using it to mark the walled compound off-limits.

"No stopping allowed," he said. "This is a crime scene."

"Jim Slater owns this home," Sam told him. "I run a youth center downtown, and he's on my board of directors."

"Is he all right?" Ana asked as she emerged from the backseat. "Please, we need to know."

"We got one body, I can tell you that. But no identification."

"A body," Raydell exclaimed.

"I can identify Jim Slater," Sam spoke up quickly. "Could I talk to the sergeant?"

"I'll bring him over. Stay back near your car. They've almost got the fire out, but the place is a mess."

"Wait, please," Ana caught his arm. "Two girls were living here. I have to know—is the body a child?"

"It's a male adult, ma'am." He paused, the roll of crime scene tape almost empty now. "Are you saying two girls may be inside the house?"

"Yes. I'd guess eight and ten years old. They speak Spanish."

He frowned. "The firemen have been able to get through part of the house but not the whole thing. I'll go tell the sergeant. Wait here."

As the officer jogged away, Raydell spoke up.

"I vote we go around back and take a look at the house ourselves." His face was lit with excitement, and the gap where his gold tooth had been knocked out gave him the look of an eager boy. "I can get into any place. It don't matter if there's cops around or nothin', I don't never get caught."

"Ain't you been in juvie, dog?" Terell asked, turning a skeptical eye on the teen. "Sounds to me like you got caught at least once."

Raydell scuffed the toe of his sneaker on the pavement. "Okay, maybe once."

"We'll wait for the sergeant," Sam said, determined to keep order despite everyone's panicked concern for the children. He didn't have to wait long. Three policemen—one in plainclothes—and a fire chief emerged from the area around the burning building and strode down the long cherub-lined walkway toward the open gate.

"You say there were children inside the building?" the chief asked as he stepped up to the group. "How many?"

"Two," Ana told him. She gave a description as Sam spoke to the police.

"If the body is the homeowner, Jim Slater, I can ID him for you," he said. "He was on my board of directors."

"Not so fast, sir. What's your name, and why are you here tonight?"

Sam knew it was time to tell the whole story. Ana joined him in outlining the most recent activities of the man they now knew as Jack Slaughter. They detailed the events of Sunday, when Slaughter and Bering had chased Flora, and she'd hidden in the garbage bin. Ana related her attempt to investigate Slaughter. As the detective took notes, she described Bering's appearance in the *Post-Dispatch* building earlier that evening and their headlong run down the stairwell. When she displayed her injured hand, the fire chief leaned closer.

"Doesn't look pretty from here," he said. "We have an ambulance right over there, ma'am. I'd recommend you let the paramedics take a look at that. You need to treat a gunshot as quickly as possible. There's often foreign matter in the wound. It can get infected."

"Yes, Ana," Sam told her. "Go to the ambulance. Let the paramedics take a look."

"But, Sam—"

"Please." He cupped her face in his palms and forced her to meet his eyes. "Do this, Ana. I care about you. A lot. I want you to be safe. Do it for me."

She lowered her gaze. "All right. But I'll be back here in a few minutes. I want to know about that body." She started to walk away, then swung around and took his arm. "Sam, find the girls."

"I will."

As the fireman and the detective led her away, Sam pressed again to be allowed access to the dead man they had found. The sergeant shrugged. "I need an ID. The coroner's here, and he's working the scene with our homicide unit. It's the two girls you saw in the house that worry me. You say this Bering was a hit man?"

"Pretty sure of it."

"But killing children? I've never heard of hiring a hit man to do that. It doesn't happen."

"These girls know all about Slater . . . Slaughter,"

Sam explained. "If we're right, they would be able to nail the man. They'd know his connections in Honduras, St. Louis, anywhere he works. They could verify everything."

The policeman made notes on a small pad he had taken from his coat. "We'll be searching the grounds in a few minutes. There are some outbuildings—staff housing, I guess. We're bringing a canine unit out here, too. Why don't you come with me, Mr. Hawke, and I'll let you speak to the coroner."

Sam glanced at Terell and Raydell. They had been talking intently a moment before, and as they lifted their heads they both looked as guilty as sin. What were they planning? Sam didn't like the sheepish grins on either man's face. Not one bit.

He gave the best warning scowl he could muster. "Stay here," he said. "I'll be back."

As Sam followed the sergeant through the gate he could almost hear the two scampering away. Great. Ana had gone off to show her hand to the paramedics. He was just about to look into the face of a dead man. And his two sidekicks were up to no good. Exactly what he didn't want—everybody scattered, nothing going by the rules.

The coroner was a small man with a bald head and piercing blue eyes. He snapped the fingers of his latex gloves one by one as he questioned Sam. After signing several forms and handing over his driver's license, Sam was ushered into the foyer of the smoldering remains of the house.

Swallowing, Sam stepped toward the prone figure of a man. Dark and stocky, he wore a surprised look in his glassy eyes. A halo of blood spread out across the marble floor tiles behind him, and a round black hole was centered in his forehead.

"This isn't the man we're looking for," Sam said. "This is Don Bering."

Sam stepped into the cool night air, found a smoke-free spot near a grove of tall oak trees and drew down a deep breath. He had seen dead men before. Many times. He'd seen dead women. Dead children. Even dead babies. And he'd never gotten used to it.

His stomach churning, he bent over and closed his eyes. Don't see the girl, he told himself. Don't see her. Don't look at the small white dress and the bloody scarf and the thin arms with their baby hands reaching for help. But she was there before him again, her brown eyes staring into his face. Big brown eyes.

He had shot her. He knew his bullet had been the one that had pierced her tiny body and snuffed out her life. His fault. His guilt. He had held her close, begging her to come back. Breathe, breathe! But she lay unmoving in his arms, looking up at him with her empty brown eyes.

He had sat in the base clinic in Basra, trying to tell the story, swallowing the medication, listening to the psychiatrist talk about post-traumatic stress syndrome, hearing the cold facts. And knowing that no matter how long he lived, no matter how many times he told the story, no matter how much medication he took, she would stay in his mind forever. The little girl with the big brown eyes. The dead brown eyes.

"I got her!" The shout rang out through the darkness. "I got one, and T-Rex has the other! We got 'em both!"

Sam straightened, blinking, trying to remember where he was. He could see someone now, running across the lawn, skirting fallen concrete cherubs, and dancing around the policemen who surrounded him. In his arms, Raydell cradled a child—small, curled into herself, sobbing.

"Sam? Hey, Sam!" Terell's voice called, and he emerged in the artificial light around the burned house. "Sam, we found them! The girls are all right. Where are you, man?"

Sam staggered forward, out from the copse of trees where he had hidden himself and his shame. The two children he and Ana had seen inside the house were alive. Police and paramedics blended with the silhouettes of his two friends and their fearful burdens. Shouts echoed amid the confusion.

Sam could see that one policeman had drawn his gun, and then another. He broke through the ring. "Terell," he called out. "Sergeant, tell these men to put away their weapons. Raydell, give the little girl to the paramedic."

"They was in the pool house." Clearly giddy, Raydell handed off the child and then jumped up and down, whooping with joy. "They had ropes and all, but we cut 'em loose. We did it, me and T-Rex."

The sergeant supervising the investigation approached Sam, who quickly explained the situation. Terell apologized for disobeying the order to stay with the car, but the broad smile on his face belied every word from his mouth.

"Don Bering didn't kill them," he said, taking Sam's shoulder in his big hand. "I had a feeling he couldn't do it. What man would? Not even a hit man could have a heart that bad."

"Thank God. They'll go into legitimate foster care until INS locates their family in Honduras."

"Two little girls," Terell said. "Look at them, Sam. Just look at that."

Female paramedics were checking out the children, gently rubbing ointment on the rope burns on their wrists. Someone brought a couple of teddy bears from the box policemen kept in their trunks for emergencies involving children. Both girls took one look at the toys, stiffened and burst into tears all over again.

"You need to get a victim's advocate out here right away," Sam told the sergeant. "They have to be taken to a hospital immediately and examined for signs of abuse. If what we suspect about Jack Slaughter is true, then . . . then . . ."

"They've been molested," Terell filled in.

"The man was keeping them in this house until he could send them to a client. Sell them, maybe. He was a predator. These children are his prey."

The sergeant shook his head. "I've read newspaper

accounts about this fellow you're calling Jack Slaughter. The guy I know as Jim Slater is in the society column nearly every week—going to one charity event or another. He's a big donor, and I've heard he does good work through his adoption agency. Now you're telling me he's supplying pedophiles with children from Honduras?"

"Everything I know about the man points to that conclusion," Sam said.

"Where is he then?"

"No idea."

"Look, I know who Jim Slater is," the sergeant said, "but I don't have a clue who you guys are. I'm half inclined to arrest you on suspicion of involvement in a crime. And you—" he pointed at Terell "—you and that kid are guilty of trespassing."

"Sir, we couldn't just stand by—"

"Save it," the sergeant cut in. "I'm not in the mood for excuses."

"I need to see about Ana," Sam said. "May I go?"

The man eyed him for a moment. "The coroner's got your identification, but I'm going to need names and contact information for your two pals here."

Sam produced a business card and jotted Terell's and Raydell's names on the back. "We all work at Haven downtown," he said, handing the card to the officer.

"Haven." He inspected it for a moment. "I know the place. You do good work there. Okay, get out of here, all three of you."

The sergeant brushed them aside and stalked off. Sam and Terell grabbed the teenager by the arms.

"But what about the little girls we found?" Raydell protested. "That lady is taking them away."

"They're going to be all right." Sam propelled him down the walkway, through the gate and back toward the car. "And you'd better not ever do anything like that again."

"I'm gonna be a cop," Raydell announced. "I decided it tonight. I'm going to the police academy after I graduate."

"You got a record, dog," Terell reminded him.

"But I was a minor. It was juvie, and that don't hardly count. They'll take me."

"I thought you dropped out of high school after eleventh grade."

"I'll get my GED, T-Rex. I can pass. I want to be a detective and do investigations."

Sam paused near a fireman who was winding a hose. "Where's the ambulance that was right here? Did you see a woman with a bandaged hand?"

"Sorry," the man said.

Sam asked a group of policemen standing nearby. The officers shook their heads and resumed their conversation.

Sam stood in the street and stared at the place where she was supposed to be. Ana was missing.

I hold my sister's hand. It is cold, and her fingers feel small and thin. She puts her head on my shoulder. She is tired. Her eyelids slide shut.

"Aurelia," I whisper. "Wake up. Wake up and talk to me."

"No," she says.

She's been saying no for many years now. No, she will not go to school. No, she will not go to church. No, she will not eat her food. No, she will not wear that dress. No, she will not walk on the beach or gather seashells or dance in the sunshine.

But Aurelia says yes, too. All her yeses are wrong. I try to tell her this. She must not say yes to bad things. But Aurelia no longer listens to me. I can't comb her hair and braid it into a long plait down her back. I can't sing to her and make her laugh. I can't talk to her or touch her. I can't even love her.

But I do. I'm desperate with love for Aurelia. I'm so desperate that I have decided I will tell. I've asked Mama and Papa to sit with us now and listen, because I have something very important to say. They stare at me. They ask why Aurelia will not open her eyes. Why will she not look at them?

I don't answer these questions, because I am going to say something more important. I am going to tell about the man.

First, I swallow. I can feel fear rising inside me like a volcano. I'm grown-up now, and I know in my heart that the man lied. But I still believe him. I'm sure I should not tell. I feel dirty. I'm ashamed.

But I'm also desperate. Desperate for Aurelia, who is dying from the filth and the shame and the pain.

I can't swallow down the fear. It spews into my mouth,

filled with bitterness and anger. I had planned everything so well, but now it boils out of me in words that rage and sting and blame.

"You must have known!" I hear myself shout. "Why didn't you protect us from him?" I cry. I remember the years of the goodbad man. They were the same years my parents almost lost their marriage. It was the time Papa found another woman. The time Mama drank too much. Which came first, and whose fault was it? They had blamed each other, fighting and shouting, until the night when Mama went after Papa with the broken bottle.

"You weren't paying attention to us!" I scream at them, throwing the accusation the way Mama had thrown the bottle. "You were too busy to notice what was happening to your own daughters."

"No, no," they tell me as they sit together on the sofa, holding hands, secure in the marital unity they achieved by heaping great mounds of denial to cover all that had happened between them. "What you're saying can't be right."

"Yes, it was him. He was the one. He did this thing to me. And then he did it to Aurelia." I'm sobbing now, and my parents are still staring.

My sister is silent against my shoulder, her mind numbed and her body deadened by all it has been subjected to year after year. She is Sleeping Beauty, sleeping for a hundred years, and no prince will come for her. Or for me. We know this. We do not expect him. We do not want him.

"No," my father says finally. "I can't believe you. You must have imagined this."

My mother's eyes are full of tears, but she agrees with him. "It can't be true," she says. "He was our friend. He took good care of you when we were away. He loved you."

Yes. No. He was the lovehate man, I remember. He was the goodbad man. He confused me. He built a game in my mind, and he played with my thoughts until I was not sure what I could believe. Sometimes I think he is still inside my brain, mixing everything up, telling me lies, assuring me that what he says is true, and then lying again.

"How can you not believe me?" I ask my parents. "It is true."

"No," they say, shaking their heads. "He would never do such a thing. Why do you desecrate the memory of our dear friend?"

I stare back at them, and I understand now that he was right. He said they would not believe me, and he was right. They don't believe it. They will never accept it. They can't, even though they see their two daughters before them, ruined and broken and without hope.

"I told you," Aurelia mumbles. "I told you not to tell." She hasn't been sleeping on my shoulder as I thought.

She heard. She knows I told, and she knows no one will believe us. Ever.

We are lost.

I look up and see the lightbulb. It cannot take me away now. I am too old, too full of sickness and scars and disease. My heart is already dead. My body is dying. I want to die.

Aurelia wants to die, too. She will.

Chapter Eighteen

Ana sat in the darkness and held the hand of the small child. She had come so far, all the way to this place, and now she saw only impenetrable night surrounding her.

What seemed like many years ago, she had walked away from Sam Hawke. A paramedic had unwrapped her hand and exclaimed in dismay. A policeman had insisted that she must do what they told her. She was a gunshot victim. A victim, they both called her.

You are a victim.

They needed reports and information. She needed X-rays and surgery. And so she found herself in the ambulance, and then in the emergency room at Barnes Hospital, and then at a police station, and then—many, many hours later—in a taxi on the way to her apartment.

It was three in the morning, and when she opened the door, she saw that someone had been there already. Her couch had been slit with a knife, and its downy filling covered the floor like snow. Her new dishes lay in pieces on the floor. Her sheets lay tangled at the foot of her bed, and a huge X had been slashed into her mattress.

This was not a robbery. She knew at once who had

been there, coming in the darkness to violate her privacy. Not Don Bering. He would hardly take the time to wreak such havoc. Jack Slaughter, enraged by her discovery, had come after her. She had found him out.

She had told.

And someone had believed her.

Fear rising inside her, Ana backed away from the apartment and staggered down the polished oak steps. She had hammered on the door of her elderly landlady, who stood on the other side and confessed that she had let the man in. A friend, he had told her. Ana had been injured and was in the hospital. She needed clothes and a few personal items. The landlady had thought he looked so kind and sounded quite worried. She was concerned, too. Was Ana all right? Why was she out of the hospital already?

Ana had turned away, running down the hall and out into the night. And then she had heard the cry.

"Señorita!" The voice came from behind the yew bushes that grew close to the foundation of the old house. "Señorita Ana . . ."

And the child arose, small and frightened, her face skeletal under the streetlight. "It is me. Flora."

Ana walked between the yews, where there was no path, waded straight into the tangled limbs and shrubbery. She caught the child in her arms and began to weep. Both of them, sobbing now.

The two sat for a while together in the darkness, Ana aware of the heat of sun-baked bricks pressing into her back and the pain returning to her hand as the anesthetic wore off. Where could they go? Not the apartment. He had been there, torn into it, ripped away the protection it had offered. Haven? But perhaps he was there—Slaughter with his knife. Maybe Bering and his gun, too. The men would hide there and wait for Ana and Flora, the two they were sure would come.

Holding Flora close, Ana searched her mind for safety. There was nothing. No place in the world that could cradle them. The police had listened to her story and written it down. But she had seen the skepticism in their eyes. Jim Slater was an alias? He was selling children from his adoption agency? Jim Slater—so admired and respected? That Jim Slater?

Who are you to say such a thing?

He's a good, kind man. A man of integrity. He would never do this.

The police would not protect her. Sam wanted to save her, but he could do nothing. Bering had gotten into the newspaper building. Slaughter had been inside Haven and her apartment. Every place she believed had been secure was open now, vulnerable.

She and Flora couldn't hide behind the yews forever. They needed a place to go. A haven of their own. Ana thought of the city bus and the heartless bus driver. Then she recalled the old man who had guided her to safety. An angel? A guardian sent by God?

Feeling sick, exhausted and frightened half out of her mind, Ana stood on a corner with Flora until a bus rolled into view. They boarded, and it was empty except for the driver. No angels. No place to go.

As they rode, Flora rested her head on Ana's shoulder and slept. That was when Ana remembered the other angel God had sent her. Perhaps not an angel. But a gift. A friend.

In silence, they left the bus and hurried through the darkness to her friend. Now the three of them sat together and listened to the sounds outside. Ana reflected on her articles about lead paint and had to laugh. How meaningless.

She lit a candle and took out the reporter's notebook she always carried. Someone had taken the ink cartridge from a pen, using the plastic casing as a pipe for marijuana. She held the flexible tube in her broken hand and began to write her broken story about all the broken people.

She wrote about Sam. Terell. Raydell. She wrote about Tenisha, Gerald, Antwone and golden-haired Brandy. And she wrote about Flora. All of them. She wrote until she was empty. Finally, then, she put her head on Flora's shoulder. And she slept.

"He won," Sam said the following evening. "He got her, and he got Flora. And then he escaped."

Terell rubbed his face, trying to stay awake.

"Go on to bed," Sam said. "I know you're tired."

"I'm tired, man, but I can't let you keep talking this way. You're going to have to get your head around it one way or another. Why don't we go over to Drewes and get some frozen custard? They'll still be open. C'mon. It'll be good. The air-conditioning's down, and I'm about to bake up here anyhow."

Sam shrugged. "I can't make myself care about the air-conditioning. You know we're going to have to shut the place down anyway."

"Yeah, but we've got a few days before that," Terell said, tugging on a T-shirt. "We'll get one of the volunteers to work on the AC tomorrow. Besides, I'm not giving up on Haven, Sam."

"You heard the lady. We don't have the money to fix our lead paint, so the health department is shutting us down. Nobody gave up, T-Rex. I fought hard to get that money. But Jim Slater—or whoever he really is—disappeared along with the promise of that five grand. The rest isn't enough."

"Okay, here's what we'll do." Terell stood by the door. "I've been holding out on this, because I thought we could take care of it some other way. But there you go."

He slipped the gold Rolex off his wrist and tossed it onto Sam's mattress. "We can sell that. And I'll call my mama tomorrow to see if she'll take out a second mortgage on the house I bought her. How's that?"

Sam sighed. "You can't, Terell. Your mother isn't making the payments on that house as it is."

The big man turned away, pain obvious in the tilt of his shoulders. "I meant to pay it off for her. I did, Sam. I thought I could."

"You know, that frozen custard is sounding pretty good after all." Sam stood and handed his friend the watch. “Keep your Rolex, man. It’s a reminder of better times.”

“Worse times.” They walked down the stairs of the empty, darkened building. “Bad as things are right now, Sam, this is better than it was in the old days. I thought I was happy with all my ladies and my blow and my big NBA contract. Buying a house for my mama and daddy, buying a boat, buying a Mercedes and a big Harley . . . Man, I was crazy.”

Sam had to laugh. “I think I’m glad I was in Iraq.”

“Glad you didn’t see me messing up so bad? Me, too. But how about the war? You think you’re ever going to heal from what went down there?”

Stepping out into the night, they both instinctively looked up into the star-sprinkled sky. “No,” Sam said. “I’m pretty sure nobody gets complete healing until heaven. That’s just how it is.”

“You’re gonna carry that little dead girl with you everywhere?”

“Probably.” He struggled to swallow the knot in his throat. “And now Ana.”

“Sam, I don’t think Slaughter got her. I really don’t. He wasn’t the killer type. That’s why he hired Bering.”

“Slaughter shot Bering, Terell. You know that. He’s probably the one who trashed Ana’s apartment, too. Yesterday, when I saw what he’d done to the place, I couldn’t believe it. I have no doubt he’d do whatever it took to stop her.” Sam jammed his hands down into his pockets. “I keep expecting the police to call me.

They'll find her body in the river. Or lying in a parking lot somewhere."

"Nah, she's too mean."

Sam tried to chuckle.

"She's probably just hiding out," Terell said.

"She would have called me by now. It sounds crazy, but we had something, Ana and me. There was something between us. I know she'd tell me if she was okay."

They walked side by side in silence, Sam fighting the overwhelming sense of loss that dogged him. Ana, Flora, Haven—all gone. He had no idea what he would do with himself. They would put the building up for sale, of course. But the chances of a quick turnaround were slim. They would both be broke and jobless.

"Wasn't this the place Raydell's thugs attacked Ana?" Terell asked as they passed a boarded-up storefront.

Sam studied the graffiti. "Yeah. She lost her shoes in there. She's always losing her shoes."

"Wears them dumb little high-heel things."

Sam smiled. "Hey, you want to meet somebody? Homeless geezer named Glen lives in there. Crazy coot. Let's take him out for frozen custard."

"You're the crazy one," Terell said. "This is a crack house."

"Nah. It's pretty much deserted. Except for Glen."

"You first, dog. I ain't going in there by myself." Sam pushed open the door and stepped into the darkness.

"Glen?" he called out. "Are you in here?"

The silence stretched on for so long that Sam decided the building must be empty. Then a voice answered him.

"Sam?" A woman's voice, soft and familiar. "Is that you?"

"Ana?" He hit Terell on the shoulder so hard the man nearly fell over. "It's her! Ana! Ana, where are you?"

A match flickered to life in a far corner. Sam spotted the collection of cardboard boxes and paper bags that made up Glen's home. Illuminated in the glow of a candle flame was Ana's face.

"Sam!" she called. "It's me. And Flora. We're both here."

"Look at her eating that frozen custard," Terell said as the five sat around a table on the sidewalk outside Drewes. "You'd think she hadn't eaten in a week."

Ana looked up from her cup. "We haven't had much. A can of beans last night."

"Now then." Glen pursed his lips. "You bein' fussy about my cookin'?"

"Yes, I am," Ana said.

She felt strange, almost otherworldly sitting out under the stars with Sam and Terell. For so many hours, she had hidden away with Flora—too frightened to come out. Too confused to think her way to a solution. Whose dead body was in the Ladue mansion? Where was Slaughter? What had become of Bering? Where could she turn?

And then the darkness inside the old building became a friend. She and Flora talked for hours. Glen joined in, his story even more confusing than theirs. He was a man, abused as a small child, molested by adult men, stripped of his innocence and dignity. He had taken a common path. Used drugs to escape the pain. Paid for his drugs by selling himself. And in the end, he had lost what shred might have been left of the person he should have become. He was a shell now, riddled with disease, his mind half-gone, but his soul still alive. He had wept when Flora wept. He patted her head and gave her his necklace of keys.

Ana had written out the articles due at the newspaper. Not the way Carl Webster wanted them—but the way they demanded to be written. And then, somehow, Sam and Terell found her. Bering was dead. Slaughter was missing. Haven was lost. But in the group gathered around the wrought-iron table, she sensed a joy. A dawning hope.

"Beans," Glen said. "Well, sugar, you do the best you can with what you got."

Ana sucked down a mouthful of frozen custard, enjoying the feel of the cool treat sliding all the way to her stomach as she pulled a folded sheaf of tattered pages from her pocket. "I need to drop these off at the paper. And then . . . well, I don't know where to go. I don't know what to do about Flora."

"Your apartment's been cleaned already," Sam told her. "The landlady has called me at least twice. She's frantic. You should be safe there now."

Ana considered it. She wasn't sure she would ever feel safe anywhere. "And Flora? Are we supposed to turn her over to the Division of Family Services? Give her away to strangers?"

"Does she know where her family is?"

"In La Ceiba." Ana took Flora's hand when the child glanced up at the familiar name. "She told me that her father is poor. They live not far from the beach. Jack Slaughter has a large house in an exclusive waterfront area. The children all know the place. He has several TVs, a lot of toys, baskets of candy. Kids go there and hang out to watch TV and eat candy. Slaughter—the man she calls Primero—doesn't touch them. Sometimes he asks if they will let his friend take their picture . . . ."

She paused, trying to go on.

"Slaughter has a studio on the property," she continued. "Several men work there, photographing children and sending the images to customers all over the world. He also runs a travel agency that brings wealthy men down to his property for a weekend vacation. Sometimes they stay for a week or more, Flora says. Slaughter and his employees pay the children to do whatever the men want. Flora had been to the house and eaten chocolate candy several times. But she knew nothing about the other things before the day her father took her and her sister to Slaughter and sold them."

"Sold them?" Terell said. "Like slaves?"

"Flora saw the exchange of money, and she understood that her father had no other choice. He cried, but he told her that Primero had promised to take her to America and find her a good new family who would take care of her and love her and give her plenty of chocolate candies every day. Flora and her sister stayed at the compound in Honduras for two days, and then he accompanied them on an airplane to St. Louis. They stayed in his mansion, and he was the first to abuse them. Then a man came and took Flora's sister away. Another man came and got Flora. This man—the one she calls Segundo—took her to his home. She stayed with him there for a while. And then one night, she escaped."

"A truck driver picked her up on the highway and took her to St. Louis. So she ended up back in the same city where she'd started. On the street, she met Gypsy, who took her to Haven. And then one day, Jack Slaughter walked into the building."

"Is that what happened?" Glen asked. "Wowee, girl. I never could get the whole thing straight when you was talkin' about it. So, where this bad man now? We gots to put him in jail."

"We don't know where he is." Ana had noted that Flora was watching as she told the story. Concerned about the fear on the child's face, Ana paused to explain in Spanish. "We're talking about Primero," she said. "We don't know where he is."

"I know where he is," Flora said in a soft voice. "He's in his favorite place. That room in his house where he always goes. There's a door. Inside is a special closet where he keeps the medicine. And the dolls."

A chill washed down Ana's spine. "The basement," she told the men in English. "Flora says Slaughter is in his basement."

"But the house burned down," Terell said.

"Not the basement." Sam reached out and touched Ana's shoulder. "I was in the foyer when I gave the coroner the ID on Bering. Part of the first floor and most of the second were gone. But the basement is intact."

"Surely he wouldn't be there," Terell spoke up. "By now the police have been through that place with a fine-tooth comb."

"I agree." Sam nodded at his friend. "Slaughter is too sophisticated to do something that stupid. Obviously he has a huge organization. He probably set up all kinds of safeguards and escape routes. I'll bet he's sitting on a beach in Costa Rica or Monte Carlo. The last thing he would do is go back to his house in Ladue."

"But he would, Sam," Ana insisted.

"*Sí*," Flora joined in, as if she understood the importance of convincing the others.

"It's what they do. Slaughter's collections are in the basement. His dolls. His files. Pedophiles love their collections. They can't give them up. They'll risk anything to keep the images and pictures. They build up their files for years . . . computer files and photo albums . . . ."

She paused, suddenly unable to speak. Tears filled her eyes and spilled down her cheeks as she thought of the secret she had kept so long. The deep, unmentionable, horrifying truth had eaten at her, trying to kill her, despite all the love with which God had enfolded her. She knew even now—even with the new understanding that her Lord was an invincible victor over sin—that the pain would always lurk. It would always live inside her, slowly drying her up, eventually killing her.

"Ana." Sam brushed a finger across her cheek. "What is it? Talk to us."

She shook her head, biting her lip and trying to stem the tears. Flora leaned against her, large brown eyes gazing up in compassion. And then Sam spoke.

"It happened to you, too, Ana," he said in a low voice. "That's how you know so much. That's why you couldn't stop yourself from trying to save Flora."

"Oh, sugar, this world is an evil place," Glen murmured, patting Ana's back. "You got to let it all out now, or it'll eat you up like it done me. I told you what happened when I was a boy. It's your turn now."

Ana cradled her injured arm, the wounded hand. She tried to bring out the words, but they wouldn't come. How she express what had been done to her? Yet, here were people who cared. People who would *believe* her.

"He had them, too," she managed. "The man who hurt me. He had magazine pictures, photographs, videotapes all filed in his own particular order. He made me look at them, and he . . . he . . ."

Flora's thin arm slipped around Ana's waist. On her other side, Sam's large, well-muscled arm circled her shoulders. And all at once, she felt safe. Secure. Touched by compassion. Protected by love.

"I was a little girl like Flora," Ana whispered, her focus on the table. "He was my father's best friend. He and his wife took care of us when my parents were traveling for my father's business. That's when . . . that's when it happened. The man's wife would leave the house—shopping, visiting friends, checking on her mother—and he would take me into a room, a place he had added to their garage. He always locked the door."

At that, Terell groaned in sympathy. "Mmm, if I could get my hands on that guy, he'd regret the day he was born."

Ana sniffled and forced herself to continue. "Afterward, he told me that we had a special secret, just the two of us. He insisted that I had wanted the . . . the terrible thing . . . that I had asked for it. If I mentioned it to my parents or anyone else, he assured me, they wouldn't believe it. But I wasn't to say a word. If I did, he would kill my family. He showed me a gun. He had . . . he had bullets, and he would . . . he would hold the gun to my head."

"Sugar, that man didn't need no gun," Glen said. "He was killin' you anyhow."

"What about your sister?" Sam asked.

"Yes," she sobbed. "He hurt her, too. Just like Flora's sister. We couldn't help them. Couldn't save them. And now they're lost."

She surrendered as Sam lifted her out of her chair and drew her into his arms. Holding her close, he spoke gently. "We'll find Flora's sister, Ana. I promise you that. Slaughter kept files and computer records. He has a place in Honduras. He has clients. The man is traceable. This is what I did in the military, Ana. I'll find Flora's sister, and we'll bring her back. We'll make sure they can live with their parents again—with money to support the family."

"You don't even have enough money to keep Haven open." She wept. "It's hopeless, Sam."

"No, Ana." He stroked his hand down her back, and she could feel Flora's small fingers woven through hers. "With God all things are possible. We'll find Flora's sister, I promise you that."

"But my sister," she murmured. "My sister is gone. My beautiful Aurelia."

Speaking the name loosed a flood inside Ana, and she wrapped her arms around Sam's strong shoulders and sobbed into his neck.

The yellow crime scene tape fluttered in the evening breeze as Sam ducked under it. He and Terell had agreed to bring Ana and Flora to the burned mansion because the child claimed she could show them Primero's special room. But Sam wasn't about to go unprepared.

First they drove to the newspaper building and walked Ana to her desk. She scribbled a note to her editor and slipped her articles under his door. Then they found Raydell's building. He insisted on coming, too. That meant there were six—too many for Sam's liking.

Most of them were all but useless. Terell was strong, but the big doofus wouldn't hurt a fly. Ana had finally expressed the pain in her past and now couldn't seem to stop crying. Glen could barely walk upright, and Flora, of course, was a child.

Only Raydell seemed like an asset. Though the young man was too full of bluster and bravado, Sam couldn't help but glow with pride at the progress Raydell had made since Haven became a part of his life. And so the six trudged across the lawn, skirting fallen concrete cherubs as they headed for the back door.

They found it open. Sam's heart leaped with hope. No doubt the police would have secured the building. A thief would have broken a window. But the door stood ajar—as though the owner had unlocked it with a key and simply walked in.

"I think Flora may be right," Sam whispered. "Slaughter could be here. Everyone stay quiet."

He took the child's hand. She pointed down the hall. They descended a flight of steps that led to the basement and stepped into a large entertainment room. The walls held countless shelves—each lined with a row of dolls. Sam ushered the others across the thickly padded carpet toward a light that shone from under a door in the distance.

He held a finger over his lips. Motioning Ana, Flora and Glen to one side, he beckoned the others. Then he kicked the door open.

"Give it up, Slaughter," he shouted.

"Don't shoot!" The man lifted his head from the pile of pillows and blankets where he had been sleeping. Blinking, he held up both hands. The room was lined with oak filing cabinets, above which rose shelves filled with toys.

"Sam?" He sounded baffled. "What are you—? And Terell?"

"Stand up, Slaughter." Sam stepped into the room.

"Now seriously, Sam. This is ridiculous." He got to his feet. Unsteady, he leaned a hand against one of the cabinets. Sam noted the bottles of vodka lining the wall.

"Turn around," Sam said. "Put your hands behind your back."

"Don't do something you'll regret, Sam." He took a step forward. "You know who I am."

"Jack Slaughter."

He peeked around Sam. "Ana, is that you? What is going on? Why is everyone here?"

"We know all about you, Jack," she spoke up. "You sell children to pedophiles. You run a sex tourism business. You trade in Internet pornography. We know who you are—and so do the police. We told them everything."

"Police?" He looked at Sam with a confused expression. "Wait a minute. I'm here because my house burned. Somebody set my house on fire while I was out of the country. I'd gone down to Venezuela to see about some children. I have two families waiting anxiously for them. Then when I got back, I found that my house—"

"Stop it!" Ana screamed. "Stop lying!"

"Primero!" Flora cried out. Jerking her hand from Ana's she hurtled at Slaughter, throwing herself into him, pummeling him with her fists. "Primero! Primero! *Donde está Maria?*"

"Where's her sister?" Ana shouted, stepping up to the man and jabbing a finger into his chest. "Where is Maria? What have you done with her?"

Sam moved between the man and Ana as Terell swept Flora into his arms. Raydell grabbed Slaughter in a headlock.

With duct tape, Sam and Raydell bound their enemy's hands behind his back. As they led him across the entertainment room and up the stairs, he continued to protest. "This is a misunderstanding. I'm telling you, Sam Hawke, you're going to regret what you've done to me. I'll shut down Haven so fast it'll make your head spin. As for you, Ana Burns, you can forget your job. I'm a personal friend of your publisher."

He was still insisting on his innocence, making threats, sticking to his alibi when Sam phoned the police. The Haven six could see his mouth moving, denying everything as the squad car drove him away.

Epilogue

Ana's suitcases stood just inside the front door of her apartment. Though the landlady had apologized and offered two months' free rent, Ana knew she couldn't stay. She had phoned her parents and told them she was coming home.

She tugged an antibacterial cloth from the small pack she kept in the pocket of her jeans. In preparation for her departure, she wiped the countertop and range hood. Though she hadn't heard from Carl Webster, Ana knew the job had ended. Since the night they had found Jack Slaughter in his basement, Ana had been unable to return to work. For an entire week, she had stayed in a hotel with Flora. Sam had visited. So had the police and various state and federal agents.

The following Friday, an FBI agent had arrived at the hotel room with Maria. The sisters silently touched hands and then, weeping, fell into each other's arms. The U.S. Embassy in Honduras had located their parents and provided tickets for the sisters' return to their homeland. And so they went away with nearly every cent from Ana's bank account, promises to write and many, many tears. As Sam had hoped, the authorities penetrated Jack Slaughter's web, and unraveled his complex organization.

They arrested men in nine states and raided the compound at La Ceiba.

Now Ana would go back to Brownsville. She shook

powdered cleanser over her spotless stainless steel sink as she pondered the long drive. It wasn't as bad as she had imagined, really. For one thing, she had told her story.

Telling was good.

Very good.

Always tell, she reminded herself. Her parents had refused to believe her on that day when she and Aurelia had confronted them about their friend. But Sam had believed her about Jack Slaughter. Even though he hadn't wanted to accept that the man who could rescue Haven was a pedophile, he believed her. Terell had believed her, too. In fact, everyone believed her—Raydell, Glen, the landlady, the police, the FBI. Even she herself—who had listened to Jack Slaughter's denials in the basement and wondered if she had made a mistake—Ana believed what she knew in her heart.

For the first time in years, she fully trusted what her mind told her was true. She trusted herself. She knew bad from good and darkness from light.

So this was a positive thing, she thought as she scrubbed her sink. Ana and Flora had told on the bad man, and now he was locked away. The two little girls from Honduras were in legitimate foster care as authorities worked on their case. Flora had found her sister, Maria. And something else good had happened, too.

Ana had discovered that what Sam told her about God was true. He was her shield and defender. No, she hadn't been completely healed. She knew she never would be until heaven. But she was no longer a victim.

Ana was a survivor.

Turning on the hot water, she rinsed the cleanser residue down the drain. She would go back to Brownsville and get a job at the old newspaper and face her parents. They would listen to her tell the story of Aurelia. Even if they still refused to believe ill of their friend who had died years ago, they would hear why their younger daughter had hanged herself from the wooden beam in the guest cottage.

Ana would tell on him. *Always tell.*

She bent down and tied up her trash bag—the last thing to be done before her trip. All was well, she assured herself as she carried the sack to the door. Only one part of her heart would hold an emptiness. But then, she had never wanted a man's love. The memory of Sam Hawke would fade.

As she turned to survey the empty apartment, the intercom buzzed, surprising her. "Yes?" she called down.

"It's me."

Sam's voice filled Ana's heart. She shook her head, willing away the pain.

"So what do you want? I'm busy up here."

"Open the door, woman."

Smiling, she pressed the button to let him in. He could help her carry down her luggage anyway. A man was good for that.

And then he was standing in her door, his broad grin with its deep parentheses reminding her that a man could be good for other things, as well. Without meaning to, she wrapped her arms around him and held him close.

"I'm going, Sam," she whispered. "I was planning to call, but then . . ."

"Going where?"

"Brownsville. If I start this afternoon, I'll get as far as—"

"Texas? No way. No possible way." He tugged a newspaper from his hip pocket. "You're leaving St. Louis when you're on page one? I thought that was the big goal. I came over to congratulate you. Future Pulitzer winner and all that."

"What are you talking about?" She took the paper in her good hand and unfolded it to find a photo of Raydell Watson standing outside the front door of Haven. She scanned the text. It was her story. The way she had written it. The information about lead paint had been woven seamlessly into the profile of a young man who had been brought up in an apartment filled with cockroaches—and whose future lay with the city of St. Louis police force.

"Part one of a four-part series," Sam said, punching the paper with his forefinger. "Right there."

"I don't believe this. I thought I was fired."

"You didn't know?"

"I called in sick. My hand . . . and Flora and the other things. I haven't talked to Carl."

His eyes held flint as he studied her. “You got your dream. I guess, now you’re leaving for sure. Chasing that prize.”

She recalled what he had told her about his mother. Following her big dream. Abandoning her children.

“Me? Chase a prize?” she asked. “How shallow do you think I am, buster?”

His mouth tugged into a grin. “Maybe you’ve changed a little.”

“I’m not chasing awards, Sam,” she said, looking into his blue eyes. “I’m chasing peace.”

“I can give you that.”

“Really?”

“Peace. Safety.” He drew her into his arms. “Maybe even a future.”

That prospect had always frightened and distressed Ana. But as Sam spoke the word, she suddenly knew a glow of joy. It began in her chest and spread through her like the sunrise.

Sam bent and brushed a kiss across her lips. “Would that be so bad?”

Sinking into him, she stroked her fingers up his arm. “I need that. I need it with you.”

When his mouth covered hers a second time, she dropped the newspaper and threaded her fingers through his hair. He kicked the door shut with his heel and pressed her against the wall.

“Ana.” As he spoke her name, his lips caressed hers. “Anamaria. Anamaria, my lady, my love.”

“Oh, Sam.” She pressed her lips to his neck,

drinking the scent of the man, knowing him as she had never allowed herself to dream. "Sam, I thought it was over. I knew I had to go. I've always run from this. From feelings. From hope. But you won't let me go, will you? Promise you won't?"

"Woman, I'll hold on to you as long as you'll let me."

"Sam, why me? You know what happened. You heard everything—"

He silenced her with another kiss. "I love you, Ana Burns. I love you exactly the way you are. If you can stand a Marine who can't get the Iraqi sand out of his head, I'll take a woman who carries a packet of antibacterial wipes in her pocket."

Pulling it from her jeans, he shook his head. "We're both a little nuts, you know."

"I think our God is big enough for that."

"Yeah. Big enough for that—and more. We've got a lot to learn about Him, Ana. He put you on page one, and guess what He did for me."

Her heart sped up. "Haven?"

"The hood put on a barbecue for us Sunday afternoon. Raydell's idea. All the families joined in. Raised two thousand bucks. On Sunday afternoon, your church came up with another five grand. Your newspaper publisher kicked in three thousand on Monday. That put us more than halfway there. When the health department showed up, I told them what we had. They gave us another month."

"Oh, Sam." She drew him close and met his lips

with hers. “A few minutes ago . . . did you mention something about a future?”

His blue eyes softened. “A future and a hope.”

Acknowledgments

Many things can happen to a book before it is opened by a reader. *Thread of Deceit* went through the refiner's fire, a process that involved abandonment by one publisher, many years languishing on a shelf, a careful revision process and finally the embrace of a true champion, Joan Marlow Golan, Executive Editor at Steeple Hill. I'm so grateful for her belief in the subject matter of this book and her willingness to publish it.

Others also played important roles in bringing *Thread of Deceit* to life. My thanks goes to each of them. While any errors in the book are my own, I particularly wish to acknowledge the time and information given to me by David Hansen, assistant attorney general in the Missouri Attorney General's Office. A former prosecutor in the Sexually Violent Predator Unit, David willingly assisted me in my effort to understand the mind and behavior of the sexual predator. I also wish to thank Angela Hirsch, former victim advocate in the Sexually Violent Predator Unit, for helping me grasp the effect that sexual crimes have on victims. Most important, she gave me the profile of a victim who is successfully dealing with the past and working toward health.

I wish also to thank the many women who shared their personal stories with me before, during and after the writing of this book. Though your names remain publicly anonymous, God knows each of you intimately. He is a God of justice. Whatever was done to you was done to Him. Knowing that, take comfort and find healing.

As always, I thank my husband, Tim, whose numerous readings and careful editing of this manuscript have helped see it into print. I love you. And, of course, I am grateful for my patient and loving sons, Geoffrey and Andrei.